HOW TO SURVIVE YOUR RETAIL JOB DURING THE HOLIDAYS

HOW TO SURVIVE YOUR RETAIL JOB DURING THE HOLIDAYS

J.L. POLANCO

Johanna Polanco

This is dedicated to all the retail workers who don't feel appreciated. I know the struggle, I know your pain and I love you.

J.L.

ALSO BY J.L. POLANCO
Love Me Again

The Lawyer & the Thief
The Lawyer & the Stalker

Flash Fiction Available on jlpolanco.com:
After The Office Party
Vampy
Jealous

I

Rule 58: Your team is like your family; we win together, we lose together. We have fun together. utilize each other's skill to achieve a common goal.

You ever wonder what a job in the fashion industry was like? Books and movies make it seem so glamourous. Montages of color-ful fabric being thrown through the air, access to the top designers, free products thrown at your feet; a beautiful, luxurious life that made you the envy of all your friends. What they failed to tell you is that to break into the industry you'd have to start at the absolute bottom, secure a human sacrifice and sell your soul to the devil himself just to sniff the same air as Anna Wintour and every other fashion idol...and still that's almost to impossible.

The climb up is a slow one. I thought the initial step of working an entry level retail job would send me in the right direction.

Wrong.

Ten years later and I'm still climbing.

Retail is like the mob; once you're in, there's no way out. You'll always be a part of it FOR THE REST OF YOUR LIFE. I know that that may sound just a tad dramatic but it's true.

I tried to leave once to be my own boss until I quickly realized that I needed food and water to survive and that involved making some form of cash money. I was selling my own designs to anyone and everyone who would buy them. The cost of fabric alone had me thinking of selling myself on a corner, but that seemed more like exercise and that just wasn't the journey I wanted to take; retail was the easiest way to make a living while I kept my fashion design as a side hustle.

My part-time sales advisor job turned into a full-time visual merchandising job. I've been at it so long that I could do this job with my eyes closed. Working at *H. Moda* was the dream; It's the world's biggest fast fashion brand. Working my way up and making it to the design team was the goal. If I can't run my own fashion brand, then I could be a part of this massive company and pitch my design ideas...at least that was the backup dream.

Le Sigh.

That never happened and honestly, I don't think it ever will. Companies want employees who will be submissive; yes men at their beck and call to make them feel like the geniuses they want to be instead of the cheats who rip off indie brands and sell it as their own original idea. I was not a yes man. I was more of the *I'll give you my true opinion even if you don't like it man*. That kind of person to those in the management position were labeled difficult.

I hate that I'm being so cynical about the company that I am still currently employed by. We can blame my sunny disposition on the fact that I was the only visual merchandiser who was scheduled the night before Thanksgiving to set up *Black Friday* signage that this billion-dollar company spent millions of dollars on to use for one day and discard as if money was disposable.

Calm down, Ginny.

I took a deep breath even though I was fuming on the inside as I stood with no shoes on in the store window putting up the vinyl. Sweat trickled down my temples under the beaming window lights.

I only agreed to come in because I thought that would put me in good favor with the store manager. But again, I was wrong.

I pressed the squeegee against the vinyl to smooth it down, making sure that there were no bubbles to be seen. A flash from this morning popped up in my head causing me to almost tear up the delicate marketing with my pent-up aggression.

I like to think that I'm an unusually optimistic person. When I was called to the office, I thought that she was going to tell me that I was going to get the raise that I asked for; the money I thought my skill and experience was worth. Instead, I was told that after ten years I will not get my annual raise because it wasn't in the budget. But these God forsaken signs told me otherwise; there was in fact money in the budget just not for the ones who slave away to make this company billions of dollars.

"Ginny, are you almost done? We were kinda hoping that we could leave by 9:30 and its already 9:45."

My store managers shrill, whiny voice pierced through my soul, making me cringe. "Maggie, we are scheduled til ten, I don't want to cut my hours because everyone else wants to go home early." I heard her as she took a breath to give me a retort, but I gave her no chance. "Plus, you gave the other visuals the night off and just scheduled me. So, what usually takes about three to four visuals to accomplish in an hour is taking this one visual almost three," I finished. It was hard to keep the snarkiness out of my response, but it was late, and my patience and sanity was worn down to the bone.

I knew she was still standing behind me; I could feel her beady little eyes boring into the back of my head. I turned slightly to give her some form of attention.

Maggie and I went way back, starting off as Sales Advisors almost a decade ago...but time and too much drama tore us apart. Now, she was the enemy disguised as a customer service-oriented store manager. "Was there anything else, Maggie?"

"No, I'll let the closing team go. I'll wait for you in the office."

I gave her my back, already knowing that come Friday this woman was going to pull me into the office to have a few words with me because of my quips that she had to take with some sense of dignity.

I continued putting up the vinyl, but I could still feel her behind me, so I began to pick up the pace; only then did I hear the click clack of her knee-high boots as she walked back to the office.

At 10:10, I finally clocked out with a disgruntled store manager tapping her foot. "I clocked out, I just have to put my coat on," I assured her.

Without another word I put on my red teddy coat and braced myself for the mind-numbing cold that was about to slap us in the face as soon as she opened the doors to let us out.

I waited as she punched in the alarm code. When she was satisfied with the confirming beep of the alarm, Maggie turned around, giving me a tightest of smiles. "Goodnight Ginny, Happy Thanksgiving. See you Friday."

I gave a curt nod in return. "Happy Thanksgiving," I mumbled.

We walked in silence to the corner, I took the steps down into the subway and she continued walking another block to her train station.

This time of night in NYC would be raging with excitement, but it was a holiday weekend, and the streets were completely quiet. I put in an Earpod and waited for my train. It was sad but the holidays were never a joyous time in my life. My luck was never good this time of year; truth was, I wanted to head home to watch *Dawson's Creek* and wallow in my own disappointing life.

My phone buzzed, interrupting the mellow dramatic music I had playing through the pods. When I saw the name, I immediately answered, "Hello, darling." I smiled to myself. My visual manager and best friend, Marvin, giggled just as the loud roar of a crowd came through.

"Listen, Meish heard from Mark who heard from Tahiri who heard from a sales advisor that you gave Maggie shit tonight," he said.

I felt my blood boil. "I did not—"

"We know that she was probably blowing it way out of proportion, you know how she does," he continued.

"We? Who's there with you?"

"The other visuals. We know you usually turn us down but come meet us! Tomorrow we're all gonna be with family that get on our nerves...might as well celebrate with the people that we see the most."

My mind kept going over all the excuses as to why I should just go home, but Marvin's seen me after a dentist appointment, higher than a kite and didn't record it on his phone, so he's one of the good ones.

My visual team are the closest people to me. We're more like siblings than co-workers. We could yell and scream at each other but an hour later we're laughing as if nothing happened. I was an only child; it was nice to have a team that felt like family. "Where are you guys?" I sighed heavy into the phone.

Twenty minutes later I walked into a dimly lit bar in Midtown. "Gin! Ginny!" I could hear Marvin's high pitch squeal over the booming music.

I waved and made my way to the high-top bar table that was overtaken by the stylish visual team of *H. Moda*.

I was kissed on the cheek by the people who I've seen consistently for eight plus hours every day for the past five years. "You made it!" Meish shouted from her spot.

"What are you wearing?" Tahiri sneered, causing me to look down at the outfit I revealed after taking my coat off— a moto jacket, white button down and distressed boyfriend jeans and Docs; an outfit I thought was semi-stylish.

"Where's Mark?"

Tahiri gestured towards the bar, where Mark was too busy talking to a group of women.

"What did you do to Maggie? I heard she was fuming," Marvin asked, his face was flushed from too much booze and too much laughter.

I laughed as he handed me a drink. "All I said was the truth! This chick was trying to hurry me up because she had places to be. Like, I'm not cutting my own hours just so you could be Betty Crocker! You should have thought of that! Plus, she only scheduled one visual to put up all the signs, that's not my fault!"

"At least you didn't bang on any tables this time," Marvin quipped, bringing up an incident where Maggie brought the whole visual team to the office to talk about our inability to complete our jobs in a timely manner, which in turn sent me on a verbal rampage and banging on a desk to get my point across...not my proudest moment but one that is often brought up when my temper begins to flare up.

They all laughed at the memory. "She just gets on my nerves!" I laughed.

"All that shit that happened back then needs to be forgotten," Marvin added.

I just wanted to change the subject. "How long have you guys been here?" I asked surveying the place.

"For about an hour," Marvin answered just as a rowdy group of guys bursts through the doors. "And look how the Gods have blessed us," he sang.

Our group all stared at the men as they pushed through the crowd to get to the bar. I made eye contact with one of the guys;

tall, auburn hair, broad shoulders, soft brown eyes, outfit tailored to his body, full lips.

Are those tattoos on his hands?

I quickly looked away. God, I hated it when I stared too long. It was one of those weird looks where your gaze happens to land on someone randomly and then you're caught staring and you look everywhere else but at that person to prove you weren't staring in the first place...it was one of those weird awkward looks that bordered on embarrassing, and I hoped no one noticed.

"He smiled at you," Marvin whispered in my ear as the others talked and giggled among themselves.

"Who?"

"The guy that you're pretending you didn't notice."

"What guy?" I tried to play it cool by sipping my drink.

"The guy you just eye fucked and then thought better of," he kept pushing.

"Marvin," I sighed. "Don't start."

"Gin, when was the last time you gotten laid. Maybe this is the perfect opportunity to let loose."

I raised an eyebrow. "I'm going to stop you right there. I am not the kind of person that can just sleep with some stranger at the drop of a dime...I'm not you." His incredulous look made me add, "I haven't even finished my first drink and you're already trying to talk me into—"

"Ginny, relax! Calm Down!" He yelled over the music. "I was just saying that maybe this is a great opportunity to get yourself back into the game. After that whole thing with Rafa TWO years ago, Ginny. TWO years—" I shot him a look. And he held up his hands in surrender. "That we are not going to talk about now. Just...you've been in a rut and you've been closing yourself off to everybody and not just men who you can possibly sleep with. Doesn't your kitty want a scratch?"

"If my kitty needed a scratch, then I'd go buy some *Monistat*."

He scrunched his face. "Don't get gross."

"Me, get gross? You're the one calling my vagina a kitty."

"But you're the one who brought up...vaginal crème," he cringed as he said it. I threw back my drink and was immediately given another by Marvin.

"What? Do you have a stash of old fashions in your back pockets?"

He laughed. "I ordered you two before you got here. Just promise me you'll be open to having fun tonight. It's been a while since we've seen fun Ginny. This grumpy, angry Ginny is starting to wear on us," he said.

"Angry, grumpy Ginny rarely makes an appearance," I pointed out.

"Well, if banging your balled fists on tables to get a point across is not angry Ginny...I'm afraid to ask what Ginny that was."

I put my drink to my lips and coyly looked behind me, immediately locking eyes with the guy who caught me staring. I gave a quick smirk and turned back to find the whole table looking at me smugly.

"What?" I asked before sipping my drink.

"He's cute," Tahiri commented with a wink.

"Oh, shit, Ginny getting her groove back," Meish exclaimed, high-fiving Tahiri as if it were a basketball game.

Marvin remained unusually silent, which caused me to turn in his direction. "And? What say you?" I asked.

He shrugged. "You do you, boo." He said with a smile.

"I don't even know what that means," I said.

"God, Virginia! It means if you think he's cute and you want to have a good time then go up to him and have a good time!" he slammed his glass down.

"I don't know why you're so worked up," I said, trying to hold my temper.

"Because you need to forget what happened with Rafa and get out of your bubble. I don't want to be your therapist whenever you're on the verge of a nervous breakdown. It's got me losing my hair." He pointed the full head of hair that showed the tiniest bit of receding. "What's gonna help you out of your two-year funk is a no mess, one-night stand with a gorgeous stranger," he finished.

"God, Marvin, take a breath."

I looked back one more time, and cute guy was still looking my way. I threw back the last bit of my drink. "Anybody wants anything?" I asked.

After everyone yelled out their drink orders, I finally worked up enough courage to walk up to the bar where Mr. Handsome was chilling with his buddies.

I caught the attention of the bartender right away. "Hey, let me get a margarita, martini, sunrise kiss and two old fashions," I ordered while the bartender nodded and began working on the orders.

"Talk to her," I heard someone say from the group, before Mr. handsome cleared his throat and threw out his first attempt at a conversation.

"Wow, you must really be thirsty," he said. His voice was gruff, rough around the edges and immediately sent chills down my spine.

The others in his group were no help as they all began to laugh at this poor guy.

I bit my lip to keep myself from laughing. When I didn't answer, he braved another attempt. "You look like a margarita kind of girl," he offered.

I gave him a quick glance. "And what kind of girl would that be?" I asked, trying my best to keep my voice from shaking. I was incredibly nervous; This wasn't me, this was a version of me that I always wanted to be; flirty, mysterious, exciting...but in all actuality, if I hadn't gotten an invite today, I would be home watching some 90's teen drama, with pimple cream on my face, eating brownies.

He scooted closer to me. "Well, it's the kind of girl that would be up to having fun," I felt his breath on my ear. I scooted away from him.

"Guess again," I said.

"Old fashion?"

"What kind of girl does that make me?" I asked, fully turning my body to face him.

He tilted his head, eyeing me up and down, pretending to think about his answer. He began to toy with his beard. "You like comfort."

I shrugged. "Don't we all," I answered.

He scooted closer. "Maybe. But you are risk-averse," he added.

"Meaning?"

"Meaning that you stick to what you know. You'd rather be around a fireplace than a place like this," he said with a smirk.

I leaned closer to him; the smell of his cologne was masculine without being overbearing. "Well, if you're so right, why am I here?"

The bartender brought all my drinks over. "Because you came looking for me."

I raised an eyebrow at his forwardness. "Is that so?"

He looked down at the drinks. "Need a hand with those?"

I eyed him suspiciously as if I was actually thinking about my answer, knowing full well that I already made up my mind. "Sure," I said and offered a shy smile.

As he grabbed some drinks, I noticed how big and strong his hands looked; a spark in the pits of my belly started to form; the two drinks I had before new the mission and they were working fast. I nervously led him to our table, while his group gave a small round of applause and whistles. My group was just as bad, all staring with knowing smiles.

"Who'd you bring, Ginny?" Mark asked. He was like the little brother I never wanted and the only straight male in our visual team.

Embarrassment flushed my cheeks as I realized I didn't get his name. I glanced at him as I passed out the drinks I had been holding. "I'm Max," he answered.

"Nice to meet you Max, I'm Gin." I said in return.

He tilted his head. "Like the drink?"

"Like a nickname, it's short for Virginia."

He stepped closer to me. "Suits you," he said with a nod.

"What do you mean?"

Max had placed the drinks he had been holding on the table. "Well, your name it sounds just as comfortable as your drink."

We stared at each as if they were in our own little bubble. I felt Max's eyes travel slowly while I did my best to slow down my breathing. *This was it*, I thought to myself. *This was pure physical attraction.* It's been a while since I felt this. Max's slow smirk told me he felt the same. That was until someone cleared his throat a little bit too aggressively. "Ginny!"

We both snapped out of the trance and turned to Marvin. "Yeah?" I said, my voice sounding too airy for my liking.

He folded his hands and cocked his head to the side. "Introduce us," Marvin insisted, punctuating his demand with a head tilt.

"Oh." I cleared my throat. "This loudmouth is Marvin, that's Tahiri over there, the curly hair beauty is Meisheko, and the one with the muscles is Mark."

"Friends? Colleagues?"

"Family. You know when you see your co-workers more than your own family? They're all like brother and sisters I never asked for," I elaborated.

"Gee, thanks," Tahiri said lamely.

"You guys I'm joking," I assured them, turning quickly to Max. "but not really."

He offered a smile that made me feel like I won the lottery. "Oh, where do you guys work?" Max asked.

Marvin opened his mouth to answer, but I answered before he could. "Retail."

Max raised an eyebrow. "That's vague."

"Well, you're a stranger."

I heard the others snicker. Max looked around the table, placing both hands on his chest. "Don't I look trustworthy?'

"You look like a snack, but Ginny's right...we don't know you," Meish replied.

"What do you do, Max?" I asked. If he answered the question, then I felt more comfortable to answer.

He cleared his throat, narrowing his eyes. "You guys are strangers too, you know."

"Interesting," I murmured as I took a sip of my drink.

Tahiri piped up. "Well, you guys can talk and get to know each other; we promise we won't listen."

"Don't listen to her, I will definitely be listening...and judging," Marvin said.

Max gestured to a table further away. "Hey, want to go talk?" he asked.

I looked at the others. "Girl, go! We'll be here if you need us," Meish said.

I nodded, picked up my drink and followed Max. I smoothed down the front of my blouse; I was nervous! I didn't know how to move my hands; should I place them neatly in front of me like some schoolgirl? Should I cradle my drink? Should I just leave them at my sides like dead anchors? Just being at the table was too complicated for me.

"Sorry about my group," I said.

He laughed. "No need to apologize, my group isn't any better."

I turned around only to find his group staring and giving a thumbs up. "Well, that's subtle."

Max began to unbutton his sleeves and roll them up. "Is it hot in here?" Max revealed his tatted arms. I rolled my eyes at his attempt at seduction.

"Nice tattoos. But, I've seen guys with tattoos...try to seduce me another way."

Max began to laugh. "I'm sorry, I'm just overthinking everything. My friends, dummies that they are, said that if I rolled up my sleeves you would be impressed."

"With?"

"How bad ass I look." His face turned red as the words left his lips. "I'm sorry...that was such a douchey thing to say."

I shrugged. "At least you recognize it and now we can move on." I looked back at Max who was grinning. "So, what brings you out tonight, Max?"

"This is my last night of freedom."

I felt the pit of my stomach sink deeper into my soul. "Listen, I don't want to be some kind of cheap thrill you get the night before your wedding. And just so you know you'd have to be some kind of dick to—"

"No, no...Geez, it's not like that."

"Then what is it like?" I asked.

I began to back away with every intention of saying goodnight to my group and heading home; I had a pint of *Ben & Jerry's* waiting and they never did me wrong.

I felt his hand reach for mine, literally shocking me.

"Ow!" we both jumped a part.

I looked towards the table where my friends were; Marvin was looking over, worried, ready to pounce at the first sign of trouble. At the feel of Max's hand on my shoulder, I turned back around to face him.

"Virginia, I'm not getting married." The sound of him saying my full name sent a thrill down my spine that I didn't want...anymore.

"Oh yeah? So, what is it exactly that you're celebrating?"

Max let out a heavy sigh. "I am taking over the family business," he finally confessed.

I took a moment to let it sink in. "So...there's no soon-to-be wife?"

"No," he quirked his lips.

"Is there a girlfriend?"

"Your interest in my marital status is a good sign," he pointed out.

I felt my shoulders relax a bit as my mind settled down. "Tell me, Max, what is the family business?'

"Can we not talk about it? That's the thing that I'm out here trying to forget."

I nodded. "Noted...then what do we talk about?"

Max passed a hand down his beard. "Well, tomorrow's Thanksgiving, you have plans?"

I didn't want to tell this stranger that my parents decided they rather spend the holiday season in a tropical paradise than with me. It seemed lame that not even my parents could stand to be with their failure of a daughter; I just wanted to be the exciting stranger he met one night.

"That's the thing that I'm out here trying to forget," I countered. His eyes softened, showing me a glimpse of sympathy that I didn't ask for and didn't want. "Wipe that look off your face," I chastised. I added a smile just to soften my irritation.

His sympathy vanished, replaced with a flirty grin. "We both have secrets that we don't want to share so...what will we talk about?"

Two hours later, bar lights were dim, our groups had become one larger group at a table, and I didn't want the night to end. Max and I spent the night laughing, our conversations starting off innocently enough; our childhood holiday memories and we currently veered off into talking about our present-day dating nightmares. Our heads were huddled closer, I couldn't get close enough to him, when the annoyed bartender called out, "Guys the bar closes in five minutes."

"Max?" one of his guys called out.

"Gin?" Marvin saddled up to me and whispered in my ear, "Are you leaving with us?"

I turned to look at Max, Cheeks flushed from spirits and great conversation. "You want to go find another place to talk?" he asked.

I turned back to my friend. "I'm leaving with him."

Marvin took my phone. "I'm sharing your location with us. If I don't hear from you by 10am I'm calling every fucking station and hospital in New York City, you hear me?"

"Yes, mom," I joked. I turned back to Max. "Let's head out."

His face lit up. "Let me pay the tab." Max walked to the bar, giving me a minute to admire his style from afar. One of his friends followed clapping a hand on his back, probably confirming that I'm headed home with him.

2

Rule 10: Use common sense. The easiest solution is often the simplest. Trust your team. Don't over analyze, it will only slow you down.

While Max handled everything at the bar, I snapped around quickly to Marvin. "What does *another place to talk* mean?"

"Really, Ginny?" He rolled his eyes. "It's just code for a place to bang. Is that what you want?"

Is that what I wanted? Every time Max's hand grazed mine, I felt the heat rise in the pit of my belly, awakening urges that I have suppressed for the last two years. The combination of my team pushing me, the old fashions that kept coming, the comfortable conversation made it really easy to make a decision. I felt the warmth spread through my body at the mere thought of having a passionate night with Max. He was sweet, funny, and sexy as hell.

I glanced at Max who was walking back. I felt my lips form a smile all on their own. "I'll take that as a yes." Marvin placed a kiss on her cheek before nodding at Max and following the group outside.

I watched as my friends left me, all winking and smiling. Max's friends left with goodbyes and quick hugs. "Don't let him get into trouble!" One with black hair and features similar to Max yelled as they made their exit. *They must be related.*

I laughed at them, the drinks making my giggles come easily. We followed right behind them, the cold night air freezing my lungs and face as we stood in the middle of the sidewalk.

"Okay, Max, where are we going to go to continue this conversation?" I asked. I wanted to get out of the cold and sweat it out in the sheets. *God, why was I unbearably horny now?*

He rubbed the back of his neck nervously but didn't say anything. "Max? We are going somewhere, right? Your apartment I assume?"

His eyes darted to me. "I wasn't sure you wanted to…I thought if I suggested it that it would—"

I closed my eyes, stood on my tip toes and kissed him on the lips; hoping that it would come off sexy like it did in the movies. "I'd love to," I said.

With hooded eyes, he reached out for me, pressing his lips to mine. In the gust of the winter wind, warmth flooded my veins. I wrapped my arms around his neck, giving him easy access to my tongue. A small moan escaped my lips. Max looped his thumbs through my belt loops of my jeans, rubbing his manhood against my feminine softness.

Our coats made it harder for our bodies to get any closer. I pulled away slightly in frustration. "Where's your apartment?" I asked.

"Just a few blocks down."

"Let's get a move on before we freeze to death," I began walking in the direction he pointed to, Max quickly fell into step beside me.

"Virginia," he began, his breath coming out in small puffs.

"Yes, Maximillian."

"Want to stop and pick up some food on the way to my place?"

"What?" My steps faltered slightly at the unexpected question. After the kiss, I thought that his line of questioning would be on the rather seductive side, a little bit more PG-13 and a little less…McDonalds.

"I'm starved and as much as you love your old fashions, that orange peel isn't very filling."

"I guess you're right," I said.

We walked in pleasant silence taking in all the holiday lights the city eagerly put up only nights before. Max grabbed my hand and pulled me to a brightly lit diner in the middle of the block. "My apartment is on the next street over but let's pick up some burgers and whatever else and take them up."

I nodded and laughed at his excitement. "Do you hold stock in this diner?" I joked.

"No, but maybe someday," he said as he held the door open for me.

The diner was empty, giving us the chance to place our orders in record time. While we waited at the counter, I swiveled my chair to face him. "Besides sex, what else do you want from tonight?" I asked. The old fashions finally hit me and any filter I had just was not going to function now.

I saw his eyes widen just the tiniest bit before he cleared his throat. "I...I don't know if that's what I really want from tonight," I felt his eyes searching my face as embarrassment passed over me. "Is that something you wanted?"

I shrugged. "I honestly don't know what I wanted from tonight, but a complete stranger turning down a night of hot, sweaty, no holds bar sex is exactly what I should have expected."

"I just...I just never taken a girl back to my place."

Dread coursed through my veins. "Oh my god, are you...are you a virgin?" I whispered.

"No! I'm not a...what would make you think that?!" he laughed.

Embarrassment swept through my face and chest. "I don't know, just the way you were talking...so you're not a virgin, you just never had a one-night stand?"

He nodded.

"Well, you can relax because we are in the same boat. I don't usually go home with guys I don't know; I'm usually home with a bottle of wine watching Netflix," I admitted.

We both got lost in our thoughts, the sound of generic pop music played. I took a deep breath to say some witty line that would break whatever tension we had going on. But before I could get a word out, the waitress brought our to-go bags.

I swallowed my comment down and smiled instead.

Max grabbed my hand and pulled me into the crook of his arm. We exited the diner, into the bitter cold. Sometimes I thought about moving some place warm but New York City was...magical. Like, if I lived in Florida, the only guys who would try to take me home were probably on spring break and that was a major no...I was too old for frat boy herpes.

Max and I walked together in silence until we got to the front of a beautiful building with iron clad doors that a doorman opened for us. "Good evening, Mr. Thomas."

"Good evening, Hector," Max answered back.

I was impressed with the massive lobby that was ordained with a giant chandelier, lounging chairs and a beautiful floral painting. *This shit must be expensive. He's probably paying a buttload for a tiny room in this building.* I caught his eye through the reflection of the gold elevator doors. "Good evening, Mr. Thomas? Are you...in the mob?" I widened my eyes in amusement.

He smiled. A mischievous twinkle shone in his eye. "No."

I raised an eyebrow. "Is your family business legal?"

"For the most part," he answered.

"What does that mean?!" my voice shot up an octave.

"I'm joking, my family's business is definitely legal," he chuckled.

We got in the elevator, and he hit number ten. The ride up gave me a chance to look at him. He was beautiful. His auburn beard made him look like a mountain man and I didn't know I was into that until my body reacted to him.

Max cleared his throat. "Like what you see?"

I should be embarrassed that he caught me looking but I smiled and said, "Absolutely."

My flirtation was short lived. The elevator chimed open and my nerves were getting the best of me as we walked the long-carpeted hall down to his apartment. "You got quiet all of a sudden," he pointed out.

"Just thinking."

"About?" Max pulled out a keycard that granted us access into his apartment. When he flipped the switched, it was unbelievable. His apartment was an open concept with a stainless-steel island separating the gourmet kitchen from the large bachelor pad living room, that was equipped with a seventy-inch TV screen and leather couches. Floor to ceiling windows that showcased NYC in all its glory. As Max dropped his keys and the food on the counter, I walked to the window, taking in the view. "What are you thinking now?" his voice penetrated my thoughts.

"I'm thinking about the jump down if I need to escape, we're on the tenth floor!" I joked.

His burst of laughter sent a thrill through me. "I'm trying to figure out what you do for a living," I admitted.

He casually threw his coat on the couch. "And?"

I mimicked him and threw my coat. "And I'm thinking that it doesn't really matter because I just like talking to you and if your job is something you don't want to talk about...who am I to bring it up? You won't see me after tonight."

His lips quirked up. "Okay...are you hungry?" He brought the bags to the living room. "Would you like wine?"

"With burgers? Yes, please."

Max laughed and dropped the bags on the oak coffee table. We unwrapped everything and fell silent once again as we savored the burgers. I took that moment to examine Max, this time discreetly. His ginger beard was trimmed to perfection; not a hair out of place...which told me that he cared about his looks. His tattoos looked as if it took up all his arms and fingers...interesting. Rebel, maybe? Or just a phony that thinks that tattoos are trendy? *Gross, I hope not. That would suck.*

"Max."

"Virginia," he said mimicking my serious tone.

"Truth or dare?"

"Seriously?" he smirked.

It was the only way to get to know someone but not make it a big deal. And even though I wanted to enter my 'ho phase tonight and use him like a meat puppet, I just wanted to know more about him. Old habits die hard.

I kicked off my boots and smiled sweetly. "Yeah, seriously. What part of me don't you think is serious?"

His eyes slowly drifted up and down my body, leaving little prickles on my skin without actually touching me.

"Truth," he finally answered.

That was easy. "Scared, huh?" I giggled.

"Not scared, just curious about what you want to know," he answered smugly. His amusement brought out the laugh lines around his eyes and I noticed a faint scar by his eyebrow.

"What made you come up to me?" I asked, doing my best not to be distracted.

"Truthfully?"

"Duh, I asked for the truth," I giggled again. I was not a giggler! *Who am I right now?* I took another sip of my wine, to wash down the giggles.

"My friends. They wanted me to loosen up a bit."

"Oh, you always have a stick up your ass?" I laughed.

He kicked off his shoes and stretched out on the couch. "That's a nicer way to put it." His embarrassment spread through his face and blended a tiny bit with his beard, but Max smiled wide despite it.

"Would your friends describe you like that?" I asked. I reclined against the love seat taking him in. No longer was I concealing my interest. *He was really comfortable with himself; I found that kind of confidence sexy.*

He shook his head. "Na uh, Virginia. You only get one question. It's my turn now. Truth or dare?"

I rolled my eyes. "Truth."

"Truth? I didn't think you were a chicken."

I threw a fry at him. "I'm not! But when you wimp out and say truth...I'm not gonna reward you with allowing you to give me a dare, that's not how it works, buddy."

Max laughed. "Okay, fine. Truth. Ginny?"

"Yes, Max?" I answered with a sweet smile.

"Did you come up to the bar to talk to me?"

I rolled my eyes. He knew, I knew, we all knew why I went up to bar. "Yes, Max. I offered myself as tribune." I clapped my hands together. "Okay, now my turn!"

"Well, I'm going to say truth," he declared with a cock of his eyebrow.

"Boring, but whatever," I scoffed. "What's so bad about your day job?"

As Max chewed on his burger, he took the time to give a thoughtful answer. I regretted this game we were playing. I just wanted to lick the ketchup from his lips. "I...it's not my passion, it's not something I saw myself doing."

"What do you want to do?" Max tilted his head at me. "I know I get one question but give me this one, next round you get a twofer," I huffed.

He rolled his eyes, mimicking me from earlier. "Fine. I saw myself running a business just not my family's."

"What's the difference?"

"It'll be all mine. I want to build something from scratch and know that I accomplished something without my family's money."

"That makes sense. Is there an idea cooking?"

His slow smile told me yes. Max sat up straighter as he began to explain. "I've invested in a handful of small businesses that needed some financial assistance. Right now, we just opened a small bakery. I think it'll be profitable. The guy running it is a genius pastry chef who just needed a tiny bit of help. He was born and raised in the Bronx, trained in the best culinary schools only to—" Max ran a hand through his hair. "I'm so sorry, I feel like I'm boring you."

"No," I giggled. "I like when people talk passionately about their...passions." I laughed. "Sorry, my brain is functioning slower than usual," I said, biting my lip to keep from laughing at myself. The drinks were catching up with me.

"What about you, Gin? Are you happy at your job?"

I shrugged. "I'm not sad. I had some trouble a couple of years ago that made me want to quit, but I needed steady income just in case I really wanted to jump and pursue my passion."

"Which is?"

"I used to design."

His eyebrows shot up. "You're a designer? What do you design?"

I began to shake my head so fast that I wouldn't have been surprised if it snapped off. "No, no. I wanted to be. I tried to be. I used to design clothing. Fashion. A lifestyle." I gestured with a flourish of my hand.

"What was your aesthetic?"

I raised an eyebrow in surprise. "Aesthetic? That's a great toilet paper word." I spoke over his laughter. "Well, I would say that it was glamour punk."

"Glamour punk?"

"Yeah. Faux fur, plaid, graphic tee's, chunky jewelry, lots of leather...bright red lipstick. But then I would design these beautiful colorful pieces that you could throw a leather moto jacket over and make it cool. I just wanted women to feel badass in something I designed."

"That sounds amazing." I looked at him and sure enough...he looked sincere. "Was it profitable?"

"For a little bit. When I made the time to post on social, when I made the effort to reach out to the right people...it was good for a little bit," I smiled faintly at the memory; it all seemed like a lifetime ago instead of two years.

"What happened?" he asked. I didn't know how much information I should divulge to this stranger.

"I was with someone who I built up in my head and made him strong enough to dim me," I answered, confident that after tonight I wouldn't see Max again. The memory of it all forced me to grow quiet. Every time I thought of it, I grew angry. Angry at myself for allowing someone to hold that much power.

"If you don't want to talk about it..." Max cleared his throat.

I looked up a Max. I ran a hand down my blouse for no apparent reason but to keep my mind busy. "I really don't."

"You could start again." He tried to broach the subject again. I nodded silently; Max took the hint and the opportunity to lighten the mood. "Truth or dare?" he asked.

I laughed in relief at the sudden change. "Dare."

"I dare you to...start designing again."

"Maaax..." I whined.

"What?"

"It's not that easy." I began to pick imaginary lint off my pants in an effort to not look him directly in the eyes. This conversation with

Max was the same one that I've had with myself many times in the past couple of years. I wasn't ready to hear it from someone else.

"I know it's not but don't let some dick tell you you can't."

I couldn't help but smile at his enthusiastic pep talk. "I still design, I just keep it to myself." I shrugged and peeked at him from under my lashes. "How do you know I'm even good at it?"

"I just have a good feeling about you."

Max's eyes bore into me with so much intensity, I had to look away. *Am I blushing?* "You don't like compliments?" His head tilted with curiosity.

I shrugged. "Something tells me I could get used to it." I winked at him to let him know I was okay.

He smiled softly. "Okay, Ginny, but for real, truth or dare?"

"Dare," I sighed.

"I dare you to kiss me."

Heat rose in my body from his demand. "I thought you didn't bring me home for a one-night stand," I said.

"Doesn't mean I don't want to kiss you."

I got up from my place by the love seat, walking over to him. I was thinking too much about my walk; if it was sexy or if I looked like a deranged hooker. All of a sudden, anxiety faltered my steps. *Oh no, he's going to think I'm drunk.* Max began to get up, I placed my hand on his chest, stopping him. "I was trying to be smooth," I admitted with a small laugh. "Lay back down," I whispered before I lost my nerve.

Max studied me; when he was satisfied with what he saw, he obeyed my command. I took notice of the rise and fall of his chest; a chest that felt like steel under my touch. I swallowed the butter-flies that felt as if they were flying all over my belly and up my throat. I dared myself to straddle him where he laid. Max's big hands automatically found my waist. I lowered myself, so that we were chest to chest, nose to nose. My lips finally found his; his soft beard lightly rubbed against my face, but I didn't mind. My tongue licked his lips, urging them open. When he opened, allowing me access, I couldn't hold back a soft moan. My hips had a mind of their own as they rubbed against his manhood. Max's hands followed the path of my spine, cupping my ass, grinding himself into my softness.

As much as I didn't want to, I pulled away from his lips. "Max, truth or dare?"

"Dare," he whispered. His eyes were hooded with desire.

I was too nervous to articulate what I wanted, too scared of the rejection but determined to give into my desires. "I dare you to take me to bed," I whispered back.

Without another word, he rubbed our bodies together, my eyes fell closed as the goosebumps passed all over my body. He kept rubbing and pressing his hardness against me like we were two high schoolers. "Is this what you want, Virginia?"

I opened my eyes as best as I could. "Yes."

Max stood up, pulling me up along with him. His hand entangled mine and he led me down a small hallway to his bedroom.

In the dark, the city lights coming through the floor to ceiling window illuminated the room. There was only a second before we found each other's lips, holding nothing back. Max lifted me up, setting me down on the bureau and ripped my shirt off, revealing the lace bra that was underneath. He bent down and tasted my nipples through the thin fabric. "Max, that feels so good," I sighed.

My fingers hungrily unbuttoned his shirt, dragging my fingernails down his beautifully tattooed chest and happy trail that led to the bulge that was about to burst out if I didn't set it free. "You want me to fuck you on the bed or should I just fuck you right here?" he groaned into my belly has he kissed his way down.

I couldn't find my voice; thoughts...scrambled. "Just...oh my God, Max!"

He found his way back to my lips again. He picked me up,

throwing me on the bed, wasting no time ripping my jeans off. He stood back to observe me as I laid back with my legs open, nothing but a tiny bit of lace covering me. "Play with your pussy," he commanded.

Under normal circumstances I would probably look like a deer in headlights. But in the dark, I felt no shame. My hand trailed over my breasts as I pinched my nipple with one hand while the other traveled down my belly, pulling my own panties to the side. I looked up at Max for encouragement. Max nodded, looking dangerous against the city lights as I began to finger myself. I was nervous; there was only a slight hesitation before I passed a finger over my swollen clit.

I just...I couldn't believe what I was doing in front of a complete stranger! Never in my wildest dreams did I think this would happen. I still got uncomfortable when I go to the movie theaters and a sex scene comes up. It's like watching an unexpected sex scene with your parents...you just want out.

But right now? Between the cocktails, the dark room, this gorgeous man that I would never see again, I decided to let myself have fun. There was no shyness, no overthinking. Okay...maybe a little overthinking. Did my body look good in this lighting? What was I thinking?! I was completely naked! Who wouldn't find me attractive? *Oh, my hands knew how to get the job done.* I smiled to myself; He wanted a show, I'll give him a show. I threw my head back, arched my back knowing full well that my breasts looked good from this angle and let the pleasure take over.

I heard Max's zipper coming down against the quiet of the room. I opened my eyes to look over. Max began to take his trousers off; his boxers were next, finally freeing his massive hard on. I felt myself buckle under the pleasure of seeing him as my fingers brought me closer to the edge. "Come, Ginny," Max encouraged as he took his dick into his hand, stroking it to my rhythm.

I cried out. "Max, please," I pleaded.

A naughty thought popped into my head. I decided that if I'm going to be this sex goddess, I should take it all the way and be the thing he thinks about when he's an old man remembering the best sex he ever had. I crawled to the end of the bed to where he was. "What are you doing, baby girl?" his voice was heavy.

"I want to taste you," I whispered. A second later, I put both hands around his cock bringing it to my mouth. I could see the amazement in Max's eyes as my cherry red lips wrapped around his dick, sucking him. There was no preliminary licking or toying with him; I went straight for the gold. His hands fisted in my long hair as he drove himself deeper into my mouth. "God, that fucking mouth, Ginny," he groaned.

The sucking and licking were getting to be too much for him. Beads of sweat were falling as he tried to keep himself from coming in my mouth.

Max stopped fucking my mouth to flip me around. "I want to fuck you from behind."

"Yes," I chanted as I wiggled my ass for him. He slapped it, before gripping my hips and finally pushing into my wet pussy. Max took a moment to steady himself, biting the small of my back.

I couldn't wait, I moved against him. "Oh, you want it? You want it that bad, baby girl?"

"Max, Fuck me hard."

"Tell me what you want. I want to hear it."

Max dove a hand into my hair balling it up as he pulled my head back, his dick sinking deeper into the wetness. "I want you to feel me for a week."

"Harder!" I cried out.

Max did as he was told. Pumping faster and harder into me. He grabbed both my arms, pulling me back as deep as he could get. "I want to feel you come all over me."

"Yes! Yes!" I cried out as I pushed myself back onto him, doing my best of get my fill. Max snaked one hand around my neck while the other one traveled down to my pussy, rubbing my clit as his dick went in and out of me. That's the moment that I really lost it. My eyes closed as I cried out with the sensations of my climax raining over me. Max laughed against my ear, pumping faster as he gave himself permission to come. My pussy was still tight as he gave one final thrust, dropping his head on my shoulder and let out a loud grunt as his body went limp against mine.

I couldn't hold myself up; I fell against the soft mattress in pure satisfaction. Max fell next to me, letting out a contented sigh.

Max blindly reached for me, pulling me close. He kissed my sweaty temple. "Are you okay?"

"I'm more than okay," I purred.

"Are you falling asleep?" he whispered.

I didn't have the strength to answer him. The city lights were a blurry set of stars, twinkling around us.

3

Rule 4: Don't lose your cool!

I groaned as I stretched my arms and legs like a lazy feline against the bright sunlight that I felt across my body. With a sigh, I rolled over finally opening my eyes. The city shone bright against the cold winter day. My body felt sore, a slow smile crept to my face until I heard the traffic noise down below; my senses slowly came back as I heard the sound of a shower turning on. My eyes widened at the realization that I wasn't in my bed!

Shit!

Max!

The flashback of last night popped into my head; hot, sweaty, rough sex that happened multiple times. My heart began to race at an uncontrollable rate. It's not like I regretted what happened, I had an amazing time with Max.

The best sex of my life!

But it was supposed to be a one-night stand. Wasn't I supposed to be out of his apartment by now? I fell asleep! I'm the worst one-night stand ever. I was supposed to bang him and vanish in the dark of the night into an uber.

I jumped out of the bed, looking around for my clothes. I scanned the room, finding my jeans on top of his dresser. No time to find my underwear; God knows where those things were thrown.

I zipped my jeans, jumped across the bed to grab my bra that was sitting peacefully on the windowsill. I caught my reflection in the mirror. My long dark hair was all over the place, my chest had burn marks from his beard and my face was flushed with the memory of what transpired in this room a record breaking three times. "You whore," I whispered to myself. I shook my head, snapping out of my trance, I secured my bra and began to button my shirt. I quickly wiped my lips on the blanket, I wasn't about to walk around outside looking like the Joker, when I heard the water shut off. I ran into the living room, stubbing my toe on the coffee table. "Fu...." I swallowed the curse words along with the throbbing pain. I tried to not think of the pain, stuffing my feet into my boots. I'm missing something...my coat!

I ran to the couch, where I lunged over it to grab my coat. I wasted no time putting it on. Out of breath, I made a mental note to join a gym after New Years as I ran to the door.

"Making a getaway?" Max's voice came cheerfully from behind me, causing me to jump out of skin. I turned slowly, dusting off the catalogue of excuses that I threw away in the trash bins in my mind.

"Were you trying to escape?" Max asked with a tilt of his head. Water still glistened on his tattooed chest, I thought I was going to melt on the spot.

I let out a sigh to steady my pounding heart. I focused on his nose as to not focus on the flimsy knot of the towel. "You caught me," I put my hands up in mock surrender.

"Why?"

"I just wanted to be a perfect one-night stand for you. No hassle, no fuss."

Max sauntered closer. "You know what would be perfect?"

"What?" My voice came out in a squeak as I kept trying to focus on anything else but this fine ass man.

"If we went to the diner down the street and loaded up on pumpkin pancakes." His hand reached out to caress my hair. "There's a toothbrush and a towel in the bathroom, so you can clean up." Max pressed a light kiss against my lips.

I hung my coat back up and walked to the bathroom. "I'll be a minute," I mumbled as I passed him. I looked over my shoulder to see him checking me out.

Once in the bathroom, I rested against the closed bathroom door, gave a silent scream.

What is happening?

* * * * * *

We sat awkwardly across from each other in a booth; I toyed around with my butter knife while I felt Max observing me.

"Are you okay?" he asked while glancing at my butter knife. "You're not going to go psycho in this diner, are you?

I offered a smile. "Funny." I gestured towards the waitress. "I would never...too many witnesses. But to answer your question, yeah, I'm just a little nervous." I looked over my shoulder at the waitress behind the counter. "I think she knows that I'm wearing the same clothes from last night," I whispered.

He smirked. "I doubt it...I think we had a different waitress last night." Max assured me.

At that moment, the waitress walked over. "What can I get you...oh, hey, you guys, back again? Must've worked up an appetite, eh, honey." She winked at me. I felt my cheeks flush. I narrowed my eyes in Max's direction.

"Um, we're gonna need a minute," he said.

Thankfully the waitress nodded and walked away. Max cleared his throat. "So, you're nervous? After what we did?"

My eyes darted around the empty diner, mortified that someone heard. "That's exactly why I'm nervous. I honestly thought the best thing to do was leave without another glance, and we could be a fond memory you look back on when your grandchildren ask if you've ever had a one-night stand with a raven-haired goddess."

His lips quirked on one side. "Are grandkids really that nosey or is this a hypothetical?"

I shrugged. "Who knows? The point is..." I sat back against the vinyl seats of the booth to think about it. "...what was the point I was trying to make? Oh, yeah! That there's still a chance to keep this a one-night stand, I can just get up and leave. We didn't even order yet."

The waitress came over again. "You guys ready?"

I looked over to Max. He smirked. "Order," he said.

"So, this guy says the pumpkin pancakes is to die for, is he right?" I asked looking up at her.

"Oh! They really are." The waitress, who was old enough to be my mother, looked Max over. "Smart and handsome...you're lucky."

"He's okay, I guess," I joked. The waitress' head snapped so fast to look at me I thought her head would roll off. "I'll have the pumpkin pancakes, please." She continued to stare at me like I had two heads. "Ma'am," I added hoping that she would forgive me.

"I'll have the same. And bring orders of bacon and scrambled eggs please," Max added, saving me from the waitress' scrutiny.

"Okay, handsome, I'll only be a minute." She winked at Max and sauntered off.

"Do you guys wanna be alone?" I asked.

"Why? Jealous?"

"Of her?" I gave an unladylike snort. "Maybe, just a little."

Max smirked. This was nice, I thought to myself. The banter was good; back and forth like a volleyball. "So, you really were going to leave." Max's statement made me remember that I wasn't much of a volleyball player; now I gotta deal with reality.

"Yeah, I thought that's what you wanted. A proper one-night stand. Who am I to deprive you of that experience?"

"What I wanted was to spend the good part of Thanksgiving enjoying the company of an amazing woman that I just met." He reached for my hand over the bottle of ketchup. "But, you were bolting...didn't you like what we did?"

"Do you always ask women for feedback after a wonderfully playful, erotic outer body experience?"

He sat up straighter, his chest puffed with pride. "So, you did like it?" he asked again.

"Well, Max, if you didn't understand what I was trying to say then I'm glad this is ending right here." I threw a tissue at him. "Of course, I loved it!" I laughed.

The waitress came by with our order. "Here you guys go, if you need anything else just holler for me."

We let the silence take over. Images of last night flickered through my mind as I caught glimpses of Max innocently licking the syrup from his lips. The world went into slow motion as he ate the pancakes and licked his fork. Who would of thought that breakfast, Americas wholesome meal of the day, could be so erotic? A flash of Max licking between my breast before devouring them ran through my head.

"Gin? You, okay?" Max asked.

I shook my head lightly. "Sorry, I just hallucinated, what were you saying?"

"I was saying that later today, I have to be with my family, things are...a little unstable at the moment."

His confession made me relax a little bit. "What family isn't? My family isn't even in the country right now. They decided to spend the holiday in a tropical paradise."

"Really? Where are you going after this?" he asked around a mouthful of pumpkin pancakes.

I tried to not think about my parents. Ever since I hit puberty, we haven't seen eye to eye on a lot of things; clothing; boys; makeup; major life decisions. "Home. To sleep and relax before I have to head to work at the butt crack of dawn," I whined.

"Why so early?"

"Because my employers are a bunch of assholes who want to cash in on a family holiday by depriving those of us who have families to miss out on the screaming matches that take place during these said holidays."

"Take a breath," he joked. "God, you really hate where you work."

"Hate is such a strong word."

"I'm not going to ask where you work even though I earned that privilege multiple times." Max cocked an eyebrow at me, causing me to smile like a crazy person. "But if you don't like it, why don't you just quit?"

I shrugged. "I did like it, in the beginning," I confessed. I finally bit into the pancakes and melted on the spot. "Oh my god, these are delicious."

"I know, I order these every Sunday but since this is a special occasion I thought why not," he laughed.

"Good choice."

"Why don't you like your job now?" he asked. My diversion didn't work as good as I hoped.

I gave a heavy, dramatic sigh. "I love my team; I see them more than my blood relatives...it's just sometimes...you want more and...I spend a lot of time at work. Time that I could devote back to designing...if I wanted to."

He nodded. "I get it."

"Do you? Because the mob and retail are quite similar but just a tad different. You were born into the business; I chose this life."

"Yeah, but the thing about the mob is once you're in, it seems like there's no way out."

I narrowed my eyes in his direction. "On second thought, maybe I do work in the mob." Max was amazing; he was more than amazing. He was sexy, smart, funny and him laughing at my dumb jokes and jabs just added to his appeal. Under normal circumstances he would warrant a second date. But this is real life; the reality of it was that we didn't have a first date and I slept with him, ruining my chances of us ever having a real relationship. Granted, it was amazing, mind-blowing, universe-altering sex that you only read about in dirty romance novels that have billionaires getting off on dominating some meek girl.

Scratch that; the sex was beyond the stuff you read about in those novels.

And I ruined my chances.

Max settled his fork on this nearly empty plate, drummed his hands against the table in the most endearing way and cleared his throat.

"Yes? What are your trying to tell me? You don't want to see me after this? Surprise, I already knew that. That's the textbook definition of a—"

"I want to see you again," he spat out.

"Why?"

His eyes darted upwards as he tried to find the words. "I don't understand your question," he said with a slight brow raise.

My heart fluttered at the thought of seeing him again. But this was new territory. A terrain I never travelled before. A one-night stand turning into a date? That was just stuff dreams were made of. "I'm sorry, I was nervous. I didn't mean to ask why. I mean...are you sure?" I asked. My eyes couldn't quite meet his and I had focused on his nose.

"Am I sure? Yes! You're amazing!"

My eyes widened in surprise at his exclamation. "Amazing? That's great, keep going. What else?" I teased.

"You're funny, smart, charming."

"What about beautiful? Tell me I'm beautiful."

"Stunning. Gorgeous," Max laughed so hard the corners of his eyes crinkled a tiny bit.

"Damn, Max, keep going and I just might to have to cover you in syrup next," I winked.

"I don't know if it was just me, but I thought we had an amazing night. We talked, we laughed and we...I mean I don't have to spell it out for you, you were there," he wiggled his eyebrows which made me burst out with laughter. The few people in the restaurant turned to look at us.

I felt myself blush. "Yes, okay...hand me your phone." I reached out my hand.

I added my name and number to his phone and dialed. My phone vibrated and I held it up to show him. "This is you?" I asked.

He nodded and held his hand out. "Give me yours."

I handed him my phone with no questions asked. When he handed it back, I raised an eyebrow in his direction. "Big daddy? My, aren't we full of ourselves," I teased.

Max lowered his voice. "Should I not be?"

My phone began to buzz. "Did you butt dial me? Just couldn't wait, could you?" I teased.

"Nope, not me. Must be one of your other suitors" he said as he continued eating his breakfast.

"Oh, I give you my phone number and you upgraded yourself to suitor? Interesting."

"Just answer your phone." he gestured at the phone, happy and content at this moment.

I looked at the screen. "It's Marvin, can you give me a minute while I talk to him?"

"You can take the call here, I don't mind," he said.

"I do mind, he'll say something inappropriate, and I will get embarrassed even though you didn't hear what he said," I explained.

"Fine," he laughed and waved a hand. "But hurry back."

I walked away from the booth and picked up the call. "I'm fine and safe, Marvin," I said in lieu of a greeting.

"I knew you would be. How was Mr. handsome from last night?"

"Um..." I looked behind me to see Max scrolling through his phone as he waited for me to finish with my call.

"You left him in front of the restaurant and went home alone, didn't you?"

"I'm actually still with him," I whispered.

"Come again."

"We went back to his place and then we went to get breakfast together."

Marvin fell silent and I glanced at my phone to make sure he hadn't hung up. "Hello?"

"Ginny, what happened in between all that?"

"Mind your business," I spat out. I didn't want to over analyze what happened last night because I would talk myself out of the present and the present was going really well.

"Are you extending your 'one-night stand' time into a whole entire morning? Leave the man alone and head home, you're bordering on the line of stalker." Marvin's tone was a bit too aggressive for my liking.

"He said he wanted to see me again," I added to prove that I wasn't some psycho you'd hear about on one of those true crime shows.

"Probably for a booty call." Skepticism dripped from is voice.

"Marvin! Shut up for a second. Do not get in my head and ruin this for me. He's sweet, he's kind, he's funny and I had an amazing time."

"And he's got you rhyming?"

"Shut up!" I scolded through clenched teeth. I just wanted someone to be happy for me because no matter how positive I tried to be it always seemed like the universe really didn't want me to win. I just needed a win. Max made me feel like I just won the lottery. "I want to see him again too," I confessed. The dating seen was just like finding random socks in the laundry, you're like WTF until you find the right match and jump for joy because your life's a mess but at least your socks match.

I heard a sigh come through. "Ginny, why couldn't you just have a normal one-night stand like the other single people in New York City? How do you come out of it with a boyfriend?"

"Do you want me to give you details?" I quipped.

"No, you don't have to get nasty. I'm just looking out for you; I don't want you to get hurt like—"

"I know!" I shrieked. I looked behind me to see Max staring at me with curiosity. I waved at him with a phony smile to assure him all was well and that I wasn't as crazy as my outburst made me seem.

"For someone who had sex last night, you're really wound up," Marvin said.

"Marvin, I'm okay, I'm all good. Was there anything else?"

"Happy Thanksgiving. I love you."

"Happy Thanksgiving. Love you too. I'll call you later." I hung up before he could answer. I power walked back to the table, hoping to get back to the easy conversation.

"Was everything okay?" Max asked as I took my seat at the booth.

"Just peachy."

"Your conversation looked kind of animated," he pointed out.

I smiled, shrugging off the insane friendship that Marvin and I shared. "Just a friend making sure I didn't go home with a serial killer, that's all." I narrowed my eyes in his direction. "I told him that you had no intention to take me and hide my body...I was right?"

"Oh, yeah, sure...let me just call off the van I had picking us up."

I laughed. "Okay, I like that you're not as straight as you seem."

"Excuse me? After last night you question my sexuality?"

"No...definitely not. But if you're bi...that's your business..." I stammered. I averted my eyes. *Why did I have to talk out my ass? Wait, was he laughing at me?* "I hate you." Max's laughter grew louder. "I just meant that I like that you get my oddness, it's nice."

"I like that you're odd."

"Thank you?" I picked up my fork to continue eating but something that Marvin said was taking up space in my mind; I had to get it off my chest. "Max, I know we just met, but...do you want to see me again because you like my company or because you're looking for a booty call?" My question came out in a rush. I met his gaze head on.

Max let out a small laugh.

"You can be honest," I added so he didn't lie to spare my feelings. My eyes narrowed in his direction. "Are you laughing at me?" I couldn't control the pounding in my chest as color rose to my cheeks. *This is embarrassing; he's got a penis so of course he just wants a booty call. I gave him the milk for free, why would he want the cow? No, that doesn't sound right...*my eyes darted back to him, ready for an explanation. If he wasn't careful, I was ready to throw my pancake at him.

Max's eyes widened and his laughter vanished almost instantly as he realized that I was being serious. He laid his hand on top of mine. "I'm not laughing at you," he whispered.

"Then what are you laughing at?" I whispered back.

"Why are you whispering?"

"Because you are!" My voice rose, drawing attention from the one other customer in the diner.

"I was giggling because I thought the way you asked your question was cute...endearing."

"Men giggle?"

"Only those who are comfortable in their masculinity," he wiggled his eyebrows, breaking the tension that arose out of nowhere. "I don't know what just happened, but I want to see you for you. I thought we had a good time," he said. Max sat his fork down as he smoothed out a wrinkled napkin. "Did...you only want a booty call?" His pointed look gave me no indication of what kind of answer he was looking for.

"Honestly?"

"Always."

I slid my hand out of his hold, covering my face. "I don't know what I want. I just know that I had a good time with you, and I wouldn't mind seeing you again," I admitted.

"Good." His smile reached his mocha eyes.

The subject was settled for the moment and before we knew it, time flew by as we enjoyed the rest of our holiday breakfast. It was peaceful, fun, and easy; the flirting was exceptional. If we were in a romantic comedy, this would be the part of the movie that everyone swoons over. The easy before the drama. After Max paid the bill, we were outside, saying our goodbyes. He leaned in, pressing a kiss on my lips. I moaned against him, not caring that we were in the middle of the street holding up foot traffic.

This was New York City, even if they were walking, people would still find some reason to be upset. His lips pressed harder; I savored the taste of syrup that lingered on his lips.

I reluctantly pulled back, casting glances all around. "Max, we can't do this here in broad daylight."

"Come back to my place," he said, still holding on to me.

It was tempting, but I knew that this wasn't reality. "I would love to but I gotta get back to my life...you got family to see."

He kissed me one more time before letting go. "Meet me Friday."

I laughed at his urgency. "I work Friday. In retail we call it black Friday." His disappointment was almost laughable, but I didn't want to break his heart even more. "How about I meet you after work around six? Give me some time to work, get home, shower and ready to see you."

Max kissed me one more time. "Sounds great. Let me get you an Uber." I gave him my address to punch in. We waited in front of Max's building despite the cold temperature and gusts of wind. Our linked hands held tight; both dreading the arrival of my ride. When it finally came, we both rushed to say our goodbyes.

"Thank you for an amazing night and morning," I giggled.

"Ginny, I—" Max smiled when he finally heard what I said. "It was my pleasure," he whispered.

We met halfway; Max leaned down while I stood on my tippy toes to give him a kiss that should be illegal during this time of day.

"See you tomorrow," I said one more time before the door shut behind me and I headed back to real life.

4

Rule 10: Believe in your team, through belief anything's possible. The company loves to challenge you from day one; When the team develops, the company as a whole develops.

I sunk into the leather seats of the SUV, not really sure what just went on in the last ten hours. I went through the events in my head; I had a shitty day at work, met my friends for drinks, went home with a stranger, had amazing sex, my body soreness was a great reminder of that. I wish that the morning lasted longer, but it was a holiday and normal people visited family and friends. I, on the other hand, was going home to nap and try to forget the familial drama that I've been running away from since I turned eighteen. Not to mention forgetting about the great backstab of 2019, where I found out my boyfriend of two years was married. I found out I was the other woman on Thanksgiving Day when I surprised him at his apartment...it was his wife who opened the door.

What made that situation even worse was that we all worked together and...let's just say it wasn't my shining moment.

The Uber pulled to a stop in front of my building, bringing me out of the vicious memory. I sighed as I began to climb the stairs to the fifth floor; huffing and puffing, pausing on the third floor to catch my breath.

Apartment 3C creaked open. I cringed as the wrinkled face of Mrs. Pierce peeked out at me. "Hello," I waved at her.

"Don't wave at me," she spat out. Mrs. Pierce has never welcomed me in this building with open arms. I always tried to be nice and greet her but there was always something about me that ticked her off. If it wasn't my outfit, it was my make-up or my shoes or the people who came to visit me.

Usually, I entertained her hostility with a quick joke or a small jab at her floral nightgowns, but as I entered the building into my reality where sometimes the hot water goes out and the super only fixes things when you call 311, I couldn't keep my sour mood from coming out. "If you don't want to say hi then why'd you open the door?"

"I can't with the attitude of this generation," she muttered.

"You're commenting on my attitude? You're the one who opened the door to scold me for no reason," I pointed out.

"Women who go out all night and return in the morning with the same outfit she left with are called whores," Mrs. Pierce was in a foul mood.

"Aww...that's nice...well, gotta go!" I yelled out.

"Go! Continue ruining your life!" she yelled behind me before slamming the door.

I continued my journey to the fifth floor. Without stopping I yelled in my sweetest voice. "Happy Thanksgiving, Mrs. Pierce!" I yelled from my floor.

I walked into my quiet apartment. Just standing there, in the emptiness. After the chaos of the bar, the humming of the city streets, this was the first time in a long time my apartment felt lonely. This was one of the times that I wish I had a sibling or a close cousin...dare I say, I wish my parents were around?

I peeled off my coat and let it fall to the floor, kicked off my boots on my way to the couch, throwing myself in a sexually exhausted heap as if I were Cleopatra. All I needed was a bowl of grapes or something. I shook my head to shake out the image of Max feeding a naked me grapes. My mind was a funny thing; it replayed everything, especially the sexy stuff in slow motion.

But what was getting in the way of me enjoying my fantasy was the fact that I was spending this holiday alone.

I sighed.

I picked up the phone to call my parents. The phone rang a billion times before going to voicemail. I sighed; I don't know why I got my hopes up. "Hey...guys—I mean mom and dad...just thinking of you and just wanted to wish you a Happy Thanksgiving. Enjoy the beach, the sun, the tequila or whatever your heart's desire. Talk to you guys soon," I finished. I felt the lump in my throat and tried to clear it away. The lump was still there, and I felt the sting of tears before they fell.

I curled up in a ball, in the comfort of my apartment, and let go of the tears that I held back since yesterday morning; tears I thought I would cry after work yesterday. Tears that I held back because my friends distracted me; tears that I cried every Thanksgiving just like clockwork. It was just me pitying myself. I pride myself in being Ms. Optimistic, but sometimes I just needed to let it out.

Afternoon turned to night; I took a bath to calm my nerves, ordered enough Chinese food for an army and settled on the couch accompanied with a glass of wine to watch a cheesy love story to get my mind out of the holidays.

I glanced at the clock on my bookshelf, although the darkness came earlier, the clocked showed that it was only seven. Sighing, I pressed play on *Pride & Prejudice* and filled my wine glass again. I can easily lose myself in the love struggles of Elizabeth and Mr. Darcy.

The soft buzz of my phone forced me to stretch to the coffee table. *Big Daddy* appeared on the screen. My heart began to race, the phone fumbled out of my shaking hands. "Hello?" I answered, completely out of breath as I struggled to get out of my blanket cocoon.

"Am I interrupting something?" I could hear a hint of laughter in Max's voice.

"No, why would you ask that?"

"You sound like you were running."

"Just from the voices," I joked.

"Excuse me?"

"Nothing, what's up, Max?" I sat up straight, waiting for his reply. Eager to hear that last night's enjoyments wasn't one-sided.

"Um...I'm downstairs."

"What?!" I jumped up from my spot on the couch. I knocked over my wine glass. "Shit!"

"Are you okay?"

"Uh, yeah, how do you know where I live?"

Max cleared his throat; I smiled at his nervousness. I found it endearing and sexy. "I ordered you an Uber earlier today...I hope this was okay...what am I saying? I know it's not okay, this is borderline stalkerish," he muttered to himself. I did my best to suppress a giggle.

"Are you really in front of my building?" I asked. I walked over to the window, looking down as he nervously ran a hand through his slicked back hair, disheveling it as he did.

"Yes, I'm sorry. I'll go home now; I don't know what I was thinking." I witnessed his indecisiveness as he turned to leave and immediately turned to come back to the building.

"I'll put you out of your misery," I laughed. "I'll be right down." I continued to laugh as I witnessed the fist pump he gave the air.

I went on a scavenger hunt for a bra and something suitable to wear that says I was relaxing but cared what I looked like but didn't really put a lot of effort. Once I was satisfied with the effortless chic look that high waisted denim and a graphic t-shirt afforded me, I ripped my hair out of the messy bun and fluffed it out, I headed down to let Max in.

"So, what do I owe the pleasure?" I did my best at a flirtatious greeting.

"I left my family dinner," he started.

"And?" I bit the inside of my cheek to keep from smiling.

"And I couldn't stop thinking of a certain raven-haired beauty I met last night."

"And she wasn't available?" I joked.

"Ha ha." He gave a quick eye roll that I found very charming.

I held the door open wide. "You coming up?"

He eagerly followed me to my apartment. I thought we would pass the third floor with no problem...I was mistaken. Mrs. Pierce cracked her door open, just the shadow of her bloodshot eyeballs were visible. "Hello, Mrs. Pierce! Meet my gentleman caller, Max. He was the one I was 'hoing around with last night," I said without a backwards glace. She immediately slammed the door at the same time Max's steps faltered behind me. "What? Why'd you say that?" he asked, his eyes darting between her door and me.

"Don't worry, it's our thing," I called behind me.

We made it to my apartment where a wave of embarrassment washed over me. Compared to his place, mine was tiny and crowded with knick knacks collected throughout the six years I've been in this apartment. To the average person, it looked chaotic and unorganized; to me, it was cozy; shabby chic. Why was my mind worried about what this guy, that I just met yesterday, thought?!

I watched as he walked slowly through my kitchen into my living room, looking at pictures as he went. He held up a black and white photo. "Who's this?"

"That was my grandma," I said, taking the photo and placing it back on the shelf.

"Sorry, I didn't mean to—"

"No, don't worry about it. It's very rare that I have friends over, very rare to have a man that I've...well, you know."

Max smiled sheepishly. "Yeah, I guess I do."

"Would you like something to drink? You caught me enveloped in the love drama of *Pride & Prejudice*."

Max turned. "I honestly had no intention of coming here tonight. I just...I wanted to see you again." I felt the heat rush to my face. "I love that you blush even after all the stuff you let me do to you." His hand caressed my face; the hardness of his hands, sent the heat lower.

"I'll get you a glass," I whispered close to him. I don't know how we were so close; it was as if our bodies were pulled together like magnets. I brought back a glass in record time, pouring him a glass of merlot while he took a seat on my couch. "Enjoyed your family dinner? They all excited about your take over?" I asked. I took a seat next to him.

"They're excited but I'm not."

"Why aren't you? I would love if my parents offered me some high up position in the mob."

His deep laugh sent chills down my spine. "We're not in the mob," he said.

I shrugged. "Since the family business is a secret, I like to make believe that you dabble in something dangerous."

"You're dangerous, I like to dabble in you," he said with the most serious of faces that I let out a boisterous laugh that vibrated in my tiny apartment. "What? Not so smooth?" he asked, embarrassment flushed his cheeks, and I was here for it.

"You know, Max, for a mountain man, you blush easily."

"Problem?"

"Sexy," I answered.

"Noted," he averted his eyes downward.

"So, you didn't have a good time at the family shindig..." I encouraged him to continue.

"Not really, my family has a hard time with separating work from play and that kind of puts a damper on everything when you're there for quality time and everyone can't seem to stop talking about profit margins and projections for the next quarter." He glanced my way when I didn't give any input. "Virginia, how was your holiday? Enjoy some family time?"

"Oh yes, Richard Gere and Julia Roberts never seem to disappoint. And my cousin Keira Knightly seems to be falling in love with a certain Mr. Darcy." I gestured towards the TV and realization dawned on him.

"You spent Thanksgiving alone? What about your family?"

"I told you, they are enjoying their time on the white sandy beaches on some tropical island...we are kind of not on really speaking terms at the moment."

His eyes grew from warm to soft. "Do you miss them?"

"Sometimes I do," I admitted in a low whisper. When I saw the sympathy in his eyes, I sat up straighter. "But then I pour myself a glass, turn on a feel-good movie and cry my eyes out for better part of the day and that seems to numb the pain," I said partly in jest but the look in his eyes told me that he felt sorry for me and that's the look I just couldn't stand. "Wipe the look from your face," I demanded.

"What look?"

"That dopey one that says 'oh, poor little orphan girl, alone on Thanksgiving Day'," I said in a very bad British accent.

"I see your cousin hasn't really helped you perfect your accent," he quipped.

"I know, what a bitch, right?" That seemed to lighten the mood a bit.

"Okay, so tell me, why didn't you just meet up with your friends? I know they like you."

"Yeah, but they have families of their own to eat turkey with." The conversation was making me sad; I didn't want to cry in front of Max. Just like the millennial that I am, I changed the topic to avoid the subject of my family dynamics and trauma. "Want to watch something on TV?"

I passed him the remote and took the liberty of laying my head on his shoulder. He did one better and wrapped his arm around me. *Oh, this was nice,* my inner voice gave her approval. I saw small tattoos on his fingers. *Mmmm, sexy.* "Max?"

"Hmmm?"

"How many tattoos do you have?" I traced my fingers along his hand.

I felt his soft chuckle. "How many did you see?"

"Your chest, your arms...I'm just noticing the small ones on your fingers...I don't remember seeing any on your legs."

"I have too many to count."

"What do your parents say about the new mob king being tatted up?"

"They don't complain. Better for intimidating. Do you have any?"

"I don't know if I should be offended that you didn't really see mine."

He peered down at me. "Little miss sunshine has tattoos?"

"Just one."

"Where?"

I shrugged. "If you didn't see it last night then I'm not going to tell you," I teased.

"I'll find it." Max spoke under his breath loud enough for me to hear and my body felt warm just at the thought of him finding the small rose along my waist. He fell silent, probably thinking where it might be. I snuggled closer, allowing the comfort settle around us. His soft breathing was almost enough to lull me to sleep. After a few minutes of mindlessly flipping through channels, I heard a contented sigh escape his lips. "Why does this feel so natural? I don't even know you," he whispered.

"Maybe that's why. It's easier to talk to someone you don't know, they can't really judge you...I mean they can, I certainly have," I felt the chuckle vibrate through his body. "But what does it matter if I do."

"That's the thing, it matters to me what you think. I told you things last night that I've never told a soul."

I smiled against his chest. "Except where you work, or what your family does."

"The mob, did you forget?" he teased. "Virginia?"

"Yes, Max?"

"What's your last name?"

I sighed. "Perez."

"Virginia Perez?"

"Mmmhmm," I felt my eyelids falling; It was comfortable in his nook.

"Are you falling asleep?" he whispered.

"No," I answered without opening my eyes.

"Let me put you to bed," he said, kissing the top of my head.

"Well, that's pretty forward."

His pulled me from the couch. "Which way?" he asked.

"Max, this apartment is the size of a pinky nail, there's only two other doors; one is the bathroom and the other is my bedroom...choose one," I laughed.

I looked up at him; his eyes pierced through mine. "What?" I asked. Before I knew it, he threw me over his shoulder and carried me caveman style to the bedroom. I was fully awake now. "Max!" I laughed. "What are you doing?!"

"You were getting real snippy with me, Miss Perez. I had to show you who you were dealing with."

"I could think of a better way you could show me," I giggled breathlessly.

With that invitation, Max tossed me on the bed, instantly covering my body with his. His lips found mine with ease, his kisses had a hint of merlot and I was instantly intoxicated.

My hands traveled up and down his chiseled chest; his shirt was an unwanted barrier between our skin.

Against my own desires I pulled away. "Max?" I whispered.

His kisses stopped their assault on my neck. "What's wrong? Are you okay?" he asked.

"Yeah, I'm...I..." I found it hard to vocalize my fears.

"What is it?"

"What if this is it? What if your business takes over your life and this just ends up being a Thanksgiving memory?"

He rested his forehead against mine. "I promise, we'll see each other after this," he whispered.

Max kissed me as if he was sealing his promise. I kissed him back hoping that he would understand that I truly believed his promise.

5

Rule 29: Give and accept feedback. Having an open mind about people and your work environment brings positivity. Speak directly to each other; be open and honest, yet humble and respectful.

My alarm rang and it was completely dark outside. My neighborhood was dead at this time of morning. My body stretched naked against my blanket, soreness aching all over. The ringing of the phone kept going until realization hit me.

Ugh! It was Black Friday!

My arthritis began to flare up just thinking about it. I wanted to sink deeper in the bed; enjoy the warmth of the hot-blooded man that was in my bed.

"Max," I purred as I rolled over to seduce him. He was gone.

I sat up; my heart dropped to my stomach. *Really, Ginny why are you upset? He didn't promise you anything...well he did, but you know guys, didn't you learn from before?* My inner voice scolded me. I sighed; I really didn't understand my disappointment. *He was just a guy who wanted to get in my pants, nothing more.* I walked out into my dark living room. My eyes scanned the small room but again, disappointment hit me hard. *He was really gone.*

I began to get ready for my 4AM shift with a mix of emotions ranging from sexually content, hurt, sadness, to angry back to sadness. It was the best sex of my life and I didn't know how act.

I dressed in my black jeans and black button down with combat boots because it was a rule in retail to dress in all black on *Black Friday* as if it were an original concept. I pulled my hair back, applied my red lipstick as if I were getting ready for battle. Let's face it, working on Black Friday was going into battle because in about an hour people were going to fight each other to purchase a sweater that was on sale for one day and just going to be discounted more come the following week as a winter sale deal. Customers were dumb enough to really believe that it was worth it to pull themselves out the comfort of their warm beds to take advantage of a deal when in fact, their gullibility were the ones being taken advantage of. Geez! I needed to change my attitude; I knew it was too early to be so bitter, but this man that I spent the last two nights with ups and leaves turning this fantasy into the two-night stand it was always meant to be and it was taking me long to process.

I marched to the station; the bitter cold whipped me in the face as I cursed Max for deserting me without so much of a goodbye but in the same thought telling myself that he was the perfect gentleman so I shouldn't be that upset. The vibration of my phone brought me back into reality.

I peeked at the screen and the name Big Daddy flashed on the screen. Because I was a lone female in the empty streets of New York City, I tucked my phone back in and ran the rest of the way to the station. When I swiped my *Metrocard* and made it to the platform, I took my phone out to read the text.

Good Morning! I had

to leave super early for my first day in the mob, jk. I didn't want to wake you because you look so peace-ful...I know you worked to-day but I wasn't sure your schedule, so I left without saying goodbye. Is it okay if I stop by after work?

You pulled the one-night stand sneak away flawlessly, I applaud you. And yes, we can meet up after work. I'll text you before I clock out, is that okay?

My heart was racing. I felt the cheesy smile spread across my face as I texted back immediately. Then, I couldn't help but overthink; did it come off flirty enough? Did I agree to a meet up too fast? Should he have worked for it? *It's not like he really had to work hard for the good stuff*, my mind sarcastically pointed out. I felt another vibration, satisfaction rained on me at the immediate text back.

Perfect! See you then!

Hmmm. That was a little disappointing. I tucked my phone away, overthinking his last message...or lack thereof.

******

The instant high of my Max infatuation deteriorated rather quickly as I entered what I like to call Black Friday Hell. There was no time to prep, we opened our doors to customers in Christmas shopping mode.

I barely stepped a toe onto the sales floor when a customer approached me from behind. "Ma'am, where do you keep your black dresses?"

"Is there a particular dress I could help you find?"

"No, I'll just browse them if you can point me in the right direction."

I couldn't help the sigh that escaped. I don't know why customers assumed that there were designated areas for specific garment types. This was not a discount store. We were providing fashion buying suggestions. For some reason that concept was hard for some people to grasp. "Unfortunately, we don't have a specific area for dresses, we spread them throughout the store," I explained.

The Carol Baskin look alike blinked at me. "So, how am I supposed to find a black dress?"

"Well, if there is a specific dress that you're looking for I can help you find it or one that is similar."

Her round, flush face went from cluelessness to anger in a matter of seconds. She pulled her dark ski jacket closer. "How do you expect to provide customer service if you can't even tell me where the dresses are?"

I swallowed the scream that wanted to come out. Instead, I

smiled politely and pointed over my shoulder to a random section of the store. "We keep most of them over there," I said.

She nodded. "Was that so hard to do?" she scolded as she passed me in search of one random black dress. Ugh! I wish I was still in bed with Max.

That customer was just the tip of the iceberg.

In a matter of minutes, the store was in utter chaos. Black Friday in fast fashion was mind boggling to me. It wasn't as if we sold electronics; we sold clothes...garments that look like the clothes you use to steal from your mom's closet. What people failed to realize is that just like history, fashion repeats itself. But customers fool themselves into thinking they need the latest recycled style when all they need to do is chill at home on a Friday after a national holiday.

"Excuse me!" I heard a customer yell in my direction. I yelled internally before turning in that direction. What would happen if I just snuck away to the bathroom and hid there for a couple of hours? *With your luck, you would get fired for stealing company time!* my inner voice yelled at me.

"Hello, how can I help you?"

She held up her phone. "Do you have this sweater?" I nodded and proceeded to help. This kept on for a full hour.

I snuck away to the bathroom when my walkie talkie chirped. "Ginny, can you please meet me in the front of ladies?" A sales advisor called.

"Copy," I answered with a sigh.

I looked around the store as I slowly took the escalator back upstairs. It was a mess. The lines to the fitting rooms and registers where out of control. I spotted grown ass women being pulled a part by security because they thought the kids department was the perfect spot to fight over the last pair of pink polka dot leggings. Off the escalator, I passed half naked people trying clothes on in front of public mirrors, passed some teenagers posing for the 'gram.

I really hated this holiday.

I spotted the scared sales advisor who had called for me. "What's up, Cal?"

She looked nervously between the customer and me. "This lady would like the blouse off the mannequin."

"Unfortunately, we cannot undress the mannequin at this time but if you'd like, I can take your number—"

"Why can't you take that off the mannequin?"

"Today is the busiest day of the year and unfortunately—"

"Are you the manager?"

"No, ma'am." I saw the sales advisor sneaking away. So much for *we are one team.* "Thank you, Cal," I said as she hightailed it back to the fitting room to run racks back to the floor. I turned back to the customer who had her arms crossed and tapping her foot. Did I want to fight her on this and grab a manager to deal with this? It was management who told us we couldn't undress Mannequins because it would take us away from replenishing the floor. But they would be the first ones to tell us to just give it to the customer. I sighed. I took the mannequin off the platform and began to undress her.

Customers were inconsiderate sometimes. I bet if I didn't take this blouse off, she would have taken matters into her own hands, not really considering that if she broke this mannequin, we would have to replace it. To replace this mannequin would cost over three-thousand dollars and probably my job.

I handed the blouse to the customer. I plastered a smile to my face; might as well give her a good customer experience. "Here you go," I said.

My smile did not appease this customers attitude. She snatched the blouse from my hands. "And just so you know, it's rude to refuse a customer. Macys would give me a blouse off the mannequin," she scoffed. *Lie. Complete Lie, but whatever.*

I bit my check to keep from verbally dismantling this woman.

Instead, I did what years of working in retail has trained me to do. "And Merry Christmas to you too," I said with a smile. I turned my back on her to let her know I was done with this interaction. She huffed away and the sales advisor came back. "Hey, Ginny. Sorry about that."

"Next time, pretend that you don't hear them and just walk away."

"Um...Maggie walkied for you like a couple of times. She wants you in the deco room."

I spoke into my walkie. "Walkie check." There was no response. "Shit, my walkies dead." I sped walked to the deco room, which is the visual display/computer/work room.

I saw Marvin and instantly began to complain about the customers. "Guys you would not believe the audacity of customers, it really..." I noticed that my team was sitting like children who were in trouble. I looked at Marvin. "What's going on?"

He gestured behind me. I turned around and Maggie was standing in a corner behind me, arms crossed, ready to drop the hammer. "Hey, Maggie, I didn't see you there," I mumbled. I walked over and stood next to Marvin.

"Ginny, we were looking for you but since no one could find you, I started this meeting without you." Disdain fell from her voice, and I knew she was still upset from the other night.

"Yeah, sorry, I was busy providing customer service to actual customers so..." I shrugged. "There's that."

"As I was saying," she blew over my sarcasm. "We are getting a walk today from the global team."

"On Black Friday?" I asked.

Maggie made no effort to hide her irritation with me. "Yes, Gin, on Black Friday. I was not informed about this walk until about twenty minutes ago, so I need all of you to go to your respective departments and make sure all the set-ups for the week were executed per company guidelines. Make sure all signage is correct. Make sure what the mannequins are wearing are correct, those Get The Look's should be on point."

Knowing full well that she would jump across and strangle me if I interrupted her again, I raised my hand. "What is it Gin?" she asked with her arms crossed, all she needed to do was tap her toes and she would've been the spitting image of my mother.

"GTL's are not per pages right now because you told us to sell what was on the mannequins and now sizes are gone—"

"Just do the best you can do, no more changing out mannequins." I nodded but said nothing. "Apparently there is a big change happening within the company. We are going to have a new CEO and he will be one of the people walking." The fine lines on Maggie's forehead were a great indication on how stressed she really was. She kept brushing her bangs back from her face which meant on a scale of one to ten she was at an eight and a half.

"When are they coming?" Tahiri asked.

"In about an hour, they are just visiting the soho location," she informed us.

My phone buzzed and I glanced down. *Big daddy*.

"Ginny! Please pay attention," Maggie bellowed.

I put my phone away before I could read it. I sighed. "Geez, Maggie, just relax."

"Ginny..." Marvin warned.

Maggie's eyes narrowed in my direction. "I don't think you understand the importance of this walk. They want to see which stores are worth keeping open and which they want to shut down."

The team exchanged fearful glances at each other. "Are we going to lose our jobs?" Mark asked.

"I can't promise anything. Just assume that everything is in danger," Maggie answered with a solemn face.

I rolled my eyes. "They are not going to fire us."

Maggie sighed. "Go ahead, Ginny. Enlighten us with the inside scoop you have at the global offices."

"Maggie, Ginny was trying to think positive," Marvin interjected.

I snapped. "We get it Maggie. Get out, check the departments, make sure the mannequin's outfits are up to date, easy to find, easy to buy, show no mercy. Anything else?"

Despite the anger that flushed her cheeks, Maggie kept her cool. "No, that is it," she said.

I shot out the room with Marvin close behind me. When we were on the sales floor, he reached out to stop me. "Hey, you need to cool it. You're really working her up and I don't know if any of us can stop her from being a bitch to you, especially in front of the global team," he said, making sure to keep his voice low so the sales advisors and customers wouldn't hear.

"Just looking at her pisses me off. I know my job; I know what to do. And what's with her scaring everyone with that talk about people may lose their jobs."

Marvin narrowed his eyes at me. "What's up with you? You still mad about stranger danger from the other night?"

"There's nothing to be mad about." I looked around before holding up my phone.

Marvin squinted at my phone. "Big Daddy? Who's Big Daddy?" I raised my eyebrows. "Oh, really!" he squealed. "Is his nickname accurate?" he asked.

"I do not kiss and tell," I teased.

"Oh, come on, Gin. We both know you're like an old hooker. You don't kiss."

I laughed and slapped his arm. "Marvin!"

"You know I'm kidding...even hookers kiss." He joked. I laughed along with him. "I just wanted to make you laugh and bring you out of your mood."

"I know...it's just...this place. It's her. I see her and I want to—"

"Hey, Maggie!" Marvin said to our store manager.

"Is everything okay? Are we checking departments?" her voice made me want to poke myself in the eye just for fun. I refused to answer. Instead, I looked at Marvin.

"Yeah, just touching base with Gin," Marvin answered.

I turned to offer her a forced smile just so she would leave me alone. "Gin, before your shift is over, come to the office so we can have a chat."

"Sure, no problem, Maggie. I always look forward to our chats." I nodded and walked away, mentally preparing myself to do my job with a store full of people.

On a normal day, a visual merchandiser starts their shift at least four hours before the store opens because it is easier to move product around without a store full of hassling customers. Now I was trying to do this job with a million people around.

I grabbed a rack and rotated the garments in record time; what had once looked trashed because of holiday shoppers now looked as if I had done a reset; it looked beautiful. I looked down at my phone, I had fifteen minutes to fix mannequins. My hands were sore, dry, and dirty from handling all the clothes and hangers. I picked outfits for the two mannequins that I had to change. Usually, it would take more than fifteen minutes because if you worked in a city store any little wrinkle or blemish on a mannequin was called out and you were forced to wear a big red letter on your chest...just kidding. But pressing and steaming garments was a job that was taken very seriously. Our competition was *Zara, Bloomingdales*...not *Walmart* or *Bon Bini*.

That was managements words, not mine.

We had a reputation to uphold, and it begins with our mannequins and windows.

I zoomed through the steaming and pressing, making sure to get every wrinkle and crease out. I ran onto the floor, dressed the mannequins, and stepped back to review my handy work. The customer rush had died down, but I knew it was only a matter of time before a second wave would come.

Drenched in sweat, I called to Marvin over the walkie. "Marvin, I'm going on my lunch," I said.

The radio crackled. "Ginny, wait a sec, apparently the global team is down the block, I just want to have all hands-on deck in case we get feedback," he explained.

"Copy," I sighed into the walkie.

I knew the drill.

For any visit, if a visual was done with their tasks, they floated around within the department supporting with runs, clean-up, customer service...basically whatever support the store needed.

I knew the global team had arrived because the sales advisors stopped the personal chatter, hid their cell phones, and turned into robots that cleaned, sorted, and actually greeted the customers. I busied myself with folding down a table as I felt a gust of wind pass behind me. I glanced from the corner of my eye; I counted only three members of the global team all dressed in long black peacoats, and black slacks and wool caps covering their heads; two guys, one woman. Because of the mess from a couple of years I always did my best to lay low and avoid any contact with any global, regional or district teams. I like to be my usual, bubbly self but away from the scrutiny of my superiors.

I used to care; you don't give ten years of your life to a company without having some sort of dream of growing within it. As of now, I just work to pay my bills.

"Oh, did you see them? Fresh off a magazine," one of the sales advisors whispered in awe next to me.

"I saw their backs...they looked...expensive. Or at least their coats did," I answered.

Fifteen minutes later, Marvin's voice come through the walkie. "Visual team, please meet in the manager's office."

My heart began to race, *were they going to fire us immediately? Was Maggie right about us having to watch our backs?* I gave the sales advisor instructions to finish the table and made my way slowly to the office. Last time the whole visual team was called into the office at the same time, it wasn't for a pat on the back. It was to scold us for getting called out for bad garment care when the district team unexpectedly came to walk the store. If the store was not well, it was blamed on the visual team.

I took a deep breath to steady my nerves before knocking on the door. The office was crowded; A man, who looked vaguely familiar, and woman in sleek black outfit were in deep conversation with Maggie while the visual team's eyes darting nervously between them. Maggie didn't notice my arrival, so I took the chance to observe the global team. The woman was beautiful; blonde hair fell in stylish waves around her perfect delicate features. The man had dark brown hair with bits of white sprinkled around his sideburns, giving off a distinguished look, handsome, clean face...so familiar but I couldn't place him.

"What's happening?" I whispered to Marvin.

"I don't know, she sent me to get everyone, they walked for two seconds and then came back here," he explained.

Who walks a store for two seconds and immediately demands a meeting? People who are pissed and have the power to fire you, that's who. I felt dread creep up to the back of my neck.

Maggie threw back her head to give a fake laugh before turning to all of us. "Thank you for coming. I promise this won't take long. Visual team, welcome the global team."

"Hi," we all said at once.

The man smiled brightly. "I'm George Thomas. The team and I have walked most of the city stores and we are actually quite pleased at how this store is representing this company, especially on such a busy day." His voice was like butter.

Dread started to seep in my veins. *I know him.* He was one of the guys who was out with Max. I quietly surveyed my visual team; did they not remember? Were they keeping it cool? Kudos to them because I was internally freaking out. Did he say his last name was Thomas?

I scrounged up enough courage to look directly at him. He winked!

It was him.

The woman picked up on his sentiments, "Hi all, I'm Andrea Thomas-Henderson. I just wanted to add to what my brother was saying, yes, with the window representation and the execution of each department, the store is beautiful and the attention to detail is where we wished the other stores were."

My phone began to vibrate, in a quiet room, the sound was deafening. I could feel eyes looking everywhere. The global team each looked at their screens to make sure they weren't missing an important call. It took everything I had not to look because I knew who would be calling me.

A soft knock had Maggie out of her seat and running to open the door. One more member of the team came in. "Sorry, I had to make a phone call," he said, his voice sounding very familiar.

It sounded like the same voice who was growling dirty words into my ear last night.

I followed the voice.

Max?

"And welcome, Max Thomas, everyone." Maggie gestured in his direction as he nodded politely.

His beard was gone but by the way my body reacted to the mere sight of him...there was no mistaking. Our eyes connected and I had that outer body experience where you turn hot, then cold, then begin to sweat and you can't slow your heartbeat down so a heart attack is inevitable. I let out a mix between a gasp and a wheeze...I sounded like a dying giraffe.

Everyone turned to look; I could feel Maggie's glare as she tried to restrain herself from murdering me.

Max turned in search of the person responsible for the horrendous noise that came out of me. Our eyes connected and his already fair skin went from white to ghostly.

"Ginny, do you need water?" Maggie asked, her lips pursed with annoyance.

"Yes," I answered, not looking back as I made a very dramatic exit, bumping into everyone on my way out. I spared a glance in Max's direction; he looked horrified. I think that look killed me the most.

We had bomb ass sex; the kind that could set the bed on fire, there was no need to look horrified...stunned, maybe but horrified?

I could hear Max apologize and excuse himself one more time with some lame excuse about having to make a phone call. He caught up to me by the breakroom water fountain.

"Ginny, what is going on?" he whispered.

"You're asking me what's going on? You shaved your face!" my voice jumped up an octave and I was thankful for the empty breakroom. I busied myself getting water from the watercooler. Nerves and adrenaline had my hands shaking as I brought the disposable cup to my lips.

"You don't like it?" he asked rubbing his bare chin.

"It's not that I don't like it, it just takes some getting—" I shook my head. "You just walked in with the global team," I whispered, trying to keep myself from shrieking. Truth was that his clean face threw me for a loop too. He wasn't the big, gorgeous mountain man who left my bed this morning. What I was staring at was a dangerously handsome man, less Grisly Adams more James Bond.

"You work here?" he whispered.

"No, I just wear the badge and lanyard for fun. Of course, I work here!" I held a hand to my chest. "Max, I think...I think I'm genuinely having a heart attack."

"You're okay. People having heart attacks don't usually say genuinely."

"This is not funny," I growled.

"Why?" *Was he serious?!*

"Because I've seen you naked."

I wanted to slap the smirk off his face. "Thank you?"

"It's not a compliment! I'm genuinely freaking out." A few sales advisor strolled into the breakroom in search of company provided lunch. They spotted us and eyed us curiously. "You are on the global team. That's your family in there," I whispered. My voice sounded like I had sucked in helium.

"It's my family business," he confessed.

My mind was working slow, but it was starting to put two and two together. "So, you're..." my breath kept coming fast. I threw back my water. I wish it was something stronger.

"Yes, I'm the new CEO—"

I crushed my paper cup and closed my eyes in hopes that his words and my migraine would stay at bay. "No, stop." I held up my hand. "Why couldn't your family be in the mob?"

"You know with all that..." Max glanced behind us, he cleared his throat, lowering his voice from the nosey sales advisors. "...happened between us, we never really talked about our work," he explained.

"Because you didn't want to!" I was definitely loud that time.

Aware that I was on the cusp of causing a scene, I walked out of the breakroom into the stockroom, all the way to the back where I knew no one would see us. The soft taps of Max's chelsea boots assured me he followed. I looked back to make sure we were alone before finally facing him. "I told you I was a visual merchandiser, that I worked in retail; your family owns the world's largest fashion brand. You didn't think there was a possibility that I worked for the company?"

Max was so close. He ran a hand through his hair. "Ginny, I didn't know. We were just supposed to be one night, I didn't…" sensing that his voice was a bit on the loud side, he cleared his throat and continued, "Ginny, I didn't want my family's wealth to be known; you and I weren't supposed to be a thing."

"You thought I was a gold digger?"

"No!" Max reached for my hand but thought better of it. "I didn't know…I didn't know what to think."

My heart stopped; a fierce shot of hot blood ran through my veins and not the good kind. "Oh my god, you really thought I would be after your money?"

"I didn't want to take chances; you came up to me at the bar."

"Because I wanted a one-night stand not a sugar daddy."

He sighed. "I think no matter what I say, it's not going to sound right."

I shrugged. "I think you're right."

"I didn't think that we would be in this predicament."

"Neither did I."

"I know," he finally grabbed my hand, caressing it with his thumb, immediately igniting the heat that I felt the second I laid eyes on him. He stepped closer, slowly lowering his lips to mine. That electricity shot through my body; every hair on my body stood on end. I pressed harder against him causing him to moan softly.

"Ginny!" Marvin's voice called out.

We jumped apart. "Shit." I tried to wipe the lipstick off Max's lips. "Coming!"

Before I could leave, Max held on to my hand. "Can we talk about this tonight?"

All the scenarios played in my head, from good to bad to the absolute fucking worse. There wasn't anything he could say that would make this situation any better. I shook my head. "There can't be a tonight, Max. You're my boss. You're my boss' boss. Do you know what this would look like to people?"

"What would it look like?" he asked. Instead of answering, I shook my head and tried to make a graceful exit. I bumped into Marvin who was off to the side, presumably listening to the whole conversation.

His eyes fixed behind me on Max. "Hello, Big Daddy," he said with a head tilt.

Max's face flushed with embarrassment. I began to ramble, "Don't worry, Marvin was the only one I told...I didn't know you were—"

"I know," Max assured me.

Marvin pointed his finger at Max. "I think you should go first. Just head to the bathroom first and wipe that lipstick off...it's really not your color. We'll follow behind."

I watched as he walked back towards the bathroom. Marvin immediately took me by the shoulders, shaking me in his excitement. "Oh my god!" he mouthed.

"I know," I said covering my face in shame.

"He looks so good with no beard."

"I know."

"What are you going to do?" He whispered dramatically.

"Nothing."

"Are you serious?"

"Yes!" I took a deep breath to steady my nerves. "This was just supposed to be one night, it was my mistake for letting it be two and thinking it could potentially be more."

"Well, I gotta warn you, Maggie is not happy that you had a coughing fit in the middle of the meeting," Marvin warned. "She's on the hunt, any little thing will send her off."

"I could give two shits about how she feels," I spat out.

"Geez, calm down. This whole thing is stressing you out and you're stressing me out. Just relax."

I nodded and rolled my shoulders. "Okay, yeah, I'm sorry."

"Your in-laws want to talk to you," Marvin said quickly.

I stopped in my tracks. "What?!"

Marvin let out a breath. "Don't worry it's a good thing," he assured me.

We made it back to the office, the rest of the visual team had left. I felt the beads of sweat on my temples. *I'm fired. That can't be it,* Marvin said it was a good thing. *But maybe he thought getting fired would be good for me.* I tried to quiet the voice in my head, why could all three Thomas' want to see me? Marvin gestured to the seat closest to the door. *Placing me near the door?!* I knew this tactic was so that the person who was brought into the office didn't feel trapped. This was done when something had the possibility to go bad. The last time someone wasn't placed by the door, they were fired, and they destroyed the office before destroying mannequins on their way out of the building. It got ghetto real quick.

"You wanted to see me?" I said looking straight at Maggie, the Thomas' were just a blur as I tried to avoid eye contact.

"Yes, the global team were curious as to who was the merchandiser for ladies."

I looked at the group of five. "That would be me," I raised my hand hoping that they wouldn't notice the shaking.

"We just want to applaud you. It is the best execution we've seen all day," Andrea said.

I let out a sigh of relief. "Thank you. I honestly thought I was in trouble for something," I admitted.

George smiled. "Why would you be in trouble? Virginia? Is that your name?" he asked with a twinkle in his eye.

My eyes narrowed in his direction. "I prefer Gin or Ginny." I clasped my hands together to give the notion that all was well. It was gross how clammy my hands were.

"Max, do you have anything else to add?" Andrea asked.

"No, I think you guys said it. The department is amazing, and I think the customers are getting the experience that we intended for them," Max added without looking directly at me.

"Thank you." I kept the attention on my clasp hands.

"Ginny is our star visual," Maggie said. "She's been here the longest, ten years almost, isn't that right?"

I nodded as the tightness in my eye settled and the mild twitching began. I should be proud to have a consistent job for the last decade, not a lot of people can say that. But the way Maggie was going on made it sound lame, as if I wasted my life away. Her raptor-like voice penetrated my thoughts. "She actually quit for a month to dip her toe in design and then came crawling back." *This bitch! Smack her in the mouth, no one will blame you,* the devil on my shoulder insisted. I just sat there and listened to her go on. "She was in the running to be a visual manager a couple of years ago, but we had some areas of opportunities we had to work through," she explained.

My eyes shot up. This bitch was really throwing me under the bus! Maybe instead of smacking her in the mouth, I'd just push her in front of a bus.

"Areas of opportunities?" Andrea asked.

"Oh yes, Ginny has had an issue with authority in the past that we are still trying to work out."

This time I looked at Andrea. "I don't have a problem with authority. I don't litter, I don't cross between cars while the train is moving, and I stole a bag of chocolate chip cookies once and confessed to the supermarket security guard because I felt guilty." I noticed Max discreetly cover his lips to hide a smirk. Andrea and George shared a look that I couldn't decipher. "Listen, I know the ins and outs of this company as if it were my own. I don't give a company ten years of my life if there were issues." My eyes landed on Maggie; this woman was out for blood, but I wouldn't let her win without a fight. She smiled as if she smelled a bad fart.

The Thomas' remained quiet. Probably unsure on how to proceed because Maggie just made this meeting super awkward. Andrea tucked a blonde tendril behind her ear and cleared her throat. "Well, that was...great to know. Ginny, have you ever thought of applying for a visual manager position again?" Andrea asked.

I gave a simple answer. "No."

Andrea clasped her delicate hands in front of her. "We really like to promote internally and there may be an opening soon at one of the city stores. We are taking the top talent from the top earning stores and giving them this opportunity to showcase their skills." she explained.

"I thought that we don't promote during the holiday," I said confused.

"We're trying to see if we can fast track a few things because we are changing rather quickly as a company," She added.

I nodded my understanding. I was about to say a few words about how this was a lovely opportunity, but Maggie steam rolled me. "Oh, how lovely. I'll put that on Ginny's development plan," Maggie said with a smile. Her smile wasn't one of the warm your heart kind, it was the kind that looked like she was picking the best way to kill you and then asks if you'll be attending the church picnic.

That seemed to satisfy Andrea. She stood up from her seat and began grabbing her things; Max and George followed lead.

Andrea held out her hand. "It was a pleasure meeting you," she said with a smile. I took her hand.

She tilted her head in question. "I'm sorry they're so sweaty but you made me very nervous," I whispered.

Andrea blinked before nodding. "Very well, have a nice day."

Next was George. "It was nice seeing you again, Ginny," His

smile was wickedly cheeky. I rolled my eyes at him and gave him a quick nod.

Finally, there was Max. There was no hug, no handshake. "Have a good day." was all he said in passing. He didn't stop or turn around. His departure was cold, as it should be.

When the door closed behind him, I got up to leave.

"Gin, please take your seat. Now that you're here, I'd like to take the time to have a chat with you," Maggie said sweetly. *Be careful. She's got something...a hammer, a bat...stick of dynamite.*

"About?" I asked slowly taking my seat again.

Maggie came around her desk to sit on top of it like some teacher in a 90's sitcom; it immediately made me want to laugh but I'm an adult and apparently adults have great restraint. "Well, let's start with Wednesday night," she said.

I let out a heavy sigh. "What about Wednesday night, Maggie?"

She folded her hands together; all she needed was a ruler and a habit and she would be the spitting image of Sister Francis from the all-girls catholic school that I went to; I cringed at the thought.

"Ginny, you're attitude towards me, and the store is unacceptable. We were all trying—"

"To leave early when I was scheduled for—"

"Ten! You were scheduled for ten and the fact that we still left late means that I have to doc you for your time and efficiency."

"What?!" I jumped out of my seat with so much fevor that I almost knocked the chair down.

Maggie walked around the desk shuffling through paperwork. When she found the sheet she was looking for, she slid it across the desk. "I need you to sign this, it just says that we had this conversation and that you've been warned."

I felt the heat rise to my ears. "I've been warned of what? Not to care about providing quality work? For leaving...ten minutes after my scheduled time?"

"You've been warned. If you receive another doc then you go on a final. Once you go on a final and you fail to improve then it is cause for termination," she explained with a vindictive smile.

Tears burned the back of my eyeballs, frustration getting the best of me. "Maggie, in the ten years I've been in this company I have never gotten a doc. Ever. And now you want to doc me because I was ten minutes late finishing up a project that you didn't properly schedule?" I began to shake my head. "I'm sorry, but that doesn't seem fair and I'm not signing that." I pushed the paper right back towards her. I could see the fumes coming out of her ears.

She shrugged as if it didn't bother her, but the soft tick of her eye told me otherwise. "It really doesn't matter if you sign it or not, this will be in your file, and it counts as doc one."

I stood up. "Why, Maggie?"

"Why? Because rules are rules. If I don't follow up with you, everyone is going to expect the same treatment."

"What about the other times that the team has stayed or you held the night crew here an extra hour because you wanted to have a perfect close? Can we write you up for that?"

"Ginny, you take things too personal."

I knew that I should just shut up and walk away but her smug expression kept me from doing that. "Maybe because it feels personal."

"Whatever do you mean?" The slight cock of her chin told me that she wanted me to go on; that would give her more of an excuse to terminate me on the spot. I knew that I needed to pick my battles. Was this battle worth rehashing the drama and insanity from a few years ago?

"Nothing," I finally answered. I had a huge lump in my throat from holding back frustration tears, but I would rather someone walk in on me peeing in the bathroom stall on a day that I was wearing a jumpsuit than have Maggie see me cry.

I saw the smirk appear on her face. *Don't cry, Ginny. Don't cry, Ginny.* As I stared her down, the image of my imaginary resignation played in my head. I would hop on the desk, kicking all her paperwork to the ground, set the paperwork on fire and before the cops came to drag me out the store in handcuffs, I would then yell at her and let her know what a raging bitch she was and that I hoped her plants all got root rot and died.

"Was there something else, Ginny?"

I dropped back into reality. "We're done then?" I asked, I had to leave this office. I was two point five seconds away from pulling a *Carrie.*

She nodded.

When I got to the door, she called my name forcing me to turn back around. "Yes?" I asked.

"Good job today. They really loved your department."

I slammed the door like an insolent teenager being told she couldn't hang out with her friends. I stomped down the hall, straight into the bathroom, where I locked myself in the stall and I finally let the tears run down. I hated every second of it because it showed just how much power Maggie really had and how weak I felt. Two years ago, I felt on top of the world. I would do anything for this job. Now, it just seemed like I was trapped. As positive as I try to be when I'm around the team, I felt stuck; there was no light at the end of the tunnel. Maggie would always be in charge, and I would always be the girl who gave up on her dream for a guy and who was too scared to try again.

Today I realized just how much I really hated my job while at the same time trying to process the fact that the first guy that I had a connection with in a very long time is my boss and I couldn't do a thing about it.

I was wallowing in my own pity. Lost in thought, I jumped when

I heard a soft knock against my stall door. "Occupied," I yelled out, being careful not to sound like I've been crying.

"It's me," Marvin whispered.

"What are you doing in the ladies room?"

"I came to give you a message, but I guess I caught you at a bad time," he joked.

I opened the stall door and he let out a horrified gasp. "Shut up," I spat out.

"Girl, what happened to you? You look like you had an allergic reaction. You're all red and blotchy and your eyes are glassy..." he squinted. "...did you get high?"

"Shhh, don't say that. Maggie wrote me up, she'll write me up if she even thinks you're being serious about me smoking." I looked at the vent that was right above us. "She's probably in there now, taking notes."

"She wrote you up for what? She didn't tell me anything and I'm your visual manager."

I explained everything quickly to Marvin because I wanted to get to the reason why he had breached the confines of the ladies bathroom. "So, what's the message you had for me?"

"A certain member of the global team wanted me to tell you that he would like to meet you for lunch." Marvin looked down at his watch. "Which is in like ten minutes, so I suggest you put away any work you have going on so you can head out for a rendezvous." He wiggled his eyebrows.

My heart fluttered at the mere mention of Max. "I can't go."

"Yes, you can."

"I can but I won't," I said with a confident head nod.

"Why? He's gorgeous and rich—"

"And my boss. You know that's a no go for me. You saw what happened last time. Too much drama that I don't want any part of." I made my way to the sink to wash my face. When Marvin didn't say a word, I looked over to see if he was still there. "Also, maybe he just wants to meet up just to tell me that we can't see each other anymore, which I already know. I won't put myself through anymore aggravation today, I've had enough."

Marvin folded his arms. "You're done?" he asked with a head tilt.

I mimicked his stance. "Yes."

"Okay, so go clock out, sit in the back and enjoy your break."

6

Rule 27: This is your business! We want you to be creative as well as entrepreneurs; take initiative to get business moving forward.

I used up my entire lunch break walking around to the other stores in the neighborhood because I didn't want to see Maggie's face. By the time my shift was over, I was a sweaty tired mess. I was hungry and exhausted, I just wanted to shower, and order take out.

I made it to my building in a blur; I began digging through my giant bag in search of my keys. When I finally looked up, I stopped short. "What are you doing here?"

Max's shaved face made him look dapper; like the sophisticated billionaire that he really was. With his hands tucked in his black peacoat, he gave me stone cold stare. This wasn't the first time that I couldn't decipher what a man was thinking. There was one time that I went on a movie date with a guy who said that he was going to get popcorn, but he didn't have cash. I spotted him and not only did he not come back, but he also laughed about it on the socials, so maybe I never really knew what men were thinking.

"I was waiting for you during your lunch."

I began to unlock the lobby door. "I know."

"You know? Why didn't you meet me?"

I opened the door and began climbing the steps. "Because you're my boss, Max. That's a deal breaker for me."

"People don't have to know," he said from behind me.

I snapped around. "I am not hiding a relationship. That turns into lies and then the lies turn into drama."

"I want to take you out. I don't like that we didn't even get a chance to see where this goes," he admitted.

Before I could comment, Mrs. Pierce opened the door to her apartment. "Can you quiet down?"

I snapped around. "No."

Max walked over to Mrs. Pierce. "Hi, I'm Max." he held his hand out to which Mrs. Pierce immediately slammed the door in his face. "Well, okay then."

I continued walking up the steps with Max quickly following behind. "Max, go home. We had sex and let that be that." I sighed, completely exhausted from what all that has happened the last three days. I stopped at my door. "I'm not inviting you in."

He gave a curt nod. "Very well." His voice was low, smooth like good whiskey.

"Bye, Max."

"Bye, Virginia."

When I closed the door behind me it felt as if I was closing the door on something good. But I would never know; that fact alone was enough to make me want to curl up on my couch and cry at my overflowing amounts of bad luck.

With Friday being so hectic and exhausting, I was relieved that the rest of the weekend seemed to roll by at a leisurely pace. I decided to get my mind off all things H. Moda. I treated myself to a mani/pedi, took myself shopping and was now at dinner alone at this fabulous restaurant that everyone's been talking about. I brought a book as to not seem too pathetic. I was in the middle of a really sexy chapter, the kind where you lean over just a tiny bit to make sure no one is reading over your shoulder, when the waiter interrupted the scene. "Excuse me, miss. This is from the guy at the bar," he explained as he left a drink at my table. I looked up to the bar and there was George Thomas. I tipped my head at him; apparently, he took that as a sign to come one over because he made his way to my table. "May I take a seat?"

"I mean you did buy me a drink and walked all the way over here," I joked.

"Listen, I wanted to apologize for yesterday—" he began.

"There is no reason to apologize. It's no one's fault." For lack of anything better to say, I shrugged my shoulders.

"I know Max really liked you."

Liked? Did he used the word liked?

I looked down at the pages of my book; no longer reading but I couldn't look him in the eyes. "Your brother and I already spoke about it. It's all good, no hard feelings," I said.

When he didn't respond, I forced myself to look up. "What are you doing eating all alone?" he asked.

"I just wanted food that I didn't have to cook or microwave so this was my last resort."

George looked around the restaurant with its feathered chandeliers and dark lighting, giving the restaurant a romantic ambience. "Well, I say you came up with a great last resort."

I shrugged. "It's okay. My other option was to order take out, but I think the delivery guy just feels sorry for me at this point." George smiled but remained seated. "Was that it?" I asked.

He tilted his head. He was younger than Max, but his lightly salted hair made him seem more distinguished. The gleam in his eye proved that his was the youngest. "Are you trying to get rid of me?" he laughed as I fumbled for something to say. "Relax, that was it. Just wanted to apologize," he stood up, finally glancing at the book on the table. "What are you reading?"

I blushed again. "Nothing, something stupid."

"Must be. The way you were holding it to your chest," he laughed. George waved and walked back to his table where a curvy brunette was waiting for him; she eyed us curiously I knew she would ask him who I was, and he would most likely tell her it was just business which she would nod her head in understanding but in the back of her mind she would think twice because men as rich and power-ful as he was would never go to another woman's table under the pretense of business.

Would George tell Max that he saw me out? Probably. Although Max did seem hurt that we couldn't have any personal relationship, he would most likely be relieved that he wouldn't be tied down any time soon seeing that he has a lot of responsibility. I pushed thoughts of Max and everything to the farthest recesses of my mind. I quickly ate my meal instead of lingering because every time I looked up, George's date was staring at me.

But being back in my apartment did not seem to ease my mind; It just wouldn't turn off. Not even when I was laying in the dark ready for the sandman to claim me. I glanced at my phone which told me that it was barely passed two in the morning which also told me that I only had about two more hours before I had to get up and get ready for work. Instead of trying to get any rest I decided to pick up my phone and semi-stalk Max. I started with google. Scroll-ing through paparazzi photos; photos of when the announcement was made that he was taking over the company. Family photos of him with his siblings who were the ones that accompanied him to the store.

Reading through various websites I learned that he was the mid-dle of the three. Max's takeover was a surprise to everyone because he had no hand in the company before. It was his sister who ran mostly everything while their father took a backseat on the busi-ness. They didn't really go into much detail as to why Max stepped in. I eventually sank into the black hole that only the internet could provide. Then popped up the thing that I was both afraid and curious to read about, his dating life. For all the pages that I viewed, this was the only piece of evidence that he dated anyone. He was either a monk or just an expert at keeping his relationships quiet.

The girlfriend they showed was Missy Jones; Swedish socialite whose family owned some kind of chocolate empire. *Oh shit! That's the girl that was with George!* She was leggy, brunette and beautiful. Her face was spotless; the kind you get with sunscreen, good sex and money.

I stared at her picture until my eyes burned. If he went out with someone like that, why would he want to be with someone like me? My hair was long, dark, greasy when I skipped a shampoo day; my eyes weren't symmetrical, if you looked close enough you could tell one was slightly bigger than the other. Not to mention the amount of body fat that I had compared to her.

Stop! I told myself. She and I were two different people, there was no point in comparing myself to someone I didn't even know. I switched the picture back to one of Max; back to one where he had a five o'clock shadow and looking down at his phone, oblivious to the world around him.

My alarm rang jarring me out of the trance and into Monday morning. I was so startled I dropped the phone and it smacked me right on my face. "Shit." My lip was throbbing, I knew that it would leave a mark. What a way to start the day. I got dressed with a cloud hanging over my head. I grumbled to myself about stupid store managers as I brushed my teeth, I yelled at the lone pigeon singing outside my window in the dark morning only to have Mrs. Pierce bang on my floor forcing me to stomp on the floor in retaliation. I put on my red lipstick and winced as I applied over my swollen lip. I knew that today was going to drag but I did my best to tell myself...at least I won't see Max. That was the silver lining in such an abysmal day.

Two hours later I was rolling a rack onto the floor of the store. This was my favorite part of the day; the store was empty except for some sales associates who were processing the truck and I got to make the store look beautiful. Visual merchandisers were the look of the store while the managers worried about the money. Which I didn't mind. It satisfied any creative urges I had since designing has taken a backseat. I got started bringing back to life the color combinations and redressing mannequins that people never appreciated.

Our store was split into four big departments: Ladies, Men's, Kids and Juniors. Within those departments were subdepartments like basics, denim and classic (which was more suiting for work or special occasions). I was proud to say that I successfully ran the ladies department which holds the biggest share in the store. If profit was down in that department there was only one person to blame...but thank the baby Jesus, we were in the green.

I was in the middle of recovering my department from the holiday weekend when I heard the click clack of Maggie's kitten heeled boots. Just the sound of her shoes was enough to make my stomach turn.

"Good morning, Ginny." She sang as she walked by.

"Good morning," I muttered without looking up.

"Good morning, Ginny," another voice called out. I quickly looked up to see Max's sister walking alongside Maggie. My heart began to beat faster.

"Hi!" My voice was annoyingly high pitch. "I mean, good morning," I said, mostly to myself because both women had already breezed by me.

I scanned my department before running downstairs to look for Marvin. He was in the kid's department walking Tahiri through this week's commercial changes. "Marvin!" I yelled as I walked down the escalator.

They both looked up. "Why are you yelling at me so early in the morning?" he squinted at me. "And why is your lip swollen? Did you get Botox without telling me? I think they botched it."

I speed walked to where he was. "Shut up and answer. Why is she here?"

"Who's here?" Tahiri asked.

"Max's sister," I whispered.

Marvin shrugged. "You need to chill. I don't know why she's here."

"She walked in with Maggie."

"Ginny, I'm being so serious, I have no clue why your sister-in-law is here," he joked. Tahiri laughed along with him, and I shot daggers in their direction causing them both to shut up. Marvin handed me the kids commercial pages. "Okay, fine. I'll go and look for something in the office and see what I find out. You can walk Tahiri through the pages and give any feedback you think necessary," he said.

I nodded. It wasn't a surprise that Marvin would give me a little bit of responsibility. There was a time when we were both in line for the visual manager position in this store, he ended up on the winning side of that.

"You want to talk about it?" Tahiri asked.

"Talk about what?"

"How the guys we were hanging out with are our superiors and the toll it's taking on you mentally."

I took a deep breath to swallow the irritation that I began to feel. "I'm fine," I smiled.

"Only serial killers and people who eat bath salts smile like that. You are obviously on the verge of a mental—"

"Tahiri, I think that if we place this color combo where prio two usually lands the flow will make more sense." Her honey brown eyes and expertly shaped eyebrows arched. My eyes widened in response.

She sighed "Fine."

We walked for a good twenty minutes when my name sounded through the walkie that was clipped to my hip. "Gin, can you come to the office, please," Marvin's voice rang through the entire store.

"Copy. I'll be right there." I handed Tahiri her department pages. "Were there any questions?"

"No but tell the in-laws I said hi."

"Shut up."

I walked slowly to the office, not really sure why I was being called in there, but I was also trying to come up with any excuse for whatever thing I did to set Maggie off. I knocked, hopping from foot to foot with anxiety.

Marvin opened the door with a smile as I walked in and sat with my back towards the door while Maggie, who had decided to try and dress stylishly with a wide brim felt hat, and Andrea Thomas-Henderson quietly talked amongst themselves. Marvin took a seat next to Andrea.

Andreas blonde hair fell in stylish waves past her shoulders. She wore natural looking make-up that set me even more on edge. How can someone be rich, beautiful and assertive? The corners of her mouth kicked up in a Mona Lisa smile. Never a full smile. *Maybe that's why her skin is so smooth.* "I just wanted to tell you personally that I love what you've done to the ladies department. I've been to all the city stores and...they haven't reacted to the commercial changes as you've done. So, I applaud you for that." I nodded slowly, waiting for a *but*, or a *we regret to inform you*, or at the very least lightning to strike me dead. "I also wanted to inform you," *oh, no here we go.* "That my brothers and I will be in and out this building for the next several weeks to monitor your development."

"My development?" I asked looking between the three seated behind the tiny desk.

"I've spoken to your store and visual manager, and it seems that the company may have overlooked your skills. For the next couple of weeks, you will shadow Marvin and learn what you can and by the end of the holiday season if all goes well, you will be the visual manager of our new Soho location."

I was speechless.

There were a million thoughts flying around in my brain at a thousand miles a second. Maggie kept her eyes down; no smart remark, no trying to sabotage me. Something was up.

I looked at Marvin just to get some grounding, but he was of no help. The fool was smiling like the joker.

I glanced over to Andrea; her eyes were laser focused on me; her hands were clasped in front of her as she waited for my reaction.

"Is there any way I can talk to you?" I asked. Maggie's head shot up. "Privately, Andrea?"

Andrea looked towards Maggie then at Marvin. "Yeah, sure."

The other two got up and slowly walked out. Maggie walked slower than usual, clucking around in her knee-high boots. She looked back one more time before finally exiting. With the soft click of the door, I took a deep breath. "Although this is an amazing opportunity, I don't think I'm the right person for this job."

Andrea slowly passed her small fingers through her hair, securing pieces behind her ear. She tilted her head, examining me. It was as if she were taking in every minor detail; red lips, chipped nails, denim, combat boots, oversized blouse... I began to fidget under the scrutiny. Her eyes finally settled back at my face, and I prayed to God that my red lipstick wasn't all over my teeth.

"Is there any particular reason as to why you would pass on this?"

Yeah, I've bumped uglies with your brother. "No," I squeaked.

She rolled her eyes and her pressed her lips tightly as she searched for her words. Andrea let out an exhausted sigh as if I was the one who had originally called the meeting and was now wasting her time. "The fact of the matter is that our company, although is very successful, needs a little shaking up. We loved what you did with your department, we were all very aware that you took the directive and elevated it, which was what we wished for the other stores. But if you and Maggie think that you're not ready—"

My whole body snapped into attention. "What?"

"I think you and your store manager are on the same page. Now, I'm sorry that this is not the opportunity you were looking for. Hopefully, we can find a good fit for you." She smiled with her lips, and it looked like it hurt. This felt like a dismissal.

I nodded. "Oh, right." I started to rise but stopped midway. My mind tried to grasp the fact that Maggie had definitely whispered something negative in Andrea's ear and I'm wondering if Andrea was privy to what happened two years ago...Andrea cleared her throat, making me finally get up from my seat. "Sorry, my brain was overloaded for a second. I just wanted to ask...what exactly did Maggie say?"

Her eyes softened. "I don't think that's relevant," she answered diplomatically.

I nodded slowly. "Right, right." I waved behind me like a kid leaving Disney land. "Thank you, have a nice day." I practically ran out the room, almost knocking Maggie to the floor as I passed by. "Look up when you walk!" she called after me.

I stopped in my tracks. I faced Maggie. She must have seen the crazy in my eyes because she took a step back. "What did you say to Andrea?"

"Excuse me?"

"About my development. What did you say to her?"

Maggie folder her arms, smirking at me. "I don't think that's any of your business."

"If it's about me then it is my business."

She shrugged. "Fine. I told her you weren't ready. You take every-thing personal; your efficiency isn't where it should be...you don't deserve it."

I took another stepped forward before stopping myself. *Was I really going to slap her in the mouth? Was she worth the stress and aggravation and my financial stability?* The anger in my body had no form of release so I stomped out of the breakroom. I don't know where my feet were taking me, I just knew that I had to get out of the building. I passed Marvin. "I need a fifteen," I yelled out. I didn't know how much I could figure out in fifteen minutes but all I knew was that I needed some time.

"You can't! we need to clean up before—" he grabbed hold of my arm. When he saw my flushed face, he let go. "I'll tell her I sent you to get Velcro tape from the craft store."

"Thank you," I whispered. I didn't even take my coat. I hugged myself to shield me from the cold. I bumped into someone else. "Hey," Max's voice prompted me to finally look up. "Ginny? Are you crazy? It's freezing out here." He finally noticed that I had tears rolling down my face. "What's wrong?"

"I'm sorry."

His eyebrows came down heavy. "For what?"

"Bumping into you...being overly emotional...I don't think I'm giving women a good name right now. I just..." I let out a sigh as a gust of wind whipped at us. "Want to smash something!" Max pulled me back into the store through the employee entrance that was right around the corner. "Max, I need a minute because if I see Maggie's face right now, you will lose a store manager and I will be hauled off to jail screaming that the voices made me do it!"

Max looked from side to side and pulled me towards the loading dock. "What is happening?" he held my arms to steady the angry rage that caused me to shake.

"I hate her! I don't know why I stayed as long as I have!" I began to pace in the small space between Max and the doorway.

"What are you talking about? What do you mean? Who do you hate?" he took my chin in his hands and forced me to look him in the eyes.

"Maggie." My voice cracked. "I am on the verge of a mental breakdown!"

He grinned at me. "It seems you're always on the verge of some mental breakdown, you should really see a doctor."

I finally glanced around the loading dock. "Why are we here? It looks like we're going to make a drug deal."

"You needed to cool down away from...why are you looking at me like that?"

I stood on my tip toes and kissed him. I felt him give into me, softening against me. His arms let me go and fell to my waist. He moaned as my hips instinctively pressed against his. "Ginny..." he whispered.

"Mmmhmmm," I couldn't open my eyes.

"We can't do this."

"What?" My eyes snapped open. "Oh, shit. I'm sorry, Max. I had this pent-up frustration...I lost my mind; I didn't know what else to do. I'm sorry for using you."

He chuckled softly. "I'm fine. Use my body whenever you want." My heart began to race as his words tumbled out. "It's a joke...a bad one. It's just your lipstick stains like a motherfucker...excuse my French. This is going to take me an hour, bleach and the love of Christ to get this stuff off."

"I gotta get back," I spun to make my exit.

Max's touch on my shoulder stopped me. "Wait, tell me what happened."

I refused to turn back around. "I turned down the development,

Maggie doesn't think I could do it, or at least that's what she told your sister." I sighed. "I gotta get back."

"Do you want the chance?"

I looked over my shoulder. "What?"

He tucked his hands into his pockets. "Do you want the chance?"

I thought about Maggie, Marvin...my fashion designer ambitions that I let die. "I honestly don't know," I confessed.

"I can talk to Andrea."

"Your sister is an ice princess. I'm afraid when she finally smiles, she'll shatter."

"My sister can be scary," he admitted. "Let me talk to her and make it right."

"Max, I don't want you doing me favors. It just feels icky and wrong and like strings."

"Strings?"

I finally faced him again. "Like you're Geppetto, I'm Pinocchio..."

"That's not sexy at all," he joked. I sighed but he continued, "I get it. But speaking as your boss and not the guy who has your lipstick setting on his face...your merchandising is good and from what the staff said, you're really good at your job. Fuck what Maggie thinks, what do you want?"

"Fine, do whatever." I began to walk back to the store from the loading dock.

"Is that a yes?" he yelled behind me.

"Yes," I yelled back without slowing my stride. Maggie ignited a fire of determination that I didn't think I wanted to devote to this company. I busied myself making coffee. The *Keurig* churned as I thought of a way to get Maggie to fall to her knees as I made her my bitch...figuratively.

"Is this your fifteen? Because if it's not you're stealing company time," Maggie's voice sang behind me.

"If this billion dollar company is worried about me stealing a couple of minutes, then it has bigger issues to worry about," I muttered.

"What was that?" She stopped mid stride.

"I said there's nothing to worry about, I'm on a fifteen." She squinted at me, assessing me from head to toe but didn't say a word. I began to add sugar and creamer to my cup as she stewed in her silence. "Are you going to watch me drink the coffee? I promise you it's not that interesting."

"I'm just wondering why you turned down the visual manager opportunity. Too much for you?" In her attempt to act if she cared, her nose scrunched up in a smug expression.

"It's just not the direction I want to go in," I offered.

"Well, any direction you want to go in this company needs you to have managerial experience, as I recall you don't have any, do you?"

I took a tentative sip of my coffee before answering. "No, I don't."

"I knew that." she shrugged. I could see the corner of her lips quirk up slightly; it was the only sign of her joy at my inadequacy.

"If you don't mind, I'd like to drink my coffee in peace." I slowly lowered myself to the seat as Andrea called out my name. I bit my lip, swallowing the sigh that was ready to come out. "I'm in here," I heard myself call back.

Her blonde head poked through the open doorway of the break-room. "Can we just have a quick chat in the office?"

"Absolutely," I said brightly. Surely if my voice sounded happy, my mood would change.

"I'll be right in," Maggie said from behind us.

Andrea looked over her shoulder. "That won't be necessary, Maggie. This will only take a minute."

I locked eyes with Maggie and smiled sweetly. "Don't worry, I won't extend my fifteen."

There was no seating me in the proper place this time, there was me and Andrea.

"My brother, Max, said he ran into you, and you expressed that you wanted another chance."

Wow, he worked fast.

I blew out a stream of laughter. "Yes. I was just trying to process everything when I bumped into him and thought I had lost the opportunity."

Andrea's face softened with understanding. "You can still be in the running if you want it." She glanced at me from under her lashes. "You *do* want it, right?"

My mind was an indecisive bitch, and I hated that Andrea was standing in front of me witnessing it. I decided honesty was the best choice. "I don't know."

She did her little head tilt again. "Forget Maggie. Forget me. Is this what *you* want? A step forward in your career?"

Yes. No. Yes. No. I can always quit. Oh, shit. Where the hell did that thought come from?! "What if I say no?" Oh, shit what did I just ask? I inwardly cringed at my question because I already knew the answer and I felt like an asshole for even asking such a dumb question.

"This offer disappears once I leave this room. Another person would get a shot." Andrea's demeanor changed quickly back to ice princess. Deep down in my gut I knew that this woman hated me. Did I want to stay at H. Moda? If I stayed here, would a different position make me happy? Or was this a way for me to avoid taking a leap with something I really wanted to do.

The silence was overwhelming, it was shocking when Andrea's cold voice cut through. "Well, if this meeting is over, please send in—"

"I'll do it." I had no other choice. Or at least I felt like I didn't.

Andrea's head snapped around. "Really?"

"Yes." My heart beat a mile a minute.

"Well, then, you'll have a month to prove that this is the job for you. You'll shadow Marvin, but you are still a visual so you will have to keep up with your own department as well as give feedback when needed, partner with Maggie if you need support, and you will have to be in store for the holidays. So, if you have any obligations—"

"I don't."

"Well, great. We'll start tomorrow—" Andrea was cut off by a knock on the office door. "Come in!" she yelled out.

"Hey, sorry I'm late. Waking up at this time takes some getting used to..." Max stopped short at the sight of me. "Hello, Virginia." This man should get an award for how smooth he was being.

"Hey, Max." Our eyes were locked on each other; I still felt his lips on mine, the feel of him hard against my belly only minutes before had my blood running hot. Then I remembered that his sister was watching us. "Listen Andrea, it was great talking to you. I gotta get out on the floor." I thumbed in the direction of the door and began to back out.

There was another knock on the door, without consent Maggie poked her head in, stopping me in my tracks. "How are we all doing?" In her all-black outfit, she reminded me of a witch out on rodeo. The wide brim felt hat she wore was just ridiculous.

"Gin has just agreed to shadow Marvin. If all goes well, she will be the visual manager of our Soho store," Andrea explained. As she said the words, my heart raced. I felt like I just committed myself for life. There will be no more time to be a half assed fashion designer that I've been for the last two years.

"What about that doc that she has on her record?" Maggie asked, feigning worry. My head shot up; she didn't just throw me under the bus, she was driving the damn thing.

"Why do you have a doc?" Max asked.

"Because I—"

"Because she was stealing company time the night before thanks-giving," Maggie spoke over me, and I shook my head at her audacity.

"How much time?" Andrea asked.

"Ten minutes!" I yelled. When Max's and Andrea's eyes widened, I cleared my throat as a way to settle my nerves down. "It was only ten minutes. I was the only visual scheduled to put up all the posters and signage and window vinyl's. I clocked out ten minutes later and got a doc."

Andrea looked at Maggie. "I think we can excuse that doc; it will just be a verbal warning and you can start your shadowing tomorrow."

"Congratulations, Gin." Maggie whispered, as she offered me a tight smile.

"Thank you," I replied to her. "Okay, now I'm going to go because I have some things to finish." I rushed out of the room, closing the door gently behind me. Closing my eyes and leaning against it to get my bearings. That was until it opened, and I fell backwards. I let out a yelp as strong arms caught me. "Are you okay?"

I stood straight up, stepping out of his hold as if his hands were on fire. "Yeah, I'm cool." I waved one hand up, to assure Andrea and Maggie who was looking from behind him that I was fine. Max shut the door. "That was real smooth."

"How was I supposed to know you were going to open the door two seconds after I left?"

He smirked. "So, you said yes."

"That I did. Thank you for that." I began to walk away to go hide in the deco room. I heard Max's quick footsteps as he followed me. I glanced over my shoulder. "Are you following me?"

He placed a hand on my shoulder to stop me. "Hey," when I turned around, he glanced around before he spoke. "How about you let me take you out for dinner? Lunch, if you think dinners too much."

I wanted to say yes but I knew that that wasn't the right choice. "I don't think so, Max."

"It'll be as friends celebrating a step forward in your career."

"You know we wouldn't keep it friendly," I sighed. When he smiled and shrugged, it irked something inside of me and I knew that I had to take drastic measures. "Max, I'm seeing someone." There was a tick in his jaw as he clenched it. His silence was deafening as he processed the information. I could see the questions rolling around in his mind. Before he could ask me anything I squeezed my eyes closed and foraged on. "I know I should've told you sooner but I—" I felt his hand fall from my shoulder as he turned and walked away from me.

Did I do the right thing? Somewhere in the pit of my stomach it didn't feel like I did.

7

Rule 10: Believe in your team, through belief anything's possible. The company loves to challenge you from day one; When the team develops the company as a whole develops.

I did my best to avoid Max the rest of the day, which wasn't hard because he was holed up in the office. I left with no goodbyes to anyone just a quick wave and a grunt before I escaped into the cold winter evening. On the long subway ride home, I got to reflect on the day; I replayed the look of betrayal on Max's face. To be honest, I didn't think he was going to take it that badly. But if the tables were reversed and he was the one to tell me that he slept with me while being in a relationship with someone else, I wouldn't have just left in silence. I think security would've had to escort me out. My past had taught me a couple of lessons; one, don't date anyone from work and two, being cheated on didn't feel good. I sighed and closed my eyes.

I made it home in one piece, but my mind was still a jumbled mess. I ran up the stairs so I could avoid Mrs. Pierces verbal assaults and immediately went to take a warm bath. Not even that could clear my mind. The realization on just how sore my body was hit me like a ton of bricks, and I let myself melt into the water.

Being a visual merchandiser was like being a slave. Okay, maybe slave is too harsh a term but at times that's what it felt like. We weren't managers, so our pay wasn't as high. Regardless of that fact, we were supposed to execute the moves, adjust to any feedback, we were expected to run the new production garments along with replenishment if the sales associates ran everything wrong. If the lines were long, we were still expected to hop on register, work the fitting rooms. If there were empty or messy tables, we were expected to fill or tidy up. I was on my feet eight plus hours a day at work, non-stop moving. My bones were developing arthritis, and at the ripe old age of twenty-nine, my sciatica was becoming a problem. This job took everything I had but for some reason, I kept devoting my life to it. I was a masochist.

When the bath got cold and my body resembled a prune, I got myself out and dried. I looked out the bathroom across the hall into my bedroom at my sewing machine covered in dust. Like a magnet I was pulled towards it. It was a long time since I even turned the damn thing on. How lame is it that I let a man and all the insecurities of that relationship fizzle me out? *He didn't fizzle me out, I did.*

A few successful shows and some steady orders and I thought that I was on my way. Then it all came back at me in a flash. *"So you rather spend time working on that than spending time with me?" Rafas voice was low but sharp. I just didn't want to fight.*

"What do you want me to do? Give it up?"

"Yes!" My tiny apartment shook from the strength of his voice. My heart beat fast, I've never seen Rafa so angry. He stepped closer, reaching out his hand. "Ginny, I didn't mean to yell. But you know I expect a certain amount of time and attention."

"My business does too." I fired back.

"What business?! You have a couple of crazies buying some of your designs...you think that's enough to pay bills? Is that what's going to give you a future and kids?"

I wanted love. I wanted someone who could give me those things. I wanted someone to believe in my passion. But I kept those thoughts to myself because the realization that I could lose him and be alone was not something I wanted to think about. Rafa pulled me into his arms; I kept my spine stiff and my eyes dry. I felt him sigh. "Why don't you just do this as a hobby?"

The buzz of my phone brought me out of the bitter memory. How stupid I had been. I looked down; Marvin's name appeared. "Yes?" I answered.

"You just ran off today."

"I couldn't deal." I gingerly touched the sewing machine. *Maybe it's time to start again.*

"She wants you out."

That snapped me out of my melancholy. "What? Who?"

"Maggie. She told Andrea that if there is even a hiccup in this whole development of yours, she will terminate you. No job."

"What did Andrea say?"

"She agreed. I tried to object but you know how Maggie is...she let them in on what happened...you have a reputation."

"They know about Rafa?"

"Andrea doesn't know specifics but what she does know doesn't put you in the best light. She thinks that you were given an opportunity last time because you had a thing with Rafa." I felt my body tighten again. I sighed and laid down in my bed. "Max doesn't know, if that's what you're worried about."

That hadn't been what I was worried about. "I don't know if I even want the fucking job."

"Whether you want it or not...stay away from Max Thomas. You know I'm on your side every time. But, if you want to keep your job, your dignity...don't go near that man."

I smiled to myself, thinking about how absurd all of this was. "Marvin..."

"Are you smiling? I could hear you smiling. This is not funny, Virginia. If you don't want to be unemployed, no more kissing him—"

I sat up. "You saw us kissing?"

"You know I did, remember when I…did you kiss him again?!"

I groaned and threw myself back onto my pillows. "Yes."

"What is wrong with you?"

"I don't know. But there will be no more kissing Max Thomas. He is my boss and I need to keep my job."

"Good, keep repeating it to yourself. I gotta go, I'm hosting tonight." There was no formal goodbye, just a hang-up.

"No more kissing Max Thomas," I said to me, myself, and my sewing machine.

8

Rule #43: Don't take feedback personally.

"Ginny, report to the office once you clock in."

I hadn't even taken off my coat and I was already called into the office. I groaned as I locked my locker in the breakroom and sat in the god-awful chair closest to the door. Maggie leisurely typed away as I fantasied about the coffee I was going to make and throw back once I left this room.

When five minutes passed and she still hadn't said a word, my patience began to wear off and the caffeine withdrawal was taking over. That is the little patience I had at six in the morning. "Maggie, what is this all about?"

She didn't answer. Instead, her typing slowed down and I threw my head back in exhaustion. This woman was in fact exhausting. This game we always played was exhausting. Maggie gave one last stab at the keyboard when she finally chose to answer. "Marvin has to support another store, last minute, so you will oversee the visual team."

"Me? But how is that possible? I was supposed to shadow Marvin, not do his job."

Maggie picked up her phone to glance at it, even though I knew that it didn't ring or vibrate, the damn thing didn't even light up. She wanted to mess with me, and she knew how to do it. She played with her phone, ignoring me as if I were no one. In her world, I was no one. I opened my mouth to speak when she spoke over me. "You can run the visual team, can't you?" her long acrylic nail traced against her chin lightly and I knew she was toying with me.

"With my eyes closed," I answered with a smile.

"I love your confidence, but you'll need to keep your eyes wide open. Do you value your job, Ginny?"

This felt like a trap, and I refused to fall into it. I wanted nothing more than to prove I can do this job better than she even thought. I wanted to stand on the edge of a cliff with my hands stretched out and yell like a savage, bad ass woman that I can do this job better than anyone in this company. Instead, I said nothing.

Maggie leaned forward, resting her elbows on the table. "If there is even an inkling of scandal, a minor mistake that would embarrass me in front of any Thomas family member, this job will be snatched from her calloused hands, and you will be fired. Do I make myself clear?"

My ears burned with rage. "Is this the level of leadership that you resort to? What are you trying to prove? Who do you think you are?" I asked while trying to hold my rage at bay.

"I am someone who just cares...a lot."

I got up from my seat and walked straight to the deco room where the visual team was waiting. I stared at them blankly.

"Ginny? Are you okay?" Meish asked.

There was no way I could tell them what happened in the office. What could they do? Share my anger but no action would be taken. Not one of us in this room held any power. I swallowed the lump in my throat. "Marvin is supporting another store so I will be in charge of the visual team."

Tahiri smiled. "Wow, so now what boss lady?"

A normal person would quit on the spot. But I had no other jobs lined up. I had bills to pay. I looked at the three of them, feeling like a poser. "Let's execute the kids move. Mark, start with dressing the mannequins..." I rattled off tasks for everyone when Meish raised her hand.

"You don't have to do that," I said.

"Oh, I just wanted to say that I didn't have time to prep the signage."

I waved my hand as if it were no big deal. "I can do it."

While the others set off to start the move, I made a mad dash to get the signage done when I bumped into Max at the computer. I skidded to a stop. I did my best to not draw attention to myself. I slowly turned around with every intention of finding something else to do while I waited for the computer.

"Virginia? Did you need the computer?" he asked, stopping me in midstride. His voice sounded so silky that I felt goose pimples down my spine; I hated that.

"Mmmhmm," was all I could get out. There was something about this man that turned me into a thirteen-year-old girl and him into a teenage heart throb. I thought I would feel the wrath of his anger from what happened yesterday. Max ignored me while typing away on the computer. I stared at his fingers as they glided across the keyboard effortlessly. "Okay, all set," he said with a smirk. It's like he knew what I was thinking. Those fingers could bring me to my knees...and they have.

He stepped back as I took my place in front of the computer. I began to type out descriptions and prices of garments, but still Max stood behind me.

I looked over my shoulder. "Max? Was there something else?"

"How's your boyfriend?" he asked in a low whisper.

The back of my neck prickled. "He's home...asleep...recovering from a long night," I said as I continued to type. I cringed at my answer. I didn't want to want Max, why was I trying to make him angry jealous?

"I find it strange that you didn't mention him at all."

"Max," I groaned. I didn't want to have this conversation right here, right now.

"It can't be serious if you were with me two nights in a row and where about to go on a date with me before…"

"Too many drinks." I threw the excuse out there hoping that would suffice.

"That would be a great excuse if we only left it at one night. Why didn't you bring it up the second night?"

"Just drop it," I snapped.

"I just think he doesn't exist," he said. Max leaned against the computer desk, trying to look like he was unfazed, but his eyes showed the fire burning.

"He's real."

"What's his name?"

"Ziggy," I blurted out. It was the first name that came to mind and the name I gave my vibrator because it had this third setting…you get it.

His eyebrows shot up. "Ziggy?"

"Yeah, you got a problem with that?" I shot back. I wished I could type faster and be done with this.

"What's his last name?"

"Mor…ris. Ziggy Morris."

"Ziggy Morris? Sounds like the kind of guy who doesn't wash his feet in the shower."

I suppress the urge to giggle. "Well, he does. I can tell you for a fact that he's the cleanliest person I know." What I said wasn't false, I cleaned my vibrator after every use.

I saw his jaw clenched again, the tick in his cheek making me feel only slightly victorious in our battle for the upper hand.

I hit print.

"What the hell, Ginny?"

"What?" I could feel the anger rise. I didn't expect him to take all the fake boyfriend stuff as gracefully as he did yesterday, but I also didn't think he would want to have this conversation in his place of business.

"I didn't think you would be the person who would cheat on her boyfriend, it's not like you."

My eyebrows came down in an angle as irritation settled in my bones. "You don't even know me," I snapped.

"Yes, I do. With what happened between us..." He cast his eyes downward as if replaying the passionate nights we shared.

"What exactly happened between us, Max?"

In the midst of our argument, I hadn't realized that we stepped closer to each other. We were standing nose to nose, breathing heavy, hands on hips. Behind me someone cleared their throat. Max and I jumped a part. "If you really don't want people to know what happened between you guys, maybe you shouldn't stand so close," Marvin whispered. I snatched my signs from the printer and stomped away.

Marvin followed behind. "Ginny, wait!" I stopped instantly causing Marvin to ram into my back. "Shit, Ginny."

"Sorry, what are you doing here?"

"I'm here to make sure you're set up for success. Maggie sent me away to support to make your promotion harder."

"Okay. What do I do?"

"You want this job?"

I nodded slowly. "I think so."

He clapped his hands together. "I'll take that. You need to be a yes man. Say yes to Maggie, be her right hand."

I shook my head. "That's' not going to happen."

"You want this promotion? You need her off your back. Be a yes man in her face but follow your instincts when her back is turned. If your ideas are successful, she'll get credit and you'll be in her good graces."

I rolled my eyes. "It's like you're telling me to sell my soul to the devil."

He shrugged his shoulders. "The devil wears cheap knee-high leather boots and wide brim felt hats."

"She's a bitch."

"That bitch can be worse if you don't take my advice." Marvin stomped his foot. "Also…"

I folded my arms. "What now?"

"You need to be nicer to big daddy. Not jump his bones nice but just nicer. I can tell something has changed and you don't have to tell me what it is now…that's what Sunday brunch is for…just be nice. At the end of the day, he runs this company, and he has more power than any of us. He could fire you in a heartbeat." What Marvin said was true but would Max really do that? "Now, let me steal some flat bars because the midtown store has a shortage and I want to make a good impression."

The rest of the day had no bumps. The move was executed well and I pretty much steered clear of management.

Wednesday came and it was more of the same. The visual team came in at five in the morning to secure the new juniors set-up. One cup of coffee wasn't enough to curb the anxiety I had knowing that Andrea and Max were coming in. Those two would walk the store, taking notes. Every time Max was around, I felt a tiny hint of electricity that I didn't want to indulge. He was mad and I was mad that he was mad even though it was my fault that he was mad in the first place.

Our eyes briefly passed over each other. I ignored him and walked Tahiri through her set-up. "I think we need to move the blue up higher," I suggested.

She nodded, moving fast to make the change only to have Maggie stop her. "I don't think that's the best idea," her shrill voice rang through the air, causing Max and Andrea to observe.

Today Maggie's heels were higher, probably adding to her natural irritability, and her outfit was reminiscent of fashionistas of the past, faux fur vest with a turtleneck sweater and her faux leather tights. I'll give it to her; she was really trying.

I swallowed a sigh. I shouldn't be surprised. I already knew that Maggie would try to assert her dominance over me, the only shock was that she waited a whole day to do so. "What's not the best idea?" I asked.

"To move the blue higher. In the commercial pages, that specific garment is lower on the wall," she said smugly.

"I know, but because our walls aren't exactly like the pages, we have to adjust to the wall system we have."

"But it should be lower," she continued.

I clasped my hands behind my back, digging my nails into my palm. Marvin's words repeated in my head, *be a yes man!* But old habits die hard. "I understand, but these pages were made for the perfect store. Realistically, we don't have all the garments that are called for, so the ones that we do have that corresponds to this trend we showcase them higher." Maggie chewed her lip while pondering my words prompting me to continue, "Also because the blue is a pop color, this particular garment should be higher because the blue before that is sitting lower; the wall should have a wave of the pop colors," I added, showing her with hand movements so she would understand.

"Ginny, it's silly. You sound silly. That garment is shown on the pages as lower. We have to follow the pages," she said, already fuming but trying her best to keep her cool in front of the others.

I smiled wide. "Yes, Maggie," I said through clenched teeth. With a nod Maggie walked away. I ran up to Tahiri. "Put the sweater higher," I ordered.

With wide eyes, she did as ordered, continually throwing glances behind us. "Tahiri, chill out. She's not going to say anything," I assured her.

When the move was over and I walked with Andrea, Max and Maggie, we stopped in front of the wall where Maggie wanted me to stick to the pages. "This wall looks different from the pages," Max pointed out.

I could feel the daggers that Maggie was shooting at me; I could see her blurry figure from the corner of my eye, folding her arms, ready to throw me under the bus yet again. "I think this looks better; it brings the trend together, almost tightening it up. Good work, guys." Andrea approved, which left Maggie standing next to me silently stewing.

Max and Andrea wandered off to deal with more pressing business matters which left me with Maggie. "Yes?" I smiled sweetly in her direction.

She folded her arms. "Well, done. If you go behind my back and the result is everyone questioning why it was wrong and it comes down to you or me...I will serve you on a silver platter." Maggie threatened, mimicking my sweet tone. She squinted her eyes as her nose came up before sashaying away. I let out a breath of relief. I rolled my neck to release the stiffness and stress that formed every time I stepped into this building. The visual team stood, staring at me. I clapped my hands just like Marvin did. "Let's start cleaning up, we open in an hour."

When clean-up was done, I dismissed everyone for a fifteen-minute break. I passed Max on my way to the bathroom. "Great set up today, Ginny," he offered.

"Now you're talking to me?" I threw back. My heart began to skip beats at the cojones that I just grew. I shook my head, my feet not stopping. I practically ran into the bathroom stall and sat on the toilet. I let my head drop into my hands and felt a ball in my throat. Is this what I wanted? I knew that Maggie had it out for me. Did I want to deal with that? Was it going to be worth it?

"Gin?" I heard Max whisper.

I sat up straight in the stall. "What are you doing in here?" Could he hear the shakiness in my bravado?

"I was waiting for you outside the bathroom, but then that felt weird."

"And this was better?" It was hard to hide the indignation from my voice. This was violating every privacy law. Only stalkers and right-wing politicians resorted to this sort of harassment.

"Ummm..."

"Just get to it," I snapped.

"I want to take you out for a coffee. Not for anything else but to set some ground rules," he said.

"I sense that I'm in trouble and I don't like this journey for me." God, I sounded like a brat.

"You're not really using the bathroom, are you?" he asked.

"No!"

"Open the door."

I thought about it for two seconds before sliding the lock open. I peeked out; Max forced himself in the small stall. "What the hell, Max?" I hissed.

"Understand that I run this store. This is my company," He had rage in his eyes.

"I know this."

"Do you? Because it seems like you don't. You used me in some sick game that you have going on with your hippie boyfriend. And now you have the nerve to just brush me off and speak to me any way you want. That's not gonna happen."

The small stall felt smaller. We were mere inches away from

each other. The electricity was undeniable, but I messed it all up with my lie.

I pushed at his chest; he caught my wrists in one hand. "Get out, Max." I whispered; all the fight had gone out of me. This man was gorgeous, funny, smart, gentle but in this moment, he was the dominant, ruthless boss and I think seeing this side of him just added to the attraction.

"I deserve some form of respect when we are here, working together." The anger made his nostrils flair. His head rested against mine, he closed his eyes. "Do you love him?"

I felt his cool breath against my lips and my eyelids fell shut. "Love who?" I asked, utterly entranced in this man's spell. Our lips connected as if on their own. It was slow, soft. His hands let go off my wrists, I wrapped them around his neck, deepening the kiss. Max had me against the door of the stall, hiking up one of my legs and thrusting his hardness against me. "Does he make you feel like this? Does he touch you like this?" he asked as his hand slid between us and desperately rubbed me through my jeans.

"What are we doing?" I asked as I let my head rest against the door.

"Do you love him?" he asked, leaving kisses down my neck.

We heard the bathroom door open and laughter that sounded a lot like Andrea and Maggie.

I pushed Max, pointing to the toilet.

He mouthed, "What?" not grasping what I was saying.

"Stand on it," I whispered.

"Hello?" Maggie called out. Max stood on the toilet seat crouched down, while I sat on what little space that was left.

"Yes?" I answered out.

"Ginny? Are you talking to yourself?"

I wracked my brain with some excuse or valid answer, nothing seemed good enough. I rattled off the first thing that came to mind. "Um, you know sometimes, I need to give myself a pep talk."

Max snorted, trying to hold in his laughter. I threw a look at him that I hoped said *shut the fuck up*. "Okay...we'll, give you a minute alone. We just came to wash our hands anyway." Max pulled out his phone and typed away.

A phone chirped. "I gotta go, Max wants to meet me outside," Andrea said.

"Good luck!" Maggie shouted to me as they exited the bathroom. I got up, giving Max room to get down. "You need to wear different lipstick. I got red all over me," he said with no emotion in his voice.

"Does it really matter?"

He eyed me coldly. "No, it doesn't." he wiped what he could with toilet paper. Emotion washed over me as I realized he was trying to hurt me like I had done to him. I refused to let him see.

Max left with a smirk on his face as if he had won some game. I gave it five minutes before I stormed out the store past Maggie. "Where are you going?" she called out.

I didn't answer.

I walked past Andrea and Max, who were in deep conversation outside. I felt Max's eyes follow me down the block until I turned the corner. Once inside the coffeeshop, I stared at the menu as I waited for my turn.

"What's your order?" Max's voice made the back of my hairs stand up.

"What? Are you following me now? I can't order what I want now? I get it Max, you're in charge. You've put me in my place. Now leave me alone." I chastised while still looking at the menu.

"You drive me crazy, Ginny. I instantly feel regret for treating you like I did five minutes ago. It's not the person I am or want to be. I'm just jealous and hurt. But it's no excuse for what just happened."

I glanced at him from the corner of my eye. "Hot caramel latte," I mumbled.

He raised an eyebrow. "Those things have a lot of sugar in it."

"Well, that's what I want." I crossed my arms. I could feel myself frowning in his direction. "I'm going to wait at one of the tables," I replied as I walked away. I just needed distance from this man. This all felt like manipulation, the same way that Rafa did to me a couple years ago. It left a nasty taste in my mouth, a sickening feeling in my belly. I didn't want it to be this way with Max and I made it that way.

I glanced over to the counter where Max was placing the order; he smiled at the barista who blushed. My irritation only grew; I wanted to leave him in the café, but I didn't know if I was being overly sensitive because I couldn't have him or because of the morning madness with Maggie, either way I wanted to get out of there.

He walked over and placed my drink in front of me. "One latte." Max smiled.

"Thanks," I snapped.

His smile faded. "I really am sorry, Ginny. Are you okay?"

"No, I'm not okay," I raised the drink to my lips and immediately regretted it. Scolding hot coffee covered my tongue causing me to spit it out and cough in hysterics.

"Oh my God are you okay?" A customer asked from the table next to us.

I glared at them which caused them to immediately turn back around as Max pounded my back. "I'm not choking!"

"I'm so confused," Max said as he stepped back.

I began to wipe the table down. "The coffee was hot," I said. Embarrassment made me angrier.

"No, I'm confused about us. You used me to cheat on your boyfriend. You made it seem like you were alone, and I still want you. I shouldn't but I do."

I ignored the stinging on my tongue and looked him straight in the eye. "I'm a liar, a cheat and your employee...I'm heading back."

I took one step towards the exit when Max's voice stopped me. "Ginny?"

I stopped without turning to face him. "Yes?"

"What's up with you and Maggie?"

That caught my attention. I spared a glance over my shoulder. "What do you mean?"

"I see the tension. I see how she singles you out, what's the deal?" Max took a sip of his drink while waiting patiently for my answer. "Are you going to answer?" he asked when I didn't respond.

"Max, I was in line for a promotion and..." I closed my eyes as the memories came flooding back. "I don't want to risk my chance by bringing up the past."

"I'm your boss. I need to know if there are any clogs in the pipes."

"What are you talking about?" I walked back to the table.

"I need to know if there is a potential for future problems."

"Then just say that." My irritability did not seize.

Max had the audacity to smirk. "Listen, I want us to be friends." His demeanor changed like he was consoling a child.

I rolled my eyes. "No, you don't." The least he could do was be honest. With what Marvin said and the whole thing with Maggie, I felt like I needed to have my guard up.

"I thought that you might need someone to talk to because you ran to the bathroom. And then you were crying in the stall—"

"I wasn't crying," I said.

"Ok, fine. You were sniffling in the bathroom...I just wanted to make sure you were good."

I sighed. "I'm fine." There was something about Max that could get me to talk. "It's just Maggie gets under my skin; you get under my skin. Marvin's not here to be a buffer. I can't get a sense of Andrea, so that throws me off."

He cleared his throat. "I know it may not seem like it now, but you can talk to me about anything." I nodded even though I knew I wouldn't really confide in him. It was nice that he was trying to make amends. Maybe we could end up just being friends.

"It's nothing. There are no clogs in any pipes," I answered.

He studied me for a second. Max knew I was lying but let it slide. "Alright, so you won't tell me what's going on. As a way of extending an olive branch, let's talk about something else. Did you get a hold of your parents? How was your weekend?"

Thank God. Was Max really trying to be nice or was there another motive? I mean, what other motive could there be? Did someone hint at a scandal from before. Either way, I was thankful for the reprieve. "No, to the whole parent's thing. And I pampered myself. I bumped into your brother at a restaurant. He was with some curvy brunette with big lips."

"That's Missy Jones," he answered.

"Missy? What kind of name is Missy?"

Max chuckled. "Rich people are always trying to make their kids sound interesting before they develop a personality," he shrugged.

Then realization dawned on me. "Missy Jones, as in your ex-girlfriend?"

"Googled me, did you?" he teased. "Her and her family are long-time friends of ours, she's had her sights on George for a while."

"Wait, weren't you guys engaged at one point?"

"Yeah." He shrugged his shoulders as if it were no big deal.

"And she's dating your brother?"

"I wouldn't call what they do dating."

"Ewww. It just seems pretty incestuous to me," I pointed out. I braved another attempt at drinking my coffee even though I could feel the roof of my mouth already peeling.

"Be careful with that, it's hot," he said with a smile.

I narrowed my eyes I at him. "Real funny."

Our eyes lingered on each other; I was the one who decided to break the spell. "Max."

"Virginia," he said with a smirk.

"Why'd you pay for my coffee?"

"I don't know," he shrugged, looking everywhere but at me. "Why do we do half the things we do?" I nodded my understanding. "I just instantly felt guilty. I could never act like that to anyone...I'm not a bad guy."

I shrugged my shoulders. "But I am." The hurt in his eyes showed, that crushed me.

"I don't think clear when I'm around you. My thoughts are all jumbled just by the smell of your perfume." His voice and his honesty were seductive.

I looked down at my drink. "Don't say things like that," I whispered.

"I know." His voice sounded just as miserable as I felt. When I finally got the courage to look at him, he took a deep breath. "Listen, Ginny, I—"

"Well, well, well, what do we have here?" George's voice bellowed throughout the café.

I should've been mortified from the stares but knowing everyone witnessed the fire I set inside my mouth, I just didn't care, I wanted to know what Max wanted to say.

"Why are you so loud?" Max asked, making no effort to hide his annoyance.

"What are you guys doing here?" he asked.

"Gin had a rough morning and I'm trying to give her a pep talk," Max fibbed.

"Really? Then you're giving a real shitty one. You guys look like you're at a funeral," he laughed.

"I think I have to head back," I slowly began to make my exit.

"No, wait. I'm sorry, I'll get my drink and we'll all head back to the store together," George said. When he saw my hesitation. "No one's going to say anything, you're with the global team. You won't get in trouble," he added with a laugh before he went to stand in line.

"I'm sorry about George."

"It's okay." I took another sip of my drink.

"Ginny, I—"

"Max, don't. I thought I wanted to hear what you had to say but I don't. Not here, not now."

He nodded. "If you need anything from us, please feel free to let us know. If Maggie is getting too much for you..."

"Would you offer the same courtesy to someone who hasn't seen you naked?" I whispered.

His lips formed a thin line. In my defense, I wasn't going to ask my boss, who I've seen naked, for special treatment.

"Yes, I would." The look that he gave me was full of anger. "I pride our company in one that takes care of its employees."

"I'm sorry, Max. I didn't mean to assume—"

"It's fine," he said.

Before I could say anything else, George came back with his drink. When he caught the sight of us his eyebrows furrowed. "You guys really have to lighten up," he scoffed.

We all walked back in silence. I went back to the breakroom where the team was waiting to have our meeting for the big holiday window reveal. Although the holidays were upon us, we always left the reveal to the week of Christmas to get people in for last minute shopping.

While I was going over the check list, I saw Max fling his coat on. "Have a good day, everyone!" he shouted, not really making eye contact with anyone. I realized that I was quiet. I brought my attention back to the team...who were all staring at me with knowing grins. "What?" I barked.

"You a little thirsty, Gin?" Meish asked.

"What?" I rolled my eyes.

"I think she broke her neck." Mark elbowed Meish. While Tahiri laughed.

"Okay, back to the meeting. Tahiri you and Mark will do the overnight for window set up."

"Yes," she groaned.

"Meish, you and I will be here in the morning to refresh the department to get it ready for the holiday rush."

"Yes, ma'am," she answered. "But remember, I have to leave around twelve because my parents are coming into town."

I nodded. "Yes, I remember. I think I'll add a sales advisor to support just in case we fall behind."

Thank the baby Jesus and Santa Clause that the rest of the week was so busy that I had no more run ins with Maggie, which calmed my nerves down just a tiny fraction.

Max was apparently handling business outside the store and the other Thomas' where practically invisible. There was no sign of Maggie until we had a touch base Friday afternoon. After successfully walking the store with her, and by successful, I mean with minimal verbal abuse and murderous looks, Maggie dismissed me for the day. "I heard that you worked overtime, you can adjust today and leave early." She glanced at her watch as if that was enough to make me disappear. In all honesty leaving early was great because I wanted to head to the fabric store. That urge hadn't surfaced in a long time and there was adrenaline coursing through my veins just thinking about starting something new.

"Have a good weekend, Maggie," I yelled as she walked away.

I spun on my heel to leave her when I slammed into someone. I glanced up to see George's beaming face. "Ginny!" his voice boomed, I wondered if he had any control over the volume.

"Hey, George."

"Ready for the meeting?"

"Actually, I'm about to head home," I said.

"Really? I thought you were shadowing the little guy," he said.

"His name is Marvin and he's busy supporting another store. And I'm not a manager so I'm not a part of that," I said. I really wanted to leave and head to the fabric store, inspiration struck, and I needed to tend to her. I saw the determination in George's eyes that told me that I was going to attend that meeting whether I wanted to or not.

"That's bull! How else are you going to learn?" he put an arm around my shoulder and pulled me close alongside him. He leaned down so his mouth was close to my ear making the hair on the back of my neck stand up. "These meetings are boring, but I think you'll benefit from them. I usually end up dozing off," he teased as I wiggled a tiny bit to get out of his hold, but he didn't let go. We walked to the office with all eyes on us. Max, Andrea, and Maggie immediately seized conversation when we entered.

"Gin, did you need something?" Maggie asked. Distain dripped from every pore of her body as her glance focused on George's arm around me.

"Um, no. I'm sorry for interrupting," George's arm finally fell to his side as noticed the intensity of the room.

"I invited Ginny to this meeting, seeing that she is technically part of the management team, and this would be something she would have to partake in later on down the road."

I caught the look that passed between Andrea and Max, who cleared his throat. "Well, of course. Have a seat, Virginia." Max gestured towards a chair next to me. I awkwardly sat down; I knew they had been talking about me. I wasn't sure, but it was just the awkwardness of it all; Maggie practically grinning, Andrea looking unfazed while toying with her pen and Max, unblinking in my direction. Taking a seat in this room felt as if I were sitting in the electric chair. I didn't know where to place my hands; should they sit on my lap? Should I be holding a pen? Should I cross my legs? Smooth my jeans?

"Ginny, can't you just sit still?" Maggie snapped. "I mean, please, just...be still."

Embarrassment flushed my cheeks as I folded my hands neatly on my lap. I spared a glance to Max, who looked irritable and Andrea, who observed silently, her face revealing nothing.

"Sorry," I whispered.

Max sat up straight. "Virginia, it's actually good that George was so kind enough to drape his arm around you and bring you in because we have something rather urgent to discuss."

So, this was the CEO. I've seen him in action since he's been at the store regularly; being polite to the employees but never joking around or completely relaxed, that was George's role.

"How has your week gone? Have you been happy running the visual team?"

This felt like a loaded question, but I ventured on anyway, "I don't have any complaints," I answered.

"I'm just going to be straightforward with you, Virginia. Word has gone back to us that you don't want this position and that you actually don't want to be part of the H. Moda family anymore," he explained. From the corner of my eye, I could see George put his phone away as he sat up straighter.

"I've never said that." At least out loud anyways.

"I'm going to ask you straight forward...do you want to work here?"

I felt like there was no other choice to make. I felt trapped, suffocated. Max's aggressiveness was enough to make me want to curl up in a ball. I was trying to find out what happened from our sort of truce in the coffee shop until now.

I looked over to where Maggie sat with pure hatred oozing out of her eyes. She was going to be no help.

"Virginia, it's an easy yes or no," Max's voice was firm. Although he tried to cover it, the hurt and anger bubbled close to the surface and the guilt I felt because of it was overwhelming.

A squeak came out as I tried to verbalize an answer that I couldn't give.

"Of course, she wants to be here. She's already given us eleven years of her life, why wouldn't she?" George petitioned in my favor.

"You are not her spokesperson. Virginia is a grown woman, she can speak for herself or else she wouldn't be up for this job," Max's words bit into everyone in the room. If this was Max keeping his cool, I didn't want to be around him when he lost it.

"Max..." Andrea chastised while George began toying with his phone again.

"Yes, I want to be here, Mr. Thomas." I answered. This situation called for formality, the twitch in his jaw told me that he didn't like it.

Maggie adjusted in her seat, sitting forward as if she were Oprah conducting some interview. "I just think that you still have a lot to learn in this role and that you take things too personally. It's okay to admit that this job is too much for you." Her eyes were like stone while her voice was sugary sweet.

"I honestly have no clue where this is coming from, those words have never left my mouth and if I were having second thoughts, you all would be the first to know...maybe not all of you, maybe like half the room." I sliced my hand through the air as if cutting through. I felt myself grow hot, then cold, and then pure hell erupt in my body.

"We overheard some sales advisors talking..." Maggie began. "We just want to make sure we are not overlooking someone who may deserve this, someone who is committed."

"Am I undeserving? Am I not committed enough?" I asked. No sooner had the words left my lips did the Thomas' all jump in.

"Absolutely not."

"No one is saying that."

I fought the urge to roll my eyes. That's the thing with working in a close-knit store, you never knew who was listening or spying. I sat up straighter in my seat. "I've stayed late every day this week, which is not something I would do if I wasn't committed. What the sales advisors overheard and falsely reported was that I was eager to leave early today because I am working on a collection."

"Really?!" Max's excitement caused the others to look at him as if he just grown another head. As he noticed, Max slumped a bit in his seat and toyed with his phone.

I decided to plead my case. "I know I have a lot to learn. I'm only shadowing, this isn't a formal training. Isn't formal training what's going to prepare me for the role? What I'm doing now is preparing me for my official training for this role," I heard George snort which gave me a little bit more confidence to defend myself. "Also, as a company we promote a healthy work/ life balance. Am I not allowed to have interests if it doesn't happen to do with this company?" I asked. I felt my cheeks flush as I waited for someone to answer.

"I'm just concerned that your interests outside of work will interfere with your actual job. Isn't designing clothes a time-consuming hobby?" Maggie asked.

Did she just call my passion a hobby? I narrowed my eyes at her. "I am a fashion designer; it is not a hobby."

"Even more of a reason to reconsider what you're getting into." She knew which buttons to press and just couldn't stop.

"Almost all creatives have day jobs. This would be no different." I said through gritted teeth. I could feel my heart pounding in my ears. I didn't want to lose my cool in front of the others, it was proving to be a difficult feat. The others observed in silence. I turned to George. "Do you guys usually have these conversations with other candidates or am I just special?" I knew what the root of this issue was, but I didn't have the balls to say it out loud.

"Although I find you special," George began with a wink. "I do think that we are overstepping just a tad."

"I second that," a brooding Max added.

I cleared my throat. "I would like a word privately with Maggie," I said. Marvin chose that moment to walk into the office. He stopped at the doorway as he took in the full office.

"I just came to do the timesheets...should I comeback?" He stood blinking.

"Marvin, please come in, we are about to leave. Ginny, because I am sound of mind, I can't let that happen. Obviously, emotions are all over the place," Andrea added.

"Can Marvin stay as a witness?" I asked.

Andrea looked to her siblings, her look lingering on Max. Upon his curt nod, she stood up and gestured towards George. "Let's go," she said. She turned back to Maggie and me, "We will give you five minutes," she said.

When the door closed behind us, I began, "Is this how it's going to be?"

"What do you mean?" She sat back and crossed her arms. Maggie did her best to look nonchalant, but she looked as if she were uncomfortable like she was holding in gas.

"Come off it, Maggie. You're trying to sabotage—"

Maggie folded her hands on the table in front of her. "I don't think that now is the right time for your development." Her words fell out slowly as if I were some creature from another planet. As if I wouldn't or couldn't understand the words that were coming out. She always had this tendency to make certain people feel as if they were beneath her. She got off on people feeling stupid. That's the worst thing to do to me. Nothing in the world ticked me off than someone making me feel dumb.

My cheeks flushed as anger raced through my body. "That's a lie and you know it. I am more qualified that most who are already in position," I pointed out.

"I think you take things too personally," she insisted.

"I take things personally if you make them personal," I shot back.

"Why would I make them personal?" she asked.

She had called my bluff before but not now, now I had the chance to set her straight. "Because of Rafa."

I heard Marvin gasp. I forgot he was here. The room fell silent as the weight of my words settled. "What about my husband, Ginny?" she asked threw gritted teeth. She sat unmoving in her chair.

"I've tried to explain when it all happened, I didn't know he was your husband, Maggie. If I had known—"

She held up her hand to stop me. "Enough." Maggie leaned forward in her seat. "This has nothing to do with that. This is simply me being your boss and telling you I don't think you're ready."

"Were you ready when they promoted you?" I asked unable to lose this argument.

She sighed. "Everyone is different, Ginny. If you're not ready or you want to spend your time on being a fashion designer," She sighed, "then why waste everyone else's time?"

"I think she's ready," Marvin said from his spot where he sat silently taking everything in.

"What was that?" Maggie asked, her response sounding less cavity inducing and more of a growl.

"I think that Ginny is more than ready for the promotion, she's been in the company a long time, longer than most. She's ready. She has her own methods of working that might be better than what we're used to."

"You are saying that because she's your friend," she snarled.

"No. I am saying this because I am her visual manager and I see her skill."

"My opinion still stands." Maggie folded her arms stubbornly putting an end to this conversation.

A soft knock sounded. Andrea poked her head in. "Are you guys ready?"

Maggie didn't think I was ready; if I'm being honest, I wasn't even sure I wanted the job. Everyone marched into the room and took their place. "Shall we continue on with this meeting?" she asked.

"Ginny, I think you are over your time, you may clock out now," Maggie said, as she walked behind me to see me out.

Without a single word I left the office. How many times have I thought to myself, *I need to get my shit together*?

Being blatantly sabotaged in a company I gave my twenties to felt like someone kicking me straight in the kidneys. It felt like going to Starbucks for a cold brew only to find they ran out and you ask for an ice coffee, but they don't have that either, so you have to settle for tea...who wants tea?! Not I! I refused to settle for less than what I deserve! And what I deserve is a fucking venti vanilla sweet cream cold brew!

Swap the cold brew for a life as a successful designer and you'll catch my drift.

"You're going have to seduce him," a voice whispered.

"God, is that you?" I whispered as I looked behind me to find Marvin standing close. "Oh, it's just you. What are you whispering about?" I asked as I put on my coat.

He pulled me to the side. "You need to sleep with him, seduce him...we need to beat Maggie. The devil cannot win."

I rolled my eyes. "I'm not seducing him."

"You know I would never tell you to pimp yourself out for a promotion, but if you really want it, I think it's necessary," he added. I took him in. His tense posture, his arms folded, tapping his tiny feet; Marvin was serious.

I shook my head. "You're out of your mind." I began to walk away; Marvin ran up behind me.

"Maggie is in there now talking about how she doesn't think you're right for the job."

I spun on my heels almost knocking him down. "I don't care, Marvin," I hissed. "Max and I are on very thin ice; I don't want to anger him more than I already have."

"Fine," he shrugged. "Seduce George then. He's the type that probably wouldn't mind."

"That's an even worse idea than the first one," I muttered.

"Okay, seduce Andrea but I don't think she dips in that water. Although, if she did, she might be a top...all of them seem a bit aggressive."

"Marvin, I'm not using your Scorpio toxicity to get promoted. I'm not sleeping with anyone who's last name is Thomas. If this promotion is meant for me, I will have it." I sighed. "I feel as if I wasted ten years of my life on something that was supposed to be temporary," I confessed.

"Then sleep with him, give him a BJ in the office...let him see a boob, whatever it takes to get promoted."

"Did you have to do something like that?" I snapped. I walked through the breakroom and onto the sales floor.

Marvin reached out and gentle pulled me back. "Before anyone was anyone, I slept with Tim on a random Friday night at a random foam party."

"Tim..." realization hit me. "Marvin!"

"Yes, he is now the head of east coast HR."

"Marvin!"

"I know but he isn't even my type! Who is into a pervy thin mustache and no muscle definition? Whatever, I was drunk and out of all the random people to sleep with, I picked the right one. When it came down to it, I was promoted over Tanya..."

"And me," I finished for him. "It's okay to say. I fucked that chance up too."

He shook his head. "All this to say that you still have a chance, maybe not go all the way but...butter him up."

"I can't believe this is a real conversation we're having." I continued my way out the store. "I gotta go, I'm starting a new collection, I need to pick up some things."

Marvin nodded. "Go do that but think about what I said."

I gave a halfhearted wave and finally left.

Was Marvin right? Did I have to butter Max up just to get what I thought I deserved? I cringed at the thought. Just thinking about it didn't sit well in my stomach.

I was nowhere near where I wanted to be. I wanted to be a fashion designer. I am a fashion designer. I thought that I would be one of the lucky few to live their dreams. I thought that H. Moda would help me on my path. It would be easier infiltrating from the inside; start at the entry level and work my way up to the design team. Getting a promotion wasn't as easy as it looked. There was blood, sweat, tears and the promising of your first born involved.

The truth was that I missed being creative. I missed looking at the colors in a sunset and being inspired to sketch and design a beautiful piece of art. With my mind trying to process all the drama in my life at a million miles a minute my feet dragged me through the bitter New York cold to a small fabric shop only a few blocks away. Unless you were some kind of designer or fashion major, you wouldn't know about its existence. It sat in a quiet block between the major avenues, tourists and Upper West Side nannies just passing it by. That was fine by me, I let the quiet settle and my problems melt away as my hand reached out to feel the fabrics.

"How can I help...Ginny! Long time no see!" The owner was a tiny elderly man with giant owl glasses, brown trousers up to his chest. It had been a long couple of years since I've seen Samuel.

"Hi!" I went around the counter to give him a hug.

"Where have you been?!" Samuel shrilled in his European accent that I couldn't quite place or tell if it was authentic.

I smiled wide. "I've been here, toying around with some ideas, I just wanted to look around, is that okay?"

"Of course, also let me know what you want, and I'll give you a good deal."

I laughed as I walked away towards the back. I knew from past experience that's where he kept all the good stuff. I heard the small chime of the store bell.

"Can I help you, sir?"

"No, thank you." I heard someone mumble.

I reached out to feel a red satin fabric when I felt someone tap my shoulder. "What are you looking at?" I jumped almost knocking down some rolls of fabric.

I felt goosebumps spread across my arms. "Max," I said, fixing the rolls.

"I didn't mean to startle you," he said with a smirk.

I turned around. "You didn't startle me," I snapped. "Are you stalking me?"

"No," he snorted. "What makes you think that?"

"Because you're here," I raised an eyebrow. I slowly turned around in the pretense of looking at the fabric, even though that was tough because all I could think was, *Oh shit! Max is here, why?!*

"I'm sorry, I asked Marvin where you were, and he told me you would be..." I glanced over my shoulder, finally taking him in. Gone was the hyper aggressive CEO, here was the guy who took me home on Thanksgiving eve. "Why are you looking at me like that?" he asked.

Marvin's advice came back in full force. I could shut the asshole up. I kept browsing at the fabric, my hand lightly touching each roll. "First the coffee earlier in the week, then you're looking for me. If I didn't know better, I'd say you liked me." I wanted to flirt because I was attracted to Max, there was no denying that. But having Marvin's words swimming in my brain just made the whole thing icky. I quickly shook my head. "Max, forget I said that the way I did. It came off flirty and I don't want to lead you on..."

"Virginia?" Max stepped forward only to stop once he glanced towards the front of the shop and noticed Sam observing us. When he saw us looking, he jumped back behind the register and busied himself doing nothing.

"Relax, Max, no one we know works here," I pointed out.

"Hey, Ginny, you need any help?" Sam yelled from the front. Max lifted an eyebrow.

"Well, he knows me," I laughed and continued looking at the fabric. "No, I'm good Sam!" I scrunched up the fabric in my hands and sighed.

"What are you looking for?" he reached out to feel the fabric that I had just felt.

"I had this idea to make silky, sexy dresses and suits for the fashionable holiday getaway," I said absent mindedly, feeling another fabric. I took out a small notebook from my purse, showing a page to Max. "I'm thinking exaggerated cutouts and slits on this dress that I think could work with a leather jacket if I wanted to add an extra edge to it, I'm also thinking like chiffon panels to add an extra flow..." A slow smile spread across his face and made me stop.

"I wonder what changed your mind about designing." I wanted to slap that cocky grin off Max's face.

"Don't think that you had something to do with it." My anger rosed to the surface. This man made me want to jump his bones one minute and rip him to shreds, in a bad way, the next. It was all very confusing, and that fact made me angrier! "I'm doing it because by the end of the year, Maggie is going to throw me off the roof and say that I jumped. I just want to accomplish some things before that time."

Max caressed his chin as if he forgot he had shaved his beard weeks ago. "She really hates you and I still don't know why." He lowered his chin, waiting for me to answer.

"Why did you come here?" I spat out. This was too much after the long, emotionally draining day I had. This little outing for me was supposed to be unwinding, but it felt as if he was intruding my safe space and it just annoyed me.

"I...I just didn't like how you left the office," he admitted.

"If you were so concerned you could've just called," I answered quickly. I was not going to make this easy for him.

"Are you angry?" He asked.

"I'm not angry, just tired." I waved him away in hopes that that would get rid of him.

"Can I take you home?" he asked.

"Max, what are you doing?" I whined.

He sheepishly rubbed the back of his neck. "Ginny, I have no fucking clue. I wanted to see you. I had this urge to see you." Max rubbed his face like a mad man. "I don't know why; you are already taken!"

"Are you alright, Ginny?" Sam called from the front again.

I rolled my eyes. "Yes!" I shouted back. "Keep your voice down," I hissed at Max. I couldn't take this. His eyes were accusing and angry. I could see the battle his mind was in. I glanced behind him; the exit was so far. I could just leave him here and make things worse for me at work.

I sighed. "Max, I lied, okay?"

"You lied?"

"Yes, I don't have a boyfriend. I didn't play you; I didn't play anyone. I'm not a player. I wouldn't know where to begin to play someone. I just said that so you'd—"

His kiss stopped my words. It started slow; my eyes widened at the sudden kiss. After a couple seconds of initial shock, my arms instinctively wrapped around his neck bringing him closer. This is what I wanted. This felt like something I needed. He lightly bit my lip as I came to my senses and was the first to pull away. "Whoa," I sighed. My hand came to my chest to steady my heart.

Glassy eyed, I caught him observing me. "Yes?" I asked.

Max stepped closer. "Why couldn't we..." He reached for my hands.

"We could what, Max?"

"We're grown adults. I like you and you obviously like me..."

"Obviously?" I scoffed.

"You disagree?" I didn't answer, instead, I ran a hand through my hair and sighed. "There's something here, Ginny. Whether you want to admit it or not. I wanted to have you even when I thought you were with someone else."

"I know there's something here," I whispered harshly. "But I don't want people to think the reason that I'm getting a promotion is because I'm fucking the boss."

He cleared his throat. "I know...I know." He scanned the small store, pulling me into a corner. "I just want us to get what we want." I opened my mouth ready to reply just to have him continue, "Before you ask me what I want, let me just say. I want you. Although what we had was short lived—"

"Hours long."

"I don't think we got a chance to see where this could lead and I...I hate that feeling." He rested his forehead against mine. I closed my eyes as I took in his smell. It was warm, spicy...edible.

"Kiss me, again."

"What?" he glanced around the store one more time.

"Kiss me before I change my mind and go back to seeing you as—"

His hands weaved through my hair as he cradled my head.

Max's kiss was soft, leaving me longing. He pulled away and with hooded eyes began to step back. It was if my hands had a mind of their own, I pulled him back by the jacket. "Do it again," I whispered.

Without hesitation Max kissed me with so much passion, I thought the fire alarm would go off. I felt his hands move from my waist to my ass as he pulled me closer. "Max?" I said between kisses.

"Mmmm?" He continued to kiss my neck.

"We're in a fabric store, Sam sees us and call the cops on you and then I would never be allowed back in here." Those words were like a cold shower. He immediately let me go.

Taking a giant step back, Max passed a hand over his face. "I'm so sorry, Ginny."

Max had my red lipstick on his lips. I took a napkin from my bag and handed it over. "It's okay, I asked you...we just got carried away."

"You need to find another shade to wear," he joked. "Can we go back to your place?" I saw the heat in his eyes. I knew that going back to my place was going to lead to Max ruining me for other men.

"Yes," I answered without hesitation.

9

Rule #38: it's not what you say, it's how you say it.

Max wanted to Uber to my place, I insisted that we take the train with the old *where's your sense of adventure* line. In reality, I didn't want to be in such a tight space with Max Thomas. I needed witnesses to stop me from groping this man and stop me from becoming a viral clip.

It's been proven time and again that I had no self-control when I was around him.

As the train made its way out of the city into the Bronx, we sat in awkward silence. I had no clue what he was thinking but my mind couldn't help but notice how his legs spread slightly, how our shoulders touched. I finally noticed his smirk. "What?" I snapped, embarrassed that I was caught staring.

"See something you like?" Max winked.

"Just taking in how you're taking up two seats...typical man," I joked. He wrapped an arm around me, squished me to his side and gave a cocky smile. "There. Now there's more room."

I scowled at him in return. "You didn't leave with any fabric," he said.

"What?"

"You were shopping for fabric."

"Oh, yeah."

"What are you working on?"

I shrugged my shoulders. "Stuff that would positively bore you," I replied with a terrible British accent.

"I don't know much about fabric or design so I won't offer advice, but I can listen," he said.

There was a part of me that wanted to tell him about my design, but our relationship was all over the place, I didn't know where we stood, and I couldn't tell my dreams to someone I didn't trust. I also didn't think being vulnerable on the 6 train to the Bronx was what I wanted to do right now. I decided to change the subject. "Read any good books lately?" I sat back, crossing my arms, making sure to eye him slowly. "Wait don't tell me. If I had to guess...I'd bet money that you probably read books about...business. *How to Make Your Billion Dollar Company Another Billion.*"

Max scrunched his face in disgust. "First of all, that title is way too long. Second, business? You think I'm that boring?"

"No," I laughed. "Okay, since it's not business then...you're probably into some high fantasy adventure with hobbits, witches, half naked elves."

He sat back and mimicked my pose. "Really?"

"Yeah, you have dork written all over your face," I laughed.

"Virginia..." he warned.

"I'm just teasing, some of those nerds have really big d—"

"Virginia," he shushed.

"What? I was going to say they have really big descriptive imaginations. All those boys and girls into those epic stories are going to rule the world," I finished with a big smile.

"Sure, that's exactly what you were going to say."

"All joking aside, what kind of books do you read?" I asked. It was a weird thing to talk about because we've seen each other naked and spoke about our familial issues and what we hoped for the future, but never really got down to specifics. Despite my inner conflict, I wanted to know more. I wanted to know it all.

"I like all kinds of books," he answered.

"That's what everyone says." I rolled my eyes. "What's the last book you read?"

His arm wrapped around me again, bringing back the awareness that was there before. His hand rubbed my shoulder as he thought about his answer. He rolled his head and gave me a look. "I don't want to say." His slow smile made me smile in return.

"Was it a business book?"

"I like other books! I love anything by James Patterson."

"Okay, respectable."

"So, back to you. Why didn't you buy the fabric? The real shiny one? Is it because my kisses distracted you?" Max sat forward with his arms on his knees, peeking up at me.

"No, you didn't distract me."

"Then I'm not doing a good job."

I bit my lip to keep from smiling. "I just didn't like the way it felt." I shrugged. "But I also didn't really look around that long. I think I'll go back and find something. This is our stop," I pointed out. *Thank God.* Why did I agree to have him at my apartment? *Because you're sick...and horny.* Deep down inside I'm a masochist; I didn't mind the pain his company brought.

He followed me in silence, hands in his pockets. I noticed the abuelas who eyed us as we made our way through the block. The abuelas knew what was up. He was fucking gorgeous with or without the beard. I let us in the building, barely climbing up to the second floor when Mrs. Pierce poked her head out.

I kept trailing up the stairs. "Please, don't say a word to her, I don't have the energy," I warned Max behind me.

"Another man?!" disapproval dripped from her wrinkled lips.

"No, same man. I'd put ear plugs in if you don't want to hear all the moaning and groaning that happens when two people—" I heard her door slam shut.

"Does she always come out when it's you? Or does she do this to everyone?" he asked.

"Who knows? I honestly haven't seen her do it to others."

"You know we don't have to get sexy." His face was so serious, I wanted to laugh.

"I know," I assured him. "Soooo, Max," I started as I unlocked my door.

"Yes, Virginia."

I dropped my keys on my small coffee table, spinning around to face him only to catch him looking around my apartment. "Looking for something?" I asked.

"No, it's just the last time I was here...I didn't really get a good look at it."

I followed his eyes and took in my small apartment; blush walls, plants covering most surfaces, small couch, plush rug...it wasn't much but it was comfortable. "Oh no, I think you saw it just fine," I teased.

I was rewarded with his cheeks flaming red. "I didn't mean that."

"Max, relax, I know what you meant." I set my coat and purse down. "You can get comfortable if you want."

Max was examining my collection of shot glasses. "You drink much?"

"No. It's just when you tell people you collect a certain item and every time they come back from vacation, they bring it as a souvenir...my thing just happens to be shot glasses." I shook my head to get the memory of what we did in my bedroom out of my head. I wanted to have a normal conversation but I knew the things this man could do to my body. "Your siblings hate me, right?"

"Hate is such a strong word." I felt embarrassment and

mortification spread across my chest. God, I was joking. I didn't expect him to answer truthfully. "It just seems like you're a bit more problematic than they had anticipated. The whole Maggie thing has tainted their views."

I groaned. "Really? Maggie must be ecstatic about that." I poured myself a glass of wine. I would chug the whole bottle but with my shot glass collection on full display Max would think that I really had a drinking problem.

"If she was, she does a great job of hiding it." he widened his eyes, making me laugh at the absurdity that was my store manager.

"So, you didn't find the right fabric today..."

"We're back on that subject?" I was growing tired of this conversation. "What's your obsession with the fabrics I'm looking for? Is it part of some freaky fetish?"

He shrugged. "Well, I don't know, Ginny. I just want to learn everything about you. You love fashion. I want to know what you're working on."

"Fine, Max. If you must know, I want to work on a collection that I can take from day to night with minimal effort. But the dress I'm currently working on is a silky red dress with pleated chiffon panels." I let that bit of information sit but another thought popped in my head. "I want to pair it with a leather jacket that I made years ago, mix the old with the new."

When I finally worked up the nerve to see his reaction, I was blinded by Max's brilliant smile. "What?" I asked. My heart was beating a million miles a minute.

"You've designed before? On a big scale?"

"Lately, I've been making pieces just for me because I've lost my confidence...I hate admitting that." I shrugged at my own shortcomings. "I used to actually sell my creations on a website that has long collected dust."

Max followed me to the couch, his forehead furrowed with worry. "What made you stop?"

I cast my eyes downward in embarrassment. "Everything."

"The store?" his voice was full of shock.

"The store, a guy, my parents. Back then, I blamed the world."

Max's eyes widened. "That's a lot of blame."

"Honestly?"

"Always." He sat back and waited for me to continue.

"It's easier to blame others than to blame yourself. I didn't want to be a visual you know. I wanted to design clothes. I only took the job just to pay my tuition. Then I was offered the position right after college. It seemed like a safety net to help if designing didn't pan out," I admitted.

"What kind of clothes did you design?"

"Well, for the masses, I had an assortment of t-shirts, sweatshirts and hoodies that they could choose from. The other designs; dresses, blouses, skirts, blazers...where special orders. My design sketches would be up on the website and for those few who wanted them, I would make them," I explained. I focused on the tear on my jeans; the anxiety of letting another person into my world was on an astronomical level. How pathetic it all sounded, my brilliant mind and talent on the cusp of greatness only to be thwarted by the company that his family ran. I shouldn't blame the company. All I had to blame was myself and that was far worse to admit.

"This dress can be your way back in," he said with a nod.

"That's what I was thinking but I haven't posted any designs to the website in years."

"You're scared?"

I sighed. "I don't know, with my parents not talking to me, things at work being...well you know...it's not great. I'm more nervous than scared."

"What was your companies name?"

I smiled at the memory. "Gin and Tonic. Marvin helped me pick it out."

He sat back and got comfortable. "You and Marvin been friends for a while."

"Yeah, he started two weeks after me. We've been inseparable ever since."

"He got promoted before you did," he pointed out.

This was a touchy subject for me. There was no way to explain that without revealing the mess that kept me from moving forward and propelled Marvin's promotion. There were a lot of politics that went into promoting. The person didn't necessarily have to work as hard, they just had to be in good graces with the right people. Not saying that Marvin wasn't good at his job, he was great. It was just that sometimes I know deep down inside he was given the chance because I fucked up.

"Okay, fine you don't want to talk about it."

"I don't." My stubbornness jumped out.

He nodded. "Fair enough."

"What about you? You don't have to run the family business," I ventured quietly.

"Gin, I already told you, it was basically shoved down my throat."

"You always have a choice," I insisted.

"Yeah, but my choice would send my parents on a spiral. As the eldest child, I have an obligation to uphold this family legacy."

"Is that written on your birth certificate," I laughed.

"You find it funny but it's the truth."

My laughter quickly died on my lips. I don't know how our conversation turned so quickly in a matter of seconds. "I'm sorry, Max. I didn't mean to trivialize your situation."

"I always thought that Andrea would step up. She loves this business. She's knows the ins and outs of the fashion industry...of business as a whole. She breezed through business school. She's the smartest out of the three of us."

"Why doesn't she just do it?"

"She's a woman," he said so matter-of-factly that I wanted to sock him in the face.

I could feel my face turn in a snarl. "Are you serious? You better have said that as a joke." I put my glass down ready to hurl myself at him and drag him out my apartment.

Max saw the look on my face and most likely aware of what I wanted to do. He put his cup down and slowly raised his hands in surrender. "Those are not my views. My parents are old school. To them, Andrea is married with a kid, she has her place at home..."

I let out a sigh of frustration. It amazed me that people really thought this way. "You have got to be kidding me."

"If she wants the job, then she can have it. But she hasn't come forward and said anything to the contrary."

"Because she's afraid! Help her speak up! You're her older brother."

"Andrea's a grown woman, if she needed my help, she knows she can come to me."

I shook my head. "Does she? Does she really know that?"

I was so angry on her behalf. Who knew the family who owned a successful brand also held some antiquated ideals about the sexes?

"Ginny, calm down. I am just pointing out the views of the elder Thomas'."

"Fine. I think you need to go." I stood up abruptly ready to show him to the door. There was no point to stay. I know that I invited him over because my lady bits clouded my brain.

His eyebrows came down, but a corner of his mouth came up in a smirk. "Are you kicking me out?"

"I just don't see the point in you being here." I gave him the first excuse I could think of.

"We do have business to discuss."

I tilted my head, crossed my arms and tapped my toes. This man was going to be the death of me. "And what business would that be?"

"I want us to figure us out. I know we like each other. I know that I want to see you."

"But?"

"But I also have a business to protect."

"Wow, if this is supposed to be some way to confess your love for me, you're doing a swell job." I stomped to the door, practically ripping them off their hinges. "Now, if you don't mind, I'd like to prepare myself for a date with—"

"Ziggy, you're fake boyfriend?" Max crossed his arms.

I scowled at him. Again, Marvin's stupid voice echoed in my head. *Seduce him, Ginny! Get promoted!* Max sauntered over to me, tucking my hair behind my ear. My eyelids came down at half-mast as if they had a mind of their own. I felt my breathing pick up.

"Don't get cute," I whispered as he lowered his lips. "I do have someone in my life named Ziggy."

"I bet your fake boyfriend couldn't get you wet like I could?"

I felt the heat spread all over my body. "Don't flatter yourself."

I slammed the door, grabbed Max's hand and stomped over to my bedroom. "Ginny, I'm sorry we don't—" he quieted down when I yanked my side drawer open, pulling out my vibrator.

"What is that?"

"This is Ziggy. Ziggy meet Max. Max thinks he's better than you," I whispered to the inanimate pleasure wand that I held in my hand.

"Ginny I...I..." Max scratched his five o'clock shadow. "I don't know whether to laugh or throw you on that bed and show you that I am better than that thing."

I licked my lips that went dry after all the air was sucked out of me.

"Truth or dare?" he asked.

I shook my head. Without an answer, I dropped the vibrator on the floor, wrapped my arms around Max's neck and kissed his lips.

I O

Rule 87: Go with your gut.

Everything was a blur; Max kissed my neck, nipping my breasts through my shirt. A small moan escaped my lips. He kneeled before me, unbuttoning my jeans, licking my belly button.

Seduce him.

Marvin's ever-present voice kept repeating in my head. "Shut up," I whispered.

"What?" Max looked up.

Guilt took over my senses for a brief second. I have no reason to feel guilty. I'm not sexing him to get promoted. I'm sexing him because I'm horny.

"Ginny, are you okay?"

"Yeah, why?"

"You just got stiff? You, okay?" his hands held me at the waist and gently shook me. "Hey, relax. We don't have to do anything if you don't want to."

I nodded like a bobble head. "I know. I want to... you know just a little overthinking that's all." He gave a small bite on my belly, sending shivers all over. *Seduce him!* I just couldn't relax. I pushed lightly on his shoulders. "Max, what is happening?"

Max tilted his head. "What do you want to happen, Ginny? No more games."

I wiggled my hips in front of him, he rested his forehead against me. His breath was warm against my skin and the goosebumps alone was addicting.

"Do what you want to do to me." My voice was barely a whisper.

"Lay back on the bed," he commanded. I should've listened to the tiny voice in my head that said *Girl, this is not a good idea*, instead, I threw myself back. I knew the pleasure that his body could inflict on mine and I wanted it so bad I could taste it. I was like an addict. I kicked off my shoes which made it easier for him to take off my pants. I clumsily threw my top to a corner of my tiny room while Max was still fully dressed. Max was average height and build, but in my bedroom, he looked so much bigger, wider, menacing. His silence only enhanced his massive presence.

"What's wrong?" I asked, awkwardly covering myself up.

"I don't know whether to eat you or fuck you," he said matter of factly.

I tried to play it cool even though I liquified on the spot. "Go with your gut, whatever you choose won't be a wrong choice," I shrugged.

He unbuttoned his shirt slowly. Max knew that he had a great body, only made more erotic with the tattoos that fully covered his chest and arms. He encircled one of my ankles with his hands, pulling me to the edge of my bed. "I think I want to taste you." His voice was low; goosebumps rose all over my body.

The low hum of traffic and neighbors pierced the early evening. Max grabbed a pillow and threw it on the floor; he spread my legs apart. I felt his breath. He licked my inner thighs, teasing me. I felt the flicker of his tongue. I arched my back wanting him to apply more pressure. "God," I whispered.

I heard my phone begin to ring. I refused to answer it just like

I refused to open my eyes. This felt like a dream I didn't want to wake up from. He moaned his delight as he spread me apart with his fingers, licking and sucking on my clit. Max was ravenous and I was his feast.

I tried to relax my back but with each flicker of his tongue, my back arch and my nipples harden; I wanted— no, I *needed* him to bring me over the edge.

I knew Max felt my desperation when I began to move against his tongue. "Max, please."

Two of his fingers made their way inside me. His tongue continued its assault while his fingers had no mercy. With the sunset piercing through my curtains, I locked my legs around his neck as I came in his mouth. I turned into a ragdoll in an instant; my legs fell to my sides, and I stretched my arms over my head to feel every bit of my orgasm.

I heard a phone ringing in the distance. Mesmerized by all that was Max, I ignored it. Max stood up, unbuckled his belt and took out a condom. I was under a trance. He knew he had me; his smirk said it all. Max covered his long hardness with the rubber. The bed sank against his weight. I moaned at the feel of his dick entering me. I was all sensitive nerve endings. My wet pussy glided over him with ease. "God, Ginny. You feel like heaven," he groaned.

Max pushed against me, wrapping a hand around me, arching my breasts in his direction. He took my nipple in his mouth and my head feel back at the pure ecstasy that his mouth provided. He pumped faster and harder, letting me fall back to the mattress, taking hold of my iron bed posts and fucking me harder. It was pain that quickly turned into pleasure. My moans grew louder as my heartbeat faster. I came without warning, but it only fueled Max's need.

He flipped me over as if I weighed nothing. I had no time to bask in the glow of my satisfaction.

Max's tattooed hands gripped my thighs, bringing my ass higher and positioning me right where he wanted me. He rubbed his dick down my slit, teasing me.

All I could do was wiggle in front of him, encouraging him to bury himself deep inside of me. Max spank my ass before digging his fingers into my hips and bringing me down onto his cock. I cried out in pleasure. I arched my back, I just wanted more of him!

I pushed my pussy against him.

He laughed.

Max's beautiful hands dug into my hair, gripping it tight and pulling my head back. "This is what you wanted?"

"Yes!"

"Louder," he commanded.

"Yes! Yes!"

I was lost.

He kept fucking me until I heard him groan as his climax took hold of him.

Max pumped into me slowly, before finally pulling out.

He collapsed next to me, taking his body heat with him. The beads of sweat that fell from his body to mine, instantly cooled my skin.

The chill from the early winter evening seeped through my closed windows causing me to shiver. Max pulled me to him, so I laid on his chest.

My eyes grew heavy while my body still vibrated from what we did. "Ginny?"

"Hmmm?"

"What do we do now?"

"Relax and enjoy this before we go back to work Monday?"

I felt him chuckle.

Then I heard my incessant phone ringing again. "Uh, why doesn't that person take a hint?" I groaned as I got up from bed in search of that annoying device. I ran, quickly thinking it might be my parents finally returning my call. It'd be like them to pick an inconvenient time to call. I glanced at the screen and cringed. "Hello?"

Maggie's voice came through. "Hello? Ginny? I was calling to follow up about Sunday. You did schedule someone to come in and set the holiday window?"

"Maggie? I...I..." I stammered, looking behind me as I heard the bed creaking.

"With the global team here every day until New Year's I just want to make sure you have everything set." I could just imagine her eyes rolling as she explained it to me.

"We've spoken about this at least one time each day this week. Tahiri and Mark will be there on Sunday. Unless you think I should be there." I waited a beat before a sigh escaped. "Do you think I should be there Sunday?"

"If you're confident with your team then there's no need for you to be here. Have a goodnight." Maggie abruptly hung up. I had to look at the phone to make sure that she really hung up the call.

Text from Marvin appeared.

Meet me for drinks?

Can't. Maybe next time.

What could you possibly have going on?

I have company, ok?

Is it Max?

Yes...

Yes! Did you seduce him?

Good Girl!

You'll get promoted in no time! lol

"You okay?" Max asked. I felt his lips on my neck.

I threw my phone on the couch. "I'm fine. It was Maggie." I pulled away from him in search for cover because I was still very much naked and needed to think straight.

"And?" He asked. I didn't want to lay eyes on him because he was still naked too and I was beginning to realize that in any way, shape or form this man was my weakness.

"Just double checking the plans for Sunday's holiday window installation," I explained as I looked around for a shirt.

"Ginny?" Max's voice was soft but firm which forced me to finally look at him. "What's going through your mind?"

"What do you mean?" I asked, pulling a t-shirt over my head.

"You haven't looked at me."

"I'm just trying to get dressed."

"Why?"

"Because, Max. We can't do this."

His eyebrows came down. "Do what?"

"This. A relationship. Sex. We can't do it."

"I know it's a sticky situation—"

"You are my boss. You are my boss' boss. Your family owns the company...it's not a good look."

"I know...but I like you."

I bit the inside of my cheek to keep from smiling. This was not the situation that warranted a smile. I needed to be firm. "I like you too," I sighed. I hated how whiney my voice was. Not even when I wanted tickets to see *NSYNC did I whine this much.

"So, why can't we have what we want?"

Was he being purposely obtuse? "Because it's not a good look for me," I explained once again.

"It's not a good look to be with someone who's attracted to you and you to him?"

I shrugged. "You know that's not the issue."

When he didn't say anything, I decided to continue. "How does it look that I've been in the company for ten years and now I'm in line for a promotion? How does it look if I actually get the job? If we were together and someone found out...how would that make me look?"

Max took a step and reached for my hands. He squeezed them before caressing them gently with his thumbs meant to calm me but instead, I felt my blood begin to boil. "Ginny, I get it. I understand," He said with a smile. I slipped my hands out of his. My anger was building up I didn't want to escalate the situation further. I began to clean up the small mess in my living room. I couldn't just stand there anymore.

"How could you, Max? You own the company. No matter what you do, you'll still be there, and I'll be out."

He lips formed a grim line as we stared each other down. I saw how his mind was trying to make it right. "Let's keep it quiet."

I picked up a bag of chips and rolled down the opening. "Secrets have ways of coming out."

"Get dressed," he ordered. Running excitedly into the bedroom.

I shook my head in confusion. "What?" I whispered to myself in the empty living room. "What?!" I said louder so he could hear me.

"I want to take you out on a date," he said as he began putting on his jeans.

"Now?" I looked at my naked legs.

He looked up at me with a boyish smirk. "Yeah? Why not?"

"Because it's getting dark and it's freezing out."

He stood up straight with his hands on his hips, his chest and abs on full display. "What's the issue? Are you afraid you'll turn into a snowman?"

Fine. I'll give in. This is a limited time only anyways; I might as well enjoy it while I still have time. "Where are we going?" I asked suddenly matching his excitement.

"I don't know, but it's New York City during the holidays, we're bound to find something cool."

An hour later, after layering up as much as I could, we walked along fifth avenue. Beautifully brilliant lights flashed from all the stores that set up their holiday windows. Christmas scenes from each decade was displayed on each window of *Saks* as we moved among the crowd. Christmas carols played along to the different scenes; each mannequin dressed in incredibly expensive designer pieces that could be on display at *the Met*.

We stopped on a scene from the 60's. The fashion was incredible, my jaw was to the floor. "You like?" Max asked.

"I love," I said breathlessly. "I've always told myself that I would come see the holiday windows and every year I find an excuse not to go."

"Really?"

"Yup, living in the city all your life you kind of steer clear of cheesy touristy things." I saw from the corner of my eye his look of disappointment. "I'm not saying this idea is cheesy..." I turned to give him my full attention. "I'm just saying that I wouldn't have done this by myself."

A gust of wind spun the bitter cold around us causing me to shiver. Max put an arm around me and snuggled me close. Look at Mother Nature being my wingman. "You really don't like the cold."

"I like the fashion that goes along with winter; cute boots, a coat, beanies, sweaters...the actual cold I loathe."

"Loathe? You must really hate it if you use words like loathe. Only villains and mid-century wenches use that word."

"Mid-century? What am I furniture?"

He crinkled his nose. "Did I say it wrong?"

"Did you mean medieval wench?" I laughed. A chill ran down my spine, I nestled closer in his warmth. "I could stand snow for a day before it turns all nasty and dirty."

"Then why stay in New York?"

"I'm in fashion, duh. Everything is here." I sighed. "It's either here or LA…but LA has to many fake happy people and it's only a matter of time…" I raised an eyebrow.

I felt him chuckle. We walked further down taking in the other window displays. "I love this," I whispered.

"Oh, so you secretly love cheesy dates?" he laughed.

"I love the creativity, the lights…it's like magic."

"Wait til we get further down." He kissed my nose.

When we got to the 1980s Christmas scene, the lights dimmed. Max grabbed my hand, pulling me across the street. "Max, where are we going?" I asked as I ran across the street behind him hoping not to get hit by a cab.

"Wait until you see." No sooner did those words leave his lips did loud music begin to play. Against the department store, lights danced across the façade of the building in the shape of snowflakes. The crowd stared in awe at the light show, each snowflake danced and moved along to the music. Max's arm tightened around my shoulder. This is what I want; I want to go on a date with a normal guy with no secrets. But there would be a huge secret— we would be the secret. I've learned from the past secrets have ways of coming out and fucking up your world.

Applause from the crowd brought me out of my stupor, I looked up at Max who was so excited by it all. "There's more," he laughed. He spun me around and although we were at the entrance, I already knew where we were.

"Really? You brought me to see the Christmas tree?" I laughed.

"More cheesy goodness." His warm hand took hold off mine, pulling me along the massive crowd to get a better look at the Rockefeller Center Christmas tree. "I thought since we were already here, we might as well…" he shrugged.

I don't know what it is about Christmas lights that automatically makes everything pretty and put you in a good mood, but it was amazing. Max wrapped his arms around my waist as he stood behind me. I laid my head back on his chest. This felt like a movie. This felt comforting. This felt like...I shook the thought out of my head and breath in the moment. Just because I knew that this couldn't go on doesn't mean I couldn't enjoy it while it was happening.

The gust of wind worked in my favor because Max took the liberty to tighten his hold on me and I savored every minute of it. "You want some hot chocolate?" he asked.

I kept looking at the tree. "In a minute."

I felt his soft chuckle against my back. Max swayed us to the faint music while the world moved around us at a rapid pace. He loosened his hold on me a tiny bit as he fumbled for something in his pocket. "What are you doing?" I asked.

"I want a picture," he said before pulling out his phone.

"No, Max, I don't think that's a good idea," I whispered.

"Why? Am I going to take the picture and you won't be in it thus proving to me you're a vampire?"

I turned my head slightly to get a good look at him. "The way your mind works is astonishing," I laughed.

"Yeah? You should see what my mind is thinking right now," he wiggled his eyebrows at me forcing a big laugh out of me.

I saw the flash as he snapped a photo. "Okay, now this time look at the camera," he said.

I looked at the camera and smiled.

This feeling was like a drug, it was quickly becoming addictive, and I was worried. *This is too fast. He's your boss, Ginny!* My mind yelled. *All you had to do was seduce him! Not seduce yourself.* Just for tonight I turned her off.

"Ready for hot chocolate?" I asked.

"Yes, ma'am."

We walked away from the crowded streets, the lights and people slowly fading away. The cold was brutal, I could feel the burn against my cheeks. "When you said let's go for hot chocolate, did you know that we would be walking through Siberia to get there?"

"The cold makes you grumpy," he said.

"That and hunger."

"You're hangry too? Where we're going, we can order something to eat."

"Thank God."

Max reached for my hand and squeezed. "Have you spoken to your parents?"

"No," I sighed. "I called though...that's progress. I don't think they want to spend the holidays with me."

"How do you know if you don't ask?"

"Because I know. I'm such a huge disappointment to them. They wanted me to be a doctor or something and I work in retail. I don't know who's more disappointed, me or my parents."

I spared a glance in his direction. Max frowned. "I don't like you talking down to yourself." He kept his voice low but I heard the steel in it. I didn't respond. I've always been hard on myself. I've always found a reason as to why I was a big disappointment. Max cleared his throat to get my attention. "Is it really that bad?" he asked.

"I mean, the first five minutes of the phone call isn't all bad. It's when I talk about work that turns their indifference and hostility on. Then my mother makes a smart remark about my life; men, my job, how I have no kids...it's a whole thing. And then I shoot back and then my dad is telling me that they'll call back later which ends up being like a month later."

"Damn." Max squeezed my hand tight comforting me the only way he knew how.

All the arguments we've had from high school until the time I quit college to become a fashion designer replayed in my mind. I wanted to have a normal relationship with my parents. I wanted to talk to my mother about the same shit every day like a normal Puerto Rican daughter.

I wanted to visit on every holiday and when I missed a special occasion, I wanted to feel guilty about it. I know that sounds silly in the grand scheme of things. I wanted to complain about my parents' small acts of affection like everyone else at work. Shit! Even the Thomas' were close! I mean I don't want to go into business with my family but if that's what I had to do for them to talk to me, I'd do it.

"Listen, I doubt they think you're such a disappointment." I snorted before he quickly added, "And even if they were, they're still your parents."

Instead of giving a flirty rebuttal I chose to wallow in my own pity. Max took my silence as an indication to continue, "I think that maybe they're just scared because you're following your dreams."

"But am I? Sometimes I'm a bit disappointed in myself. I...I hate the fact that they may be right."

"Ginny, don't."

The soft taps of our steps hitting the pavement always sounded louder when I contemplated my life choices. The weight of it all made my steps feel heavier. I spared a look out the corner of my eye only to catch Max observing me. "Why are you disappointed?"

"Why wouldn't I be disappointed?" My breath came out in heavy puffs. "I took the easy way out, I cut back on my designing and creating because this company offered me this position ten years ago. I thought I could work my way up, be a part of the design team...create my designs but not waste my own money..." I let out a long breath. "I cut back my dream to practically nothing because this was steady income...I just got lazy."

"I understand that," he quietly admitted.

"Do you really?"

"Hell yes. I don't want to take over this company. I feel obligated. It's just easier to say yes and do it."

"I think you're being stupid."

"I'm being stupid?!" he snorted. Max immediately stopped in his tracks causing me to trip.

I stomped from foot to foot to keep from freezing. "Yes! You have the means to say no and do your thing. I'm on my own, I can't just quit. I have rent to pay, bills to pay...where would I live?"

"Who said anything about quitting? There are a lot of creators who work a full-time job and create every other second that they're not at work. Maybe the store is just an excuse?"

"An excuse for what?" I couldn't help the scowl that appeared on my face.

"For being scared." He folded his arms to shield him from the gust of wind.

"Scared of what?"

"Come on, Ginny. You're scared of failure. Of not being good enough."

"Are we ever getting hot chocolate?" I didn't want to have this conversation, especially with Max.

It made me feel dumb, worse than the self-pity that I had been feeling. When saying everything out loud to Max, it just sounded lame.

Why did I stop designing? If I'm being honest, I tuned out way before the whole mess with Rafa and Maggie. Max's assertion wasn't that far off, I wasn't ready to reflect on my own weaknesses.

Max tilted his head, not wanting to spoil the night with an argument, he gave a short nod, reached for my hand and continued our journey through the quiet streets of New York City. Two seconds later, Max came to a sudden stop in front of a small bakery. "Welcome to Casa de Cari," he announced as he held the door open for me.

"Casa de Cari?" I looked around the small, empty, dimly lit bakery. "I don't think we're supposed to be here, I think they're closed." He laughed as he went around the counter. I looked around in a panic. "Max, what are you doing?" I whispered.

"I'm getting cookies."

"I see that but—"

I closed my mouth as someone came through the back entryway.

"Max?! What are you doing here?" a slim, tall man asked. He was dressed in a black t-shirt and jeans, wiping his hands on his apron.

"Just checking up on the place...and stealing cookies and hot chocolate. You have sandwiches left?" Max answered innocently while he continued plating the cookies.

"Interesting..." he muttered. The mystery baker finally noticed me. "And you are?"

"This is Ginny. Ginny this is Roy," Max introduced.

Realization dawned on the baker. "You're the girl from the celebration night," he remembered.

I felt the color rise to my cheeks. "Yes, I am. You own the bakery? It's lovely," I remarked, taking in the small tables with daisies in the small vases. Twinkle lights strewn against windows and counters giving the small bakery a romantic feel.

"Well, I couldn't have afforded it without the help of my investors," he said sending a wink to Max.

My look of shock had both men laughing. "You invested in this bakery?"

"Yeah, a step towards doing something that doesn't have to do with the family business. It was my last investment before accepting the job."

"I have to finish in the back. You guys have what you want," Roy said as he spun around, disappearing behind the curtains.

Max came around the counter. "Here, grab the cookies. I'll grab something to drink."

"So, you had a plan before the big takeover?" I asked.

"Yeah, I was investing in a bunch of small businesses that just needed a hand. It's something that brings me joy. The thrill of helping turned an idea into reality and watching it succeed...or not...either way, it really makes me happy," he shrugged as if his joy was no big deal.

I took a big bite out of the giant chocolate chip cookie. "Oh. My. God. This shit is so good." I salivated over the one bite. Max's gaze darkened as his eyes darted to my lips. I refused to give in. "So, have you had investments fail?"

He smirked knowing that my question was a way to steer us away from the thoughts that would have us in bed in no time. "Of course, I have. There was this cab service app..."

"*Uber*?"

"Nope. It was called Ride Safe...*Uber* launched and blew up before we launched and that's how I became broke my first year of college," he laughed.

"You had your family to bail you out, didn't they help?"

"I would never allow them to. They weren't happy about any of it. I didn't tell them what I was up to until they saw it in the business section of the Times."

My eyes widened. "Are you serious?" I grimaced at the thought of my failures being plastered all over the front page, it was hard enough to go after your dream when no one knows who you are.

"One thousand percent serious. No matter what I do now, that failure sticks out to them." He cast his eyes downward and cleared his throat. "Now, what about you?"

"What about me?" I giggled around the mouthful of cookies.

"Your fashion design. Your company. I want to know."

I sighed. "I took a leap, against my parents wishes."

"I know that very well," he muttered.

"I know you do," I replied. I sighed and continued my origin story. "They didn't give me a chance to fail. For them, failure was inevitable. I wanted to prove them wrong. So, during my senior year of college, I slacked off because I was focused on designing. I started to post on the socials and that started to gain traction. I had a show at a boutique and that opened some doors. The minute I dropped out, H.Moda offered me the visual position and the rest, as they say, is history."

"You could keep doing it." Max was slouched against the chair, relaxed in the dim glow of the café. If he asked me out right, I would've confessed it all to him.

"I mean, I still design. But I only sell to a select clientele."

Max leaned forward. "But you could do so much more. Why'd you slow down?"

"Calm down, Tony Robbins. There's a couple of things that happened that cast doubts..."

"First of all, you just showed your age with that reference. Second of all, your stuff was so good!" He slammed his empty cup on the table so dramatically that I couldn't help the laugh that escaped.

"Wait. How do you know what my stuff looked like?" I raised an eyebrow.

"I googled you," he said sheepishly. The color spread across his cheeks.

"You googled me?" I was shocked. I only thought the rich and the famous were worthy enough of a google search.

"Yeah, I wanted to know more about you, and I googled."

"You liked my designs?" I wanted him to say yes. It's not like his validation would send me back into a designing spiral. But...it feels good to know that someone that I was affectionate towards liked my work.

"Yeah, I still don't understand why you cut back so much."

"Moda is demanding." I shrugged in hopes that that was enough of an answer to satisfy him.

"Yeah, but like I said, if you really wanted it, you could have still went for it."

"It just takes that one person to really get to you," I whispered. I hated that I even said that much. I didn't want to clue him in because looking back I cringed every time I thought of it.

"Your parents?"

"My parents and...a guy."

He began to nod slowly. "Ahhh, so now we get into the ex-talk."

I threw a crumb at him before taking a sip of the hot chocolate. "Yeah, there was this guy when I first started that worked at the store. It was great..."

"Then what happened?"

I shrugged. "When your light is shining brighter than others, there are those that want to snuff your light out...he just happened to be one of those."

"And this is something you don't want to talk about."

"Because it's something that I'm embarrassed about."

"Okay, well, let me just say this, fuck him."

A big, hearty laugh escaped my lips. "It's easier said than done. When you're close to someone, their voice is the loudest. I...just couldn't turn the volume down. It was the fact that I was spending way too much time on my company, or I was spending too much time at work." There was so much more to tell but I didn't think he was ready to hear it and I don't think I was ready to talk about it.

How many times did I lie awake, embarrassed on all the shit that happened; I was played and made to be the bad guy, when I just wanted to have it all. Max reached out to take my hand, his gentle caress relaxing me. "Okay, I'm officially done, I'm ready to close up," Roy yelled as he walked from behind the curtain.

"Let's take this to go," Max said with a wink.

We thanked Roy for letting us steal the cookies and cocoa. We walked down the quiet avenue towards nowhere in particular. Our linked hands was comforting, Max squeezed forcing me to look up. I offered him a soft smile. "Yes?"

"How long were you with the ex?"

"Almost three years," I admitted.

"Three years?!" his eyes practically popped out of their sockets.

"Why so shocked?"

"I just didn't think it lasted that long."

I shrugged. "The thing is when you think you're in love, nothing can prove you wrong."

"And what happened?"

"I was proven wrong," I answered hoping he would drop the subject.

"What happened?" I guess my hint didn't take.

"He lied. He lied big time. On top of not supporting my fashion designer ambitions, he was holding out on a big secret that made me a laughingstock of H. Moda for almost two years."

"What did he lie about? Was he running from the cops?"

"No."

"Was he stealing from you?"

"No."

Max came to a halt in the middle of the empty street. He was still holding onto my hand. "Max, it's freezing, let's get going. The station is right over there," I said pulling him along.

"Don't make me keep guessing," he whined.

I let out a sigh of my frustration. "He was married. He was married and didn't tell me for three years that I was the other woman."

"What?! And in three years you never knew?"

"No! I didn't until his wife came to work at my store," I confessed. "He was good at hiding things. Looking back, I realize how dumb I was. We would stay in my place all the time. I think I went to his place one time for like five minutes and it was dark. We would meet for dates on certain days or times. But I didn't think anything of it because he made it seemed like he cared." Max was dead silent, probably trying to figure a way out after all this drama that just fell onto him. I waved my hand as if was nothing. "In the end it all blew up in my face and I was the one to take the heat. I lost my chance at a promotion, my reputation...by that time my business was already collecting dust. I was just...in a bad place."

Under the weird orange glow of the city lights I could see his face fall. He finally understood. "That's the tension, the drama between you and Maggie," he whispered.

My heart began to race. "What?"

"I'm so pissed. It's Maggie's husband that played you," he said as a matter of fact.

I couldn't answer him. I couldn't tell him how stupid I'd have been to let everything slip from my grasp. How blinded I was by a smooth talker. "I know you don't want to admit but I know it was him. That's why she is hostile towards you. Why not ask for a transfer?"

I snorted at the memory of the hot mess, trouble, and grief that I went through. "I did. I had to give a reason...I couldn't. The sales advisors and managers knew what was going on, but we were all afraid of the consequences if things were taken higher. I was still in love. And I've never been vindictive." I saw how he clenched his jaw. The tension told me that he cared. This was getting heavier than I would have liked. "Can we go now?" I pulled at his hand.

We took the train back to my apartment, sitting in silence as the train made its way through underground tunnels, glimpses of light passing through; the graffiti letting me know that people can break the rules and leave a mark on the world, even if only a selected few caught it. Maybe I can break the rules. I looked down at the hand that held on to mine and I knew that I already was.

The silence followed us to my building; Max never let go of my hand, I squeezed tight. "Would you like to come up?" I asked.

"I would but I have an early morning tomorrow," he said.

I knew that he was most likely telling the truth, but my hyper sense of insecurity began to cast shadows of doubt in my mind. I nodded my understanding.

"Yeah, I need to rest up too. If you hadn't noticed, my store manager is exhausting," I joked as I fought against tears that I didn't want him to see.

Max finally let go of my hand, the cold air forced me to tuck my hands in my pockets. "May I ask, what happened to the ex?"

I sighed. Reliving the whole thing made me sad for the girl I was. I wish she knew better; I wish she could've coped with it better. "He got promoted to store manager at another location, and I have to work with a daily reminder of my biggest mistake thus far."

He shook his head. "Just thinking about it makes me so angry. Who else knows? You said the managers and sales associates?"

"Who doesn't know?" I tried another joke. When his face stayed stone cold, I continued, "Well, you guys...don't know but I assure you, people know, there was a big blow up at the store."

"Why is it just now being brought up? I doubt that my family knew about this."

I raised an eyebrow. "There is a lot about this company that your family doesn't know. I'm not surprised if they didn't hear about this incident, I probably would've lost my job."

"Did he say anything to you after?"

I felt my body sway, the bitter cold was starting to seep through my layers. "He's reached out a few times after the blow up, but I refused to give him the time," I admitted.

He looked around, sighing. "I hate that I can't do anything about it."

Max ran a hand down his face. "I mean...there's nothing you could've done," I shrugged. I stopped him before he could say anything else. "You can't do anything. Would you get involved if it was another employee? Be honest."

Max let out a heavy sigh. "I want to say yes but I don't know. I just know that I feel useless."

I braved the cold and reached to lay a hand against him. "Relax, it's in the past. I'm fine. They're fine. We're all fine."

"Fine." He leaned in and dropped a small kiss on my lips. "I had a great time," he whispered.

"I did too."

"I want to do this again. What do you say?"

The sparkle in his brown eyes made me smile. It's like when your mom tells you not to take a bite of the cake before dinner. Max made me want to eat the whole freaking cake and some cookies.

"We tell no one?" I asked. My blood began to race at the thought of us being a in any form of a relationship.

Max let out a heavy breath, resting his forehead against mine he agreed. "We tell no one...until after your promotion."

I smiled wide. "Good." I stood on my tip toes to reach his lips, stubble rubbed against me and I savored the feel...until, I felt something rub against my boot. I looked down to see a rat scurry between us. I jumped up and screamed so loud!

"What?! What's wrong?!" Max looked around to find the source of my terror.

The freaking rat danced around us as I continued to squeal with disgust. I hurried to open the lobby door. I dashed into the building, pulling Max in with all my might. "Did you see that thing?" my breath came out heavy as I tried to control my breathing.

"Of course, I saw it. He looked like he could play football!"

I peeked through the plexi glass of the door. "God, now that thing is going to remember me." I gasped as I saw a black ball of nastiness dart from the trash bags on the side of the street to the closed lobby door. I jumped back. "Ewww! He knows where I live!" I glanced behind me in hopes that Max would play knight in shining armor or at the very least be supportive of my almost fatal rat attack. Instead, I found him biting his lip to keep himself from laughing.

I scowled in his direction. "And what is so funny, Mr. Thomas? Is my fear amusing to you?"

He wiped at his tears. "I find it funny how we just ran away from a rat. Why are we hiding from Mickey?"

"Mickey?! No way. Mickey is clean cut; this rat has seen things..." I shivered.

He leaned in to plant a small kiss. "You're a tough cookie."

"Cookie?" I giggled. "I feel like you need a cigar and add the word toots to the end of that."

Max sauntered slowly to me. "That's some weird role play but I can accommodate." He winked before kissing me deeper. He pulled back slowly, resting his forehead against mine. "Now, can I see you again, soon?"

"Hmmm, I don't know. You're not a very good protector."

"Virginia..."

I rolled my eyes. "Well. If you can use your mob contacts to kill the rat and his entire family, then I'll think about it."

"Consider it done," he laughed.

We sealed it with a kiss. I was becoming addicted to this feeling. The only way to describe it was as if you were swinging high, right before you jumped off. I like the way it made my belly feel, the high pitches and even the lows. Let's pray that it'll keep feeling like the high.

I I

Rule 59: Customers are always right...unless they want an item off the mannequin.

I spent all day Saturday waiting for the anxiety inducing love texts.

They never came.

Max was either really busy as he said he would be or he was having second thoughts. I decided to not be that girl. You know the one. Most of us have been her! She's the one who waits by the phone for a call or a text and when she does get one, she answers way too quickly and eagerly for only five minutes of an intense endorphins rush. And if there is a tiny inkling of disappointment you can just count her out for the next month as she recuperates. I hated being that girl, so for the last remaining hours of Saturday, I hid my phone and worked on the dress that had been draped on my clothed torso for the better part of a week.

Putting my phone away was a liberating experience. I felt so productive. I felt as if I were off the grid! That was until I decided to finally look at my phone on Sunday afternoon.

My heart began to race as I saw a million text messages from Tahiri all saying the same thing. Mark had called out, she's been a

164

sales advisor all day and the window couldn't get done. I cursed and yelled as I threw on jeans and a t-shirt and made my way to the city.

This was all Maggie's doing! I could feel it in my bones!

The way that she kept questioning the plans for Sunday...I just knew! Ugh!

My anger was on another level. No longer did I feel the blistering winds of the November chill. I stomped all the way to the train station. The sun already saying her goodbyes for the day. An hour later, when I finally made it to the store, it was still bustling with craziness.

Sundays in the world of retail was an entirely different beast. Families took their time to wake up late and stroll pass the stores with no intentions of buying anything, until they saw everything. Visual merchandisers seldom work Sundays because they cost too much money. Instead of using one visual, stores could schedule two to three sales advisors...and they usually did. Why have a visual to clean, ring, and provide customer service when you can add more people for less?

Apparently not in Maggie's eyes. To her, business was business, and everyone was fair game. Whatever she had to do to secure the bag, she did. That meant using a visual even when she didn't have to.

I caught sight of Tahiri with a handful of garments, probably from the fitting room.

"Tahiri!" I yelled.

Her shoulders visibly deflated as she caught sight of me. "I've been texting you all day!"

"I know, I didn't have my phone. What happened?"

She set the clothes down on the already too full rack and flexed the feeling back into her hands. "Maggie, who left at three, told me about an hour into my shift that it was too busy to set the window. She had me do everything but visual tasks!"

All hell broke loose across my chest. I tried to tame the fiery flames that radiated throughout my body as I pulled out my phone. "Can you stay over time?" I asked.

Her face fell and I already knew. "I'm sorry, Gin. I have my parents waiting for me."

I nodded; it was all I could do to not scream. I dialed. And Maggie let it go to voicemail. "Hey, Maggie. Just wanted to know if I can have the master key in the safe to close the building. I want to stay late because you had Tahiri on register and running when she was here to set the window. Now, we've fallen behind a great deal and..." I sighed. "Just please call me back." I hung up, glancing at Tahiri, hoping that the desperation in my eyes would sway her into staying. My time at this company clouded my sense of familial obligations.

She shook her head. "Gin, you know I would if I could. But I can't."

I sighed. "Go. Clock out." I dialed the next person on my list.

"It's Sunday! The day of rest! This better be important," Marvin's firm irritation caused a lump to form in my throat.

"I need help," I croaked out.

"What?! What is happening? Where are you? Call the cops!"

"Marvin! Relax! I'm at the store and Maggie has screwed me...I don't know what to do."

I felt my heartbeat faster as his dead silence told me that maybe I had over reacted. "Gin, I am in the middle of something."

"I'm sorry, Marvin but Maggie isn't picking up the phone. I was going to stay and do the window."

"Did you call your boyfriend?"

I thought about calling Max, but I didn't want to ask for favors. I knew he would accommodate me, that fact didn't sit well with me. I was paranoid that Maggie would see something deeper. I was afraid of what would happen once it blew up in my face. There was an uneasiness in the pit of my stomach that I decided to ignore. "I don't have a boyfriend," I answered.

"Call him," Marvin sighed.

"Ugh!" My hands balled up. "So, you can't help? Then she wins."

"Ginny! This isn't life or death. We are not curing cancer. We work with clothes! Stop playing the victim and figure it out!"

After Marvin's abrupt hang up, I stood in the middle of the busy store, racking my brain. The lights seemed way too bright, and the music way too loud. The smell of sweat as people adjusted from outside temperature to inside temperature was nauseating. *Don't call Max. You can figure this out.* Is this what having a heart attack felt like?

I jumped as I felt a tap on my shoulder. "Gin, you, okay? Can you check my bag?" Tahiri asked on her way out.

I nodded; my mind still clouded with a too many thoughts and not enough solutions. I felt my phone begin to vibrate in my hand. My parents number appeared on the screen, I immediately sent it to voicemail.

I didn't have the time nor the energy to deal with parental issues. When my phone began to vibrate again, I immediately picked it up. "Mami, I can't talk right now."

"Hey, it's Max. Marvin said you were experiencing technical difficulties...whatever that means."

I cursed Marvin's life and wished him bodily harm. "I'm good. Don't worry about it."

"Ginny..."

I closed my eyes, taking a deep breath, I decided to clue him in. "Maggie decided that using a visual as a sales advisor was the best for the business and the window didn't get done. I want to stay and do it but she's not picking up the phone and I don't know which manager is on duty and if they'll stay with me or let me stay alone."

"I'll stay with you." I heard a horn blare in echo. I looked up to see Max stalking towards me.

My face came down in a frown. "What are you doing here?"

His smile fell. "I take it you're not happy to see me."

I glanced around as sales advisors were no longer working on their tasks, instead they were trying to discreetly be nosey. "Can we talk in the office?" I whispered.

His eyes followed mine to the corner where two sales advisors were openly staring at us. "Yeah, let's go." I followed as he led the way to the office where two department managers were watching the latest viral video.

"Hey, Gin," they said absentmindedly. Max cleared his throat forcing them to look up. They jumped to their feet. "Mr. Thomas! We didn't know you were in today."

"If you did, would you be out there securing the floor instead of watching a show?" Max's stern voice caused them to stand like toy soldiers. "Can you guys give us a minute?" he softened his voice.

"Sure." Both managers scurried out the room.

"Now, tell me why I had to get a call from Marvin and not from you?" Max kept his boss voice, but I refused to be intimidated.

"Max, don't start with me." I was taking off my coat when my phone began to vibrate again. I glanced at my phone and then to Max. "It's Maggie."

He took off his coat, throwing it over a chair. "Good, pick it up and put her on speaker."

I did as I was told. "Hello, Maggie."

"Hello, Gin, you called?"

I steadied the anger that had sprouted again. "I was informed that the window wasn't done because you had Tahiri ringing on the register."

The line was silent as she chose her words carefully. "I did what was best for business. It was busy today and we had a call out."

"We have the holiday window to set up by tomorrow morning. What do you suggest we do?"

"Really, Ginny. I think you can figure it out."

"I do have a solution. I need the key to the store and an extra body to secure the window with me."

I felt her eyeroll along with her disdain for me come clearly through the phone. "Ginny, we cannot afford to add two extra people on a Sunday," she explained in her best Cruella Deville impersonation.

I threw myself into the cold metal chair and slumped. "But there is only so much I can do alone and I—" I swallowed the lump in my throat, aware that Max was there, and I didn't want to embarrass myself any further.

"Hey, Maggie?" Max interrupted. I hadn't notice him come behind me, he began to massage my shoulders. I reluctantly began to relax.

"Who's that?" She asked quickly.

"It's Max Thomas. I have a solution to the window problem."

"Max? I didn't know you were in today. I would've stayed to meet with you." I felt a tiny sharp pain on my side and visualized Maggie running to the voodoo doll that resembled me and covering it in pins...or it could be my sciatica.

"I came in to shop and bumped into Ginny. I don't think anyone has to worry, I will stay and support Ginny with the window." He said the last bit in his boss voice and a finality that I knew Maggie wouldn't fight. I looked behind me to see Max's reaction only to have him wink at me.

"Very well. Ginny, you have my number if you need anything." Her words were slow, her voice even.

"I sure will!" I feigned excitement just to make her angry. I hung up and let out the laughter that was stuck in my throat. "That was amazing."

Max came around and sat on the corner of the desk in front of me. His hand reached out to caress my hair. "Can I ask you a question?" he began.

"Uh oh, this sounds like I'm in trouble."

The corner of his lips curved into a slow smile. "No, no trouble. Just wanted to know why didn't you call me?" His voice was low, no boss voice, no hostility.

I shrugged. "Honestly?"

"Always."

"I just didn't want to have to run to you to solve my problems. Would you stay if it were another employee?"

He let out a humorless laugh. "You're always asking that question."

"And you never seem to answer it."

His lips were set in a grim line as he reached to pull me up from my seat. "Honestly? Probably not. But this is my business and you're...you." I laughed. Max pulled me out of my chair and into his arms.

"Max..."

"Let me help. I can help. I want to help. I own the business."

I rolled my eyes. "Do you? I forgot."

Max let out an exasperated sigh before leaving a small kiss on my nose. "Woman, let me help."

"Have you ever done a window?"

"Can't say that I have."

I let my head fall back, giving him a chance to nuzzle my neck; the gesture sent chills through my body, and I wished that we were back at my apartment. "Don't think that just because that feels good, I'm going to ease up on your workload, we have equal responsibilities tonight," I teased.

"Not even if I did this?" he nuzzled my neck causing me to giggle.

"Mr. Thomas, what would the others think?" I joked.

"Those kids? They can learn a thing or two."

We threw caution to the wind and made out in the office for a solid fifteen minutes. Hands roamed, kisses trailed, and I fought the urge to call it quits for the night and head home to finish what he started.

Instead, we stood barefoot in the window, pulling down the curtains. "So, we really don't wear shoes this seems dangerous?"

I stood back hands on my hips. "I mean, we don't want to scuff or dirty the window floors and the booties that you guys provide rip easily so..."

He gave a curt nod. "Bare foot it is." Max clapped his hands together. "Where do we start?"

I picked up a packet of pages from the floor. "These are the technical pages. Anytime the window changes, your district team sends us this." I handed him the packet and watch as his forehead came down. "Don't worry, it's not rocket science. We follow the pages step by step, adjust as we go, and then we'll be done."

Max glanced up while flipping through the pages. "How long does it take?"

"Four to five hours."

"What?!"

"Maybe a little longer if it turns out to be more complicated than they led on." Max's eyes widened. I quickly tried to ease his worry. "It'll be fine. I've done this more times than you can imagine." When he didn't relax, I stepped forward to take his hand in mine. "What's up?"

His face flushed with embarrassment. "I honestly don't even know where to start."

"Now, I'm the boss," I gloated.

His eyes narrowed in my direction. "Don't get a big head Miss Perez. I still own this company." His sing songy voice made me laugh.

"Stop making me laugh! We need to get serious. We start by completely gutting the window of all the old props."

He nodded. "Start from scratch."

"Good, you see you're a quick learner."

Max wrapped his arms around my waist and nuzzled my neck. "I could think of something else you can teach me." My eyes fluttered shut as I let the warmth of his mouth stir desire throughout my body. There were no cameras in the windows, no one looking in...we could indulge if we wanted. I wrapped my arms around his neck, bringing our bodies closer. "Ginny, don't start nothing we can't finish," he warned.

I sighed. "Fine. You're right." I gave him a light tap on his lips hoping that that would be enough to satisfy me. Max pulled me in closer, deepening the kiss. Our tongues melded, our bodies rubbed closer, his hand on my ass squeezing and lightly lifting me. A small moan escaped my lips, and in that moment, I would've given this man anything and everything he wanted just for the pleasure of his touch.

I was so close to surrendering to him, but we had a job to do. "Max..." I began while taking love bites of his lips. "Max, as much as I really want to do...whatever this is, we need to get this window done."

He dropped one final kiss on my lips and stepped back. "Of course." Max lifted one big display cube and began to empty out the window. "Hey, Ginny. If you change your mind, I'm more than willing to accommodate."

"Oh, I bet you are," I laughed.

"It'll take all of five minutes, which leaves enough time to cuddle." He wiggled his eyebrows. I bit down my lip to keep from laughing.

"Just get to work."

For the next six hours we hammered, taped, constructed the holiday window.

Out came the orange and burgundy of Fall fashion, in went the wallpaper depicting a window with a wintery scene. In addition to that, we had to assemble a fake fireplace with a giant lion's head proudly displayed over it. Max was adjusting the red batwing chair, while I started to bring the mannequins into the window.

I looked over to Max who was comparing his handiwork to the technical pages that I gave him. I took the time to observe him; his brow came down in heavy concentration while he studied the page. His large, tattooed hands moved the lions head slightly to the left. My eyes traveled down his forearms, admiring the artwork that disappeared under his rolled-up sleeves. "Can I help you, Miss Perez?"

I smiled slyly. "No, Mr. Thomas, just admiring..."

He looked back, mega-watt smile in place. "I think I'm done. How about you?"

I stood up to look at our window. "I think I'm done too. We just need to spread the fake snow all over the floor and we'll be good."

Max grabbed two giant bags of the white tiny shimmery snow-flakes. We meticulously spread the tiny pieces of shimmer throughout the floor. "Whoever came up with this shit is getting fired," Max mumbled.

I giggled at his grumpiness. "I have to admit this is the most elaborate window we've had in a while."

"Ginny, look up."

"What?" I glanced up just in time for Max to blow a handful of white confetti in my face. I picked up a handful and threw it at him. Glitter fell around us as he playfully threw it at each other.

"Ow, wait, I got it in my eye!" Max exclaimed. I rushed over to make sure that he was okay only to have him throw another handful at me.

"Oh, you liar!" I laughed. I was about to throw some more at him when he pulled me into his arms. We were both out of breath as we tried to calm down. "You're gonna kiss me, or no?" I asked.

Max's arms wrapped around my waist. "I'm thinking about it."

I stood on my tip toes to beat him to the kiss. Our kiss got deeper and hotter way too fast. His hands made their way under my blouse, gently squeezing my breast. A soft moan escaped.

"Ginny!" Maggie yelled from a distance.

12

Rule 67: There's a difference between active listening and passive listening...

We jumped apart as Maggie's shrill voice vibrated through the empty store.

"What time is it?" I whispered while pushing Max's hands away and trying to dust off the shimmery snowflakes. Even the mannequins looked a mess. I busied myself with dusting them off and everything else that we messed up. Max was already halfway out the window when Maggie poked her head in. Today she resembled a New Jersey housewife with her leopard coat and matching booties, obnoxious without even speaking.

"Oh, there you guys are. I was wondering where...oh, is the window not done?" her feline smile fell down in a frown as she took in the mess.

"It was my fault, Maggie. I had no clue what I was doing so that ate up most of the time."

Maggie's frown turned into an instant smile. "I hope Ginny was understanding. She can have a short fuse when it comes to coaching others."

I sighed. "Good morning, Maggie. I'm here. I can hear you," I replied.

Her eyebrows rose high on her freshly Botox forehead. "Well, good morning to you, Ginny. Don't be mad, I'm just dishing out some constructive feedback." She winked at me as if we were long time gal pals. When I didn't reciprocate her fake friendliness, her face shrunk into itself as she pursed her lips. "How much longer? I want the curtain down around eight."

I glanced at my watch. "I mean seeing that there was no other visual and this was pushed back by a whole day...I will have the curtains down by then." I smiled a sugary smile that I hoped told her to fuck off.

"Ginny, I already explained that I did what I had to do for the good of the business," she sighed. She spoke down to me as if I were a child. My adrenaline began to pump as I thought about all the smart ass remarks I could never dish out, especially if I wanted to keep my job.

"If we're talking about the good of the business, I would think that setting up a holiday window would take priority, it showcases our new garments and gift ideas so we can maximize sales. So, in the future I hope we can think twice on how we use our staff. Especially the ones on the higher end of the pay scale." Max's voice was stern. It was intimidating how he could go from gentle, sexy, funny guy to...the Hulk. The way he went to bat for me made me love him even more.

Love? Who said anything about love? Girl, you need to calm down. Big dick energy does not equate to love. I felt like cold water wash over me. Was I in love? *No! you are just hypnotized by the amazing sex, great banter, and even better conversation.*

"Ginny, are you okay?" Max's voice penetrated my thoughts.

I shook my head. "Yeah, I'm fine. I think the exhaustion just hit me." I ran my sweaty hands down my jeans. "I need coffee." I stepped down from the window, passing between them. "Excuse me, I'll be right back." I slipped my sneakers on, and power walked to the employee entrance. I didn't stop to grab my coat, I should've but I just felt like the air was sucked out of me. The cold gust of wind smacked me right in the face. I ran to the coffee cart.

"Are you immune to the cold?" George Thomas' voice called out as he approached the coffee cart.

"The way I'm shaking makes me question my sanity." I smiled at the cart guy. "One large coffee, milk, two sugars please."

"Make that two." George slid a five-dollar bill through the window of the cart.

"George, you don't have to do that."

He smiled. "How would it look if I let the lady pay?" George shook off his long brown trench and threw it over my shoulders. How could two brothers be so different? George's smile was accessorized with dimples on each cheek which made him seem more charming and handsome. Where Max was rough, George was smooth, no laugh lines. Less lines means he didn't worry much. I glanced down at his hands...those were smooth too.

"What are you looking at?"

"You're hands. You don't have tattoos?"

He shook his head. "Nope, Max has enough for the both of us." I knew all too well. "Do you have tattoos?" he asked in return.

I nodded. "A couple," I answered.

"I love a challenge." His voice was low, as if we were sharing a secret. I didn't even want to share a pencil with him. George's grin went from friendly to flirty in a blink of an eye and I cleared my throat. "You're going to like the window."

He shrugged. "I don't care about that stuff."

"Oh, well...then..."

George laughed at my clumsy attempt to save the conversation. "I just like the money it brings."

I felt the sinking feeling in the pit of my stomach that I got when everything was about to go wrong. "Here you go." The coffee cart guy handed us our drinks.

I began to shake off George's trench coat. "You don't have to do that; we can walk to the store together. I'm fine." He replied.

I reluctantly nodded and began to walk back to the store. We turned the corner to see Maggie, Andrea and Max were observing the window. Max eyed us curiously. If it was jealousy I was sensing, it came as a surprise. Max always came off as a man secure in his own skin. I smiled to assure him that all was good when George wrapped an arm around me. "I bumped into Ginny. Max, you shouldn't let your star employee outside without her coat, she could catch a cold and then where would be?" George laughed.

"You're late," Max answered. He crossed his arms, looking more like a stern father than George's brother.

"Yeah, well, I was out late last night."

"Ginny, the window came out great. Max said he learned a lot about the window process and had some feedback that we'll bring back to the office. Good work," Andrea nodded.

"Thank you," I muttered. I shrugged off George's arm, stepping further out to explain the process. "This is fashion for the whole family. The process was a tiny bit consuming because of the construction of the mantel and fireplace. I think the outfit suggestions are great." I bullshitted my way through, taking tiny steps towards the employee entrance.

All three Thomas' and Maggie eyed me quizzically.

"That's lovely, Ginny," Maggie replied with her teeth set in a deranged smile. "I bet you would have finished faster if you weren't throwing prop snow at our new CEO."

This was worse than the dream where you're naked and everyone laughs and point and you wake up in a cold sweat only to realize that you're alone in life, fully dressed in long johns.

Andrea tilted her head to the side while eyeing her brother. George had a stupid grin and Max looked...well he didn't look happy. His faced was flushed and his brown eyes were dark like coal.

"Maggie, I didn't take you as a sour patch. I accidentally ripped a bag causing the snow to fall everywhere. We were having a bit of fun in the long hours we just worked with no breaks to secure a window that wasn't going to be set if we hadn't stepped in."

It was Maggie's turn to look sheepish. "Oh, I'm sorry, Max. I just assumed that—"

"It would do you some good to start assuming the best of your staff instead of the worse."

"We can continue this discussion in the office," Andrea stepped between Max and Maggie, grabbing her brothers arm tightly as she led him away into the building. Maggie followed behind without looking at me. George clapped his arm around me again, leading us behind. "The window is really, great. Good job, Ginny," George muttered close to my ear. Max looked over his shoulder laying eyes on us. His eyebrows came down heavy and that feeling in the pit of my stomach made me nauseas.

******

After cleaning up whatever mess we had left, I slipped my coat on, peeking at the closed office door before finally leaving.

"What's going on?" Tahiri said from behind me. I jumped out of my skin! I spun around only to be confronted by the visual team.

"I don't know. I'm too tired to go in and check."

"Too tired or too chicken?" Meisheko asked with arms crossed.

"Fine, I'm too chicken."

Mark nodded knowingly. "You didn't have to tell us that, we already know."

My eyes narrowed in his direction. He looked down in remorse. "Ginny, I'm sorry..."

"It's fine. The window is set. Please do weekend recovery and I'll see you guys tomorrow."

Their solemn faces were enough to make me angry, but I said nothing. What could I say? I was angry, tired and the little interaction with everybody had me on edge for no particular reason. Could they see my breakdown slowly setting in? I sighed and walked past them. Instead of walking straight to the station, I walked into the coffee shop for my second pick me up in less than an hour.

"How can I help you today?" The barista offered me a smile.

"You have any openings?"

"Actually, we do but you'd have to apply online."

I let out a faint laugh. "I was joking but you would save my life if you got me a vat of coffee, milk, two sugars."

"You're the girl who burned her mouth the other day," she pointed out with a tilt of her head.

I closed my eye to keep that pin in the head feeling from evolving. "Yes, yes that was me. I'm glad you caught the show," I said.

She politely smiled, all sympathy and set out to get my order.

I moved to the side and thought about what my next move should be. I began to think about the time I needed to make up with my collection.

Last night was an unforeseen emergency and I lost time. My phone vibrated and when I looked, it was my parents calling. I sent it to voicemail. I reasoned that I was going on the train soon, didn't want to cut our conversation short.

My mind jumped exhaustingly from my sometimes-forgotten collection to my parents and then to Maggie. She took up space in my mind when there was already a ton of clutter in there. I know Maggie was clearly trying to sabotage my promotion.

This was a losing battle.

"Here you go," the barista handed me my drink. "If you were serious about applying, the managers usually do interviews on Thursday mornings," she added.

"Thank you." I mean, if I got fired or decided to quit, I could always be a barista. Not my life's calling but surely not as crazy as H. Moda. I began to wonder what if. *What if I quit my job today? What if I had gone home the night before Thanksgiving? What if I hadn't met Max or What if he wasn't my boss?*

I knew that was a dangerous game to play. But I was living on the edge lately, I felt okay indulging in the game a tiny bit.

13

Rule #41: Ask for help! There will be times when the store is super busy, but team up with your managers for help or delegation.

I woke up in drooling mess in a sea of red silk and lace. I came home and went into designing mode. I was expecting a text or call from Max, and when there was none, I just went to work on the dress.

But I glanced at the sun rising and had a mild panic attack. *How long did I sleep?!*

The birds were singing their early morning song, I wished them nothing but a freezing death. I jumped up, threw on some pants, boots and coat and ran out the door. I hailed down a cab, sweating under the coat and beanie that I threw on to disguise the atrocity to fashion that I wore beneath.

I skimmed my entry card at the employee entrance, swallowing the butterflies that were floating around in my throat. I stealthily made it to the break room where I stuffed everything into a locker.

I spun around ready to blend in with the team, *maybe they won't notice I was late.*

"Are you hungover?" Maggie's voice came from behind me. I slowly spun back around.

"No, I'm not, Maggie." I glanced down to see that she finally retired her beloved knee-high boots for sneakers. "I've just had a really rough night."

She glanced at her watch. "You are over two hours late for your shift."

"I can tell time, Maggie." My irritation was short, there was no way I could hide. Missing my morning had me on edge.

"Well, we had a bunch of call outs today, I need you on register." Her face was stone. I saw the tick of her cheek as she waited for my response.

I scratched my head through my beanie. "Am I in the *Twilight Zone*?" I groaned.

"Excuse me?" her eyebrows shot up. "What was that?"

"Come on, Maggie, I thought we settled this yesterday."

"Settled what?"

"Using the visual team when we have a ton to do." She crossed her arms, threw back her head and gave a humorless laugh. "Who are you? *Cruella Deville*?" I replied.

"I'm not using the visual team. I am using the visual manager. At this point in time, that's you...until Marvin gets back." Her lips curled into a sinister smile; devils blood ran in her veins.

"I have a team to run," I pushed back.

"Who can run themselves while you ring for the next hour until the next person comes in."

"What about you?" I mimicked her stance, preparing for battle.

"What about me?"

"I see you're wearing sneakers, does that mean the district team isn't here today?"

Her cheeks flamed. "What are you implying?"

"That you only dress up when there's a visit."

Her chin rose up a notch. "I see whether there's a visit or not, you don't really put an effort." Maggie glanced down in disdain. "Another day for combat boots?"

"At least I don't get my fashion sense from the real housewives of tacky land."

Maggie's eyes widened to an abnormal size, turning bloodshot. I immediately regretted poaching the situation. "Listen, Maggie—"

"You're clocked in? Head to the register without another word," she commanded through gritted teeth. I sulked all the way to the cash point on the main floor. Walking from the escalator to the cash point was like walking the plank. A walk of shame, if you will. I could feel the stares from my colleagues, all wondering why I didn't stop in a department to remerch.

"Ginny!" Tahiri called out.

I didn't stop my stride. If I did, I would just run right home and never return again. I smiled wide in hopes that my customer service face would show to Maggie and whoever else that gave me weird stank eye that nothing could faze me. There was already a massive line for the Sunday customer who was in a hurry to make a Monday return. I swallowed a sigh as I gestured for the next customer.

"Good morning, how may I help you today?" My smile was so far stretched that I could give *Barbie* a run for her money.

"Hi, I wanted to return this." The customer pushed her shopping bag towards me. I reached in and pulled out a dress that smelled as if it were drowned in perfume. As I examined the dress, there were deodorant marks all over and it felt...wet.

"Ma'am, I'm sorry, but did you wear this?" I asked as I looked around for some sanitizer. God only knows what spilled on this dress.

"Yes, I did, but it's ruined now, and I would like my money back," she said.

I kept the smile on my face as I tried to explain the store policy. "Unfortunately, I cannot issue you a refund because you damaged the item. We only accept returns if the item is not worn or damaged."

She scrunched her face in disgust. "That's stupid."

I saw the shadow of Maggie's figure appear from the corner of my eye, watching the confrontation with the customer from hell unfold.

I shrugged. "Yeah, I know, but I don't make the rules." I pushed back the dress with one finger.

I could see the thoughts passing through the customers eyes as she stood straighter, prepared to switch tactics. "How about you excuse this just this once?" she whispered.

I looked towards the sales advisors who were ringing up on my left side and right side. They both gave me sympathetic smiles. This was just a tiny blip of what they had to deal with day in and day out. I sighed, remembering what the managers spoke about in the morning meetings; *make the customer happy. Take back that top even if they wore it to the ground. This is a billion-dollar company, we can take a hit on a dress that cost a customer twenty-five bucks.*

I looked around. "I'm going to do it this one time," I explained to her.

Her face lit up. "Oh! Thank you!"

I began to type in the item number when the hair on my arms stood up. I looked up from the register, Max was on the escalator headed down, staring at me with his arms crossed. There was no flirtatious smile, no conspirator wink. This was Max Thomas.

"Miss? Are you okay?" I heard the customer ask as the wave of crowd noise came back in full effect.

"Yes, do you have the card that you made the purchase with?" I continued with the transaction when I heard my name come over the walkie. "Ginny, can you please come to the office?"

"I think the big boss isn't happy you were on register," one of the sales advisors said.

"Who knows?" I shrugged as if I didn't know.

I took my time, passing through the crowd of people trying to come up with excuses as to why I was late, why I argued with Maggie and why I no longer needed to be on register.

I swiped my access card and pushed my way into the stockroom and quietly made my way through another door that led into the breakroom. Down the small hallway, I steadied my breath and finally knocked on the office door.

"Come in," Maggie called out.

My heart began to race when I saw Max standing off to the side with his arms crossed. "Hello, Ginny." He greeted me as if we weren't naked in each other's arms just one day ago.

"Hi." *Did I sound too breathy?* I cast my eyes toward Maggie, raising my eyebrows in silent question.

"Max just popped in to walk the window and give us feedback before he heads to the next store."

"Next store?" I asked.

"Unfortunately, there are other stores not in great shape that could use my attention. So after today I'll be in the Columbus Circle location." He explained with a monotone voice. For some odd reason he was like a robot. I couldn't tell what he was thinking, I couldn't tell if his coldness was for show because Maggie was here, or something changed between us. "So, if we could walk the store just to make sure there's nothing that needs immediate attention."

I nodded. "Yeah, sure."

Maggie stood up from the desk to follow us out. "Maggie, if you don't mind, I'd like to walk with Ginny on the visual aspect of the store and walk with you after. We can go over numbers, back of house set up and procedures and anything you may have questions about."

Maggie slowly sat back down. "Of course, I have intradays to fill out for the next couple of weeks."

"Perfect."

Max and I walked out the office. As I gave one final glance back, Maggie's face was flushed, and I could've sworn I seen her head explode.

We walked to the sales floor in silence. I tried to look from the corner of my eyes to gauge his demeanor. "Should I go and grab the department pages? Should I get a notepad?"

"No, I think this can be fast and easy."

"I kind of like it slow and hard," I joked.

He stopped immediately in his tracks. "Virginia, I hope that was a joke." Max was not in a joking mood, and I didn't know how to respond so I kept my mouth shut. "I hope next time you think twice when speaking to me that way."

I felt my spine tense up as embarrassment took over my body. I stood straight; my head held high. "For sure, Mr. Thomas."

He nodded and continued walking to the front of the store. I, like a lost puppy, followed behind. "Any notes about ladies, Mr. Thomas?" I asked, taking out my phone to open my notes app.

He squinted at the department as if he were looking at the sun. His head slowly going from left to right, presumably taking everything in. Without a word, Max walked to the left of the department, walking in between shops, examining signs...he was doing the most and my irritation was bubbling to the surface. He began to speak and noticed that I wasn't behind him. "Aren't you following?" He called out.

"I didn't know I was supposed to follow, you didn't say a word," I called back. I walked at a snail's pace to him. "Next time it'll be great to get a heads up. A grunt, sign language, anything," I commented.

"Oh, I'm sorry, Ms. Perez, do you need a moment to collect yourself before we move on?"

"I'm sorry, Mr. Thomas, I'll behave myself if you stop being an asshole," I hissed.

"Follow me," he commanded, immediately stomping away.

I shouldn't follow, I told myself. *You should! He's the boss, regardless of what he says and how he acts, you should give him the respect he deserves,* my inner voice shouted back. I swallowed the pride I had and stomped after him. We marched to the deco room in silence, curious glances from the others. I smiled and waved to those who dared to throw out a greeting, trying to release the nervous energy that I felt coursing through my veins.

Max opened the door, all the visuals scattered, busying themselves with make-believe tasks. "Can you guys give us a moment?" he asked politely. He was the boss, of course they were going to leave us.

One by one they exited the room with sympathy in their eyes. When the door gently shut, Max spun around so quickly that I got dizzy. "What the hell is wrong with you, Ginny?"

"Me? What the hell's wrong with you?

He ran a tattooed hand through his hair. "I'm treating you like everyone else."

"You're an asshole to everyone?" I muttered.

"No, but I...I don't know what I'm trying to say." He closed his eyes and tilted his head back. He let out a long breath before dropping his head back down. "My brother and sister think it's best of I put some distance between us," he confessed.

"What?"

"The whole scene with Maggie made it seem as if I favored you, like I was protecting you."

Silence fell around us as I tried to process what was just said. The tick of the giant clock above the tiny desk in this small room just sounded much louder than usual. "They know?" I asked.

"They know."

"What do we do now?"

He shrugged. "We can still see each other. Just keep it to ourselves like we had planned." Max reached out for me, but I jumped back as if his hand was on fire. "What's wrong?"

"There's a camera right behind you, it can see us." With a tilt of my chin, I gestured towards the inconspicuous camera. Max took a giant step back.

"I want to kiss you," he said in a hushed tone.

I was a ball of mixed emotions. I knew that Max was the same way. I wanted to rip his clothes off and then lay on his chest and talk about everything.

But his demeanor today alone told me that that would just remain a fantasy. I sighed and did my best to sound normal. "It's just going to have to wait," I shrugged and offered a smile.

"Do you know where the blind spot is?"

"That corner," I pointed behind him next to where we kept the shelving.

"Show me," he said.

"What?"

He rubbed his chin. I noticed a hint of stubble and I knew that meant that he was going through it. "Show. Me." He lowered both his voice and chin.

With understanding, goosebumps spread all over my body.

I walked him over to the shelves. We hit the corner and I was immediately pinned to the wall. Max's body was flushed with mine; my hips caressed his as his lips covered mine, stifling a moan.

"Mr. Thomas, am I gonna have to report you to HR?" I teased as I gave a quick peck against his lips. He let out a groan as he deepened the kiss. We heard the beep of the entry card and jumped apart just as someone walked in.

"Big brother!" George's voice sang.

My heart was beating a mile a minute. I can't believe how stupid I was to let my guard down at work. I began shifting through the clothes on a random rack to give the pretense of me doing actual work as I tried to calm myself down.

"Well, hello, Ginny." I could hear the playfulness in his voice. George wasn't stupid, he knew what was up. "Busy?"

"Just checking on the prep for tomorrow's move," I explained.

"And Max is helping by sucking your face?" He asked with a charming twinkle in his eyes. It was hard to be angry or offended by George when he was always so playful.

"Wha- what?" Max stammered.

George rolled his eyes. "Both of your faces are flushed, so you either were kissing or working really, really hard."

Max crossed his arms and glared at his brother. "What do you need Georgie? Why are you even here?"

I continued looking through the rack and pretended I wasn't listening even though it felt like my sense of hearing was heightened by all the tension.

"Just be careful with the dragon lady walking around," he warned.

"Get to it, what do you need?" Max asked.

"You left brunch so fast, and I figured you would be here, I needed to talk to you about something..." he gave a quick glance my way. "...privately."

"Ginny, will you excuse me for a sec?"

I nodded absentmindedly.

They both left and I was there thinking about the *what if's* again. *What if it was Maggie who walked in on us? Max was head of the company but what if I got fired anyway? What would happen if I was made the scapegoat to protect his career?* My heart was telling me not to dwell on the imaginary drama inside my head, but my mind was telling me it was only a matter of time before this bomb exploded.

I sighed. Two hours late for work, an intense interaction with Max...I was just waiting for something crazy to happen.

Maggie probably got to George, who was probably repeating whatever she said to Max and then I would be out of a job.

The visual team came back into the deco room a few minutes after Max left. Their questioning looks was enough for me to use some sick time and call it a day.

"Call me, text me, send messenger pigeons, whatever you have to if Maggie pulls some other insane move," I called out to the team.

They all nodded with sympathy on their faces.

Max never came back to deco. There was no call for me on the walkie. That only solidified in my mind that something big was going down and I knew it had to do with me. It always had to do with me. I don't even know why he's put up with me and my drama for these past few weeks.

If I was him, I would have jump ship way back during Black Friday.

I checked my phone just in case I hadn't felt the vibration.

Nothing.

Don't let Max take over your world. He'll do you dirty like Rafa.

I had just put on my coat when Maggie stopped in her tracks on her way to the office. "Ginny, where are you going?"

"I'm not feeling well, I'm going home to rest and come back refreshed tomorrow." I didn't want to engage with her more than I had to. She didn't move an inch; hands folded in front of her just staring at me. "Was there something else?" I asked.

"How far did the team get?"

"They rubber banded, Mark just needs to press some of the outfits."

"And signage?"

"The team will have that prepped before they leave for the day."

"It's your department, are you sure they can handle it? Although you are running the team for the time being, you're still are responsible for it."

"I know," I answered curtly.

She nodded slowly but still hadn't moved from her spot. "Are you okay, Maggie?"

"Do you know the Thomas'?"

I shrugged. "I know them just as much as you do."

"They seem to be very fond of you, I just assumed that you all had met before."

She was fishing for something, and I wasn't going to give her anything. I shook my head. "Nope."

"Very well. Go home and get some rest." She spun on her heel, practically slamming into Max.

Max stopped at the sight of Maggie. "Hello, Maggie." His eyes darted to me but gone was the heat from earlier. "Ginny, I'm so sorry about earlier but George—"

"Max, I thought you had left earlier," Maggie interrupted.

His face went from casual to boss mode. "Yes, I did. But I had promised Ginny that I would help her with whatever she needed and then I had to leave to take care of something...but I'm back. Did I miss anything?" he glanced my way.

Before I could answer, Maggie jumped in. "Ginny isn't feeling well so she's leaving work early. I was just letting Ginny know that she is still responsible for the ladies department even though she is technically running the team."

"If Ginny needs to head home early, I can stay and make sure—."

I began to shake my head. "No, it's okay Ma—Mr. Thomas."

"Please, call me Max."

"I'm confident in the team. I know they got it; I just need to rest." I nervously looked towards Maggie who was silently taking in our interaction. I could feel her eyes dissecting and scrutinizing every little eye twitch and face spasm.

"Are you sure?" Max asked. I wish he could read my mind and I could just tell him to stop giving me any attention in front of

Maggie. But alas, he was obtuse in the same way that I was when I thought *the Hills* was a legit reality show.

"Don't worry, Max. You can handle business at the other location, and I can see to it that the visual team is prepped." Maggie answered. She was sucking up to the boss and if I stayed any longer, I'd vomit from the extreme ass kissing I was witnessing.

"No, really. I think we're in a good place for tomorrow. All hands are on deck, we'll be good," I insisted. "I'll head out now."

Maggie nodded. "Very well then."

I cleared my throat. "Okay, see you guys tomorrow." I breezed by the two of them.

Past the holiday crowd that refused to obey or acknowledge the store hours all the way to the time clock. I felt the buzzing in my back pocket.

Meet me at the coffee shop, I'll be there in ten.

No.

All I needed was for Maggie or some other manager seeing us and turning it into something ugly.

I glanced down at my phone.

There go those stupid bubbles.

They kept popping up and disappearing almost as if he was trying to come up with the right reply. I tucked my phone away before his reply came up.

I snuggled into my coat, gripped my handbag around me and made my way home. The entire train ride, I refused to look at my phone. I knew there was a reply waiting for me, but I also knew he didn't have to say much to get me to change my mind. City lights passed as my train made it above ground. Everything was beautifully blurry. The quiet buzz of conversation among the passengers were almost enough to lull me into a quick nap; the thought of what Max responded kept me awake.

I took my time walking home from the station. Different types of music mingled in the air with the frost.

To others, it would sound like chaos but to me it all seemed magical under the white Christmas lights that adorned each avenue that I passed. I popped my headphones in.

The music coming from my headphones weirdly matched my current mood and had me feeling like I was in a music video walking through the city questioning my love life; Ariana Grande ain't got nothing on me.

I ran up the stairs to avoid Mrs. Pierce. I wasn't in the mood for her. Regardless of my efforts I heard her door open. "Can you stop making all that noise?!"

I kept my mouth shut and kept it moving. I locked my door, stomped my way to the couch, sank in and finally read his response:

Ok.

That was worse than nothing.

14

Rule 101: Participate in company trainings. We offer trainings that can aide your development. We love to promote from within!

I barely slept. The minute my eyes shut, it felt as if it was time to get up. It was Tuesday. As far as Tuesdays go, they were like any other days; for the most part it was okay but no one wakes up excited to participate in them…it's not like it was Friday.

I slept like hell last night, fighting with the urge to text Max but not wanting to seem needy. Love was such a hard concept.

Love? Who said anything about love?

That thought just added to my foul mood. But today specifically, I was in an extremely Grinchy mood. I quickly got dressed and started my day. The moon was still out, the wind was out of control making the air seem colder than it really was. I sat in the train car sulking.

Max literally texted nothing.

Why did that make me feel like shit? It was so easy for him to let go. For all the shit he talked about giving us a try…he didn't even insist on coming over, didn't insist on trying to figure out why I didn't want to meet up.

Girl, why are you toxic? He's not a mind reader! He has no clue what you want him to figure out.

I was too busy arguing with myself that I missed my stop! When I realized it was my stop, the doors slammed in my face. I growled, throwing my arms in the air like a mad woman. Thank God I was the only one in the car. I got off at the next stop only to see that the next train going back would arrive in another half hour. I decided to run to the store from two stations away. It felt as if I ran a hundred miles. In the cold, my cheeks were flushed from my body heat, I could feel the beads of sweat freezing on my temples. My heart was pounding against my chest and when I arrived at the store, I began to cough from exhaustion. Fuck, I had no time for coffee or a bagel. I ran down to the break room, threw my things into a locker, clocked in and ran upstairs. I was still five minutes early, but I began to bring all the prep racks out of the deco room.

"Damn, Ginny. You are really eager today," Meisheko commented as she walked towards me.

"Yeah, I just want to get this over with," I muttered.

The others began arriving; one by one like soldiers onto the battlefields...that's a bit dramatic, it was more like a football team ready to set the field on fire. I took a deep breath and began handing out copies of the map that Tahiri had made. "Good Morning, every-one. I have handed you each a map with your designated sections. I also have racks with your names on it. Your soul focus will be that section. If you are done before the four hours, please hop into assist someone who needs it..." I trailed off when I saw the Thomas' siblings huddle up.

"Don't worry about us, just keep talking," George encouraged in his relaxed way.

"This is a big one guys. This is the final ladies set up before Christmas. We are setting the example for the other stores. I want us to look better than we've ever have before. We deserve it. So, look at your maps, let Tahiri or I know if you have questions, comments, concerns. And have fun!" I finished to applause from my team.

When everyone dispersed, the Thomas' approached me.

"Great pep talk," George commented.

"Very impressive," Andrea added.

"We are here super early to be of any assistance," Max explained.

I began to shake my head. "That's not really necessary."

"Max, thought it would be a good idea to come and support that way we have a better understanding on how your methods as a store works. Also, we understand it must be overwhelming to oversee your visual team as well as be responsible for such a huge share of the business," Andrea said. Her hands where daintly clasped in front of her as she waited for my instructions.

I gave a quick glance to Max. I wanted to murder him. Or at the very least injure him in a way that won't kill him but would probably give him a permanent limp. "It's not a big deal. I delegated this task to Tahiri, so I can better focus on the team and store." Why did he feel like he had to rescue me? As if I couldn't handle this job on my own.

Because we're seeing each other and having sex.

I don't need his help or his sympathy. This whole situation has just put me in a grinchier mood and although I didn't curse or scream or get disrespectful, I was sure they could tell by the look on my face that I wasn't with the shits.

"Well, we are here and at your service," Andrea answered diplomatically that I almost felt bad that I was in such a shitty mood. "The fact is this is an important time for us because we are trying to bring this company to a new era. We want to improve on a system that is already past its prime. If there is anything here, anything that you and your team are doing that can improve our methods, we want to know," Andrea finished with a sigh. "Now, Ginny, what can we assist with?"

Fine. If they want to get their hands dirty, nails chipped, fingers cut and bruised, and cramping, then by all means, who am I to stop them?

I took a deep breath. "Well, we have two massive tables that need to get changed out. Do you guys mind folding things down?"

George clapped his hands. "That's more my speed. I'll get on that." He power walked to one of the sections and asked Meisheko what should he fold onto the table.

"I'll fold the other table," Andrea volunteered. "I think since Max is the head of global, you should really put him to work and make him sweat a little." She flipped her blonde hair and stomped away to where Mark was. I felt myself blush at her comment and hopefully she didn't notice.

Then there were two.

"Where do you want me, boss?"

I rolled my eyes at him and walked away without saying a word. I began to empty fixtures at the front of the store and placing the garments on the empty racks. Max took my lead and began to empty the other fixtures.

"Max, you really don't have to do that." I was really upset and his close proximity made it seem likely that I would kick him or trip him.

"Ginny, I know you're upset—"

"Am I?"

"But, I want to know this company in and out...after we empty everything what do we do?"

I glanced at him; he already had his shirt sleeves rolled up, revealing the tattoos I knew covered both arms and most of his chest. "Fine," I sighed. Might as well use him to get the job done. After that, I'll let him have it. "After everything is emptied, we usually take the samples that are rubberbanded and labeled with the numbers and place them to their corresponding spots." I waved the map at him. "That's where the maps come in play."

He picked up samples that were fastened together with a rubber-band. "Number one goes on this fixture here."

I nodded "You got it. If something doesn't seem clear, just let me know."

"So once I place the samples, who places the garments?"

I held back my laughter. "You do. Once you fill the fixtures with the garments, you also have to BETSZ them." Max had a look of confusion; I wanted to start on my section, but I needed to make sure he understood. "Do you have a question, Max?"

It was his turn to blush. "Who's Betsey?"

I laughed. "Not Betsey. B-E-T-S-Z. It's an acronym for garment caring everything." When he still looked confused, I swallowed the eye roll and preceded to explain. "B is for Belting or Buttoning, E is for Edging, T is for Tying, S is for sizing or stickering and Z is for Zip."

He nodded his understanding which should've assured me that he was up to speed. But when he still didn't move, I finally snapped. "What's the issue, Max?"

"Just a quick question."

"I'm kind of under a time crunch so make it quick."

"What's edging mean?"

I tilted my head at him. "Have you ever worked in one of your stores?"

Max cleared his throat and scratched his stubble that had gotten thicker overnight. "Not at this capacity."

"Edging means aligning all the pant hangers so they all line up evenly." I demonstrated quickly with a set of pants that was on my rack. "Like this. Get it?"

Max nodded, but I could tell by the way he clenched his jaw

that he wasn't happy with my demeanor towards him. "If I have any other questions, I'll ask you."

We began setting everything the team had prepped.

I was in a trance.

This was one of the best parts of the job. It was like a puzzle trying to make all the garments fit together. Garments that a customer didn't think could go together, were complimentary; I did that.

I made it appealing.

That satisfying feeling was what's kept me at this job for so long. I glanced around the room; everyone else was in the zone. Except for George who was busy flirting with Meisheko. His boisterous laughter at something she said boomed in the ladies' department.

Andrea was more reserved folding sweaters and size stickering each one.

I turned to see Max carrying an armful of different garments. After he placed it all, he began garment caring; swiping sweat from his temple as he sped walk to locate the next couple of pieces.

Two hours later, when I felt we were in a good place, I walked over to Mark. "Hey, I'm going to let Max finish setting up the department." I ignored Mark's eyebrow raise. "I'm going to dress the mannequins."

"I don't know what's going on, but I think it's safe to say that your promotion is secured," he joked.

I knew Mark was only teasing, he wouldn't say anything maliciously, but what he said didn't sit well with me. If he noticed any special treatment Max was granting me, then surely the others have as well. "Gin, I'm sorry, you know I didn't mean anything by it," Mark struggled with his apology.

I offered him a tight-lipped smile. "I know." I began to walk away. "I'll be back, I'm going to grab the Mannequin picks."

I skipped the elevator and walked down the escalators. "Ginny?"

I stopped in my tracks when I heard Maggie's voice from behind me. I turned and offered her a smile. It was fake, but it was something. "Good morning, Maggie."

"How's the move going?"

I took in her outfit of the day; liquid leggings, knee high boots, wide brim hat and an infinity scarf even though we were inside.

"The move is going great. We're actually ahead of schedule."

"Reeeeally?" She took a sip of her Starbucks. "Just a heads up, the global team might pop in today to check the progress."

I knew she threw that piece of information in just to make me nervous. She had no clue but I was not the one to mess with today. "Um, they're actually here."

She choked on her coffee, and I did a little dance inside. "What?"

"They've been here since six to help with the set-up."

Maggie's eyes narrowed. "And you let them?"

"They insisted!"

Maggie jogged up the escalator, the thud of her thick heels pounding the floors. "Good morning, everyone!" I could hear her insincere sweetness. It was the voice you used when you talked to kids under the age of five; sweet, light...almost like cotton candy. Did people really like cotton candy? No not really; all it was was sugar that looks nice but lasted two point five seconds. Not worth it. Which is what I told myself about Maggie. She's not worth it.

I did my best to set her aside and continued on what I had to get done. Eye on the prize and all that nonsense.

I rolled the rack of mannequin picks back upstairs just in time to hear Maggie say, "Maybe if we switch this around. I don't think this really makes sense."

I stopped in my tracks before racing back to find a stressed-out Tahiri surrounded by Max, Andrea, George and Maggie.

"What doesn't make sense?" I asked.

I could see Tahiri take a deep breath preparing to explain, while

Maggie continued looking at the wall. "I think that if we—" Maggie began.

"Did you look at the commercial pages?" I asked, stopping her completely before she ruined everything that we've done.

"Well, no, I didn't," she answered.

"Then before you give feedback, I suggest that you look at the pages to get a better understanding as to why things are set up the way that they are." I had lost all my patience and knew that the tone I had taken was going to cause problems.

The wall was no longer her concern, Maggie turned to look at me; her fingers toying with the fringe of her infinity scarf. Her eyes looked as if lava was spewing from it. "Excuse me?"

I couldn't take it back. The words had left my mouth. "I suggested you take a look at the department pages to fully understand the teams reasoning behind placement." In that moment, I felt all eyes on us.

Maggie and I continued our staring contest. "I think if we move—"

"Maggie!" I couldn't keep it in anymore. "Look at the pages or wait until everything is set before putting your two cents in. It'll only set us back time frame wise if we start changing things before we're done."

"Excuse me! Watch your tone!"

"Then you need to listen! Do you know how frustrating it is to have you question every little thing I do?! It doesn't feel so good."

I felt a hand on my shoulder. "Ginny, I think you need to take a fifteen," Max whispered.

"I will not be yelled at because you can't take feedback," Maggie spat out.

"To normal people what you give would not be considered feedback," I yelled back as I pushed my rack towards the mannequins at the front of the store.

"Then what would a normal person call it?" Maggie trailed behind me.

"They would call it micromanaging! But I'm not a normal person so I would call it revenge."

"Revenge? For what?" Maggie crossed her arms, tapping her toes while waiting for my answer. My rage cooled down as I remembered where I was. This was not a dream, and I couldn't tell her exactly how I felt even though that's where I was headed.

"Maggie, just leave me alone and let us work. We were fine until you came upstairs, stay in your dungeon and don't come out."

I spun around to walk away from her because I gave zero fucks at this moment. But again, I heard her thick stacked heels stomping after me. "We are not through, Gin!"

"Maggie, I'm telling you stay away from me. I just need time to cool off!"

"Okay, you two that's enough," Andrea's stern voice stopped us both. "Maggie, follow me to the office, Ginny, take a fifteen."

Without a backwards glance I practically ran to the stock room to hide in a corner.

Within minutes I heard a soft knock followed by soft footsteps. "Ginny?"

"Max, go away." I was hiding in a corner, with tears rolling down my face, I didn't want him to see me that way. I felt embarrassed that I let Maggie get under my skin. I felt extremely embarrassed that I let the Thomas' see me react the way I did.

He spotted me. "Are you crying?"

I wiped my eyes. "No."

Max smirked and sat down on a stool next to me. "I've never been more exhausted in my life," he began. "Is this what you guys really do every week?"

"Yup, multiple times a week."

"God." He fell silent for two seconds before adding, "Do we pay you guys well?"

I shrugged. "Better than most companies."

He nodded leisurely, like we had nothing else to do. "Max?"

"Yeah?"

"What are you doing here?"

Max leaned back in his seat. He held out his hands in front of him, examining them. "Look how nasty my hands are. I've cut and scrape them a million times today."

I sat down on another stool next to him, mimicking his pose. I held out my hands, I wiggled my middle finger. "You see this guy? I broke him when I was carrying a cube prop and it slipped from my hand, pulling my finger back and—"

Max held up his hand. "Please don't finish that."

"I've also busted my lip trying to remove a bow from a shop." I shook my head at the memory. "There was so much blood," I whispered.

When he didn't respond, I looked to see a horrified expression on his face. "Please don't tell me anymore."

"All that to say that I have accumulated, ten years of injuries for this company and I think it's all gonna end today." I let out a heavy sigh to keep the tears from falling.

"What do you mean?" he asked.

I fully turned to him so he could see the emotion that was wrecking me. "I mean that I have to quit this job."

"Why?" Max sat up straighter.

"Because Maggie isn't going to let up. She's gonna keep treating me like shit because of all the drama from before. I kept a pretty low profile, being overly positive and happy, until you guys magically showed up and started giving me attention and pushing me for a promotion."

"Do you know why we are pushing for your promotion?"

"Because you liked my merchandising."

"That and the fact is this company hasn't really promoted anyone for the past six years. There has been no new blood and we're trying to bring excitement into this company. Andrea researched you before giving you a promotion. You were the best candidate from all the stores that we walked."

"I know this."

"We didn't just magically show up and handed you a promotion. You earned it. Maggie knows this. You're good at your job."

"I know that too."

"But—"

"There's a but?"

"You can't let her get to you like that."

I dropped my head into my hands. "I know. But you irked me—"

"I irked you?"

"Yeah, with butting in as if I needed you to save the day. I could've taken care of things." I sighed. "Maggie does this every time to try to appeal and look good to you guys."

"You don't think we know this?"

"But she slows everything down and we are on a deadline."

"We know how much of a pain in the ass this woman is, but you don't see us losing our cool."

"That's because you guys run the place!"

"You can't quit, Ginny." He pulled my face up.

"Are you telling me as someone who you're dating or as my boss?"

It was his turn to let out an exhausted sigh. "As both. You can't give up when you're so close."

"I don't feel like I'm close. I don't want to give it up but she—"

He grabbed hold of my hand. "I know."

His thumb caressed my fingers and the stirring of something deeper began to evolve. "Max—"

His other hand reached out to caress my cheek, his thumb

caressing my bottom lip. Our eyes met and I felt my body leaning closer to him.

"I hope I'm not interrupting anything," Maggie's voice broke the spell. I jumped out of my seat so fast; I almost reached the ceiling.

Max stood up. "I came to check up on Ginny. To see if she was alright," he explained.

"Ginny...oh no, are you crying?" I could've sworn I saw a twinkle in her eye.

"No." I folded my arms in hopes that would calm my nervous shaking.

"I came to apologize and see if you're alright." Her eyes darted back and forth between Max and I, never really settling on one of us. I knew she knew something was up. My heart was pounding trying to figure out at exactly what point of the conversation she walked in on.

"Thanks, but I think we both got a little out of hand," I said. I just wanted to get this over with. This room just felt smaller by the second.

"Agreed. Can we put this behind us and move forward?" This felt like a set up. I knew that she would be nice to me until the global team stopped coming to the store or if I was transferred.

"Of course." My smile was phony, but it was the best that I could do.

"Great. I have some work to do in the office, come get me when you guys are done upstairs and we can walk it," she said with a smile just as phony as mine.

The three of us just stood there waiting for someone to move. I shoved my way out. "I'll see you guys upstairs."

I busied myself with dressing the mannequins and avoiding Max. Which was hard because he was in my section of the department...doing an amazing job. I looked around; everyone was doing great! This was probably the fastest we ever completed a floor move.

I was in the middle of styling a mannequin when Max came over, hand in pockets. "What else needs to get done?" he asked.

"I'm good over here. You can see if one of the others needs help."

"What are you doing?"

"I'm just styling the mannequins."

"Can I try?"

I narrowed my eyes at him. "Why?"

"Because I just want to know how to do it," he shrugged.

"The thing is—"

"Here we go," he said with an eye roll and a smirk.

"The thing is, there's a big difference between dressing a mannequin and styling a mannequin."

"Okay..."

"When you just plopped the clothes on her, that's just dressing—"

"Her? Is it alive?"

"But when you tuck, finesse the fabric to falling in a certain way; pin, natural creases, rolling up sleeves...that's styling."

He shrugged. "I still want to try," he said like a child asking to jump off the swing.

I handed him a page. "This is the styling pages for mannequins. She has to look exactly like this."

"She?" he leaned closer. "Do they talk to you when no ones around?" he whispered.

I felt the sides of my lips quirk up and immediately forced them down. "You really want to give it a shot?"

He stood up straighter, eyes staring into mine intently. "With every bone in my body."

I glanced around hoping that no one, especially Maggie, overheard. In that second, George slug an arm over my shoulder. "What does he want to do?" he asked innocently.

I glanced up at Max's handsome younger brother. "He wants to style a mannequin," I answered.

Max folded his arms. "I don't think it's appropriate for you to have your arm around her," Max replied, doing his best to keep his voice light.

George raised an eyebrow at him and nodded. "Sorry, I didn't know there was something still going on," he whispered.

"There isn't," Max and I responded.

George smiled big. "Sure, there isn't. Just deny at the same time and everyone will think there's nothing happening."

"What's happening?" Andrea was the next Thomas to approach.

"Max is—" George began.

"Georgie..." Max gave a subtle warning.

"Let me finish, Geez. Max wants to dress a mannequin."

"Style," I corrected.

"Well, this I gotta see." She folded her arms, just like I've seen Max do a million times; it was some kind of Thomas family trait. This was the first time I've seen Andrea be a little bit silly. And although her lips only formed a faint smile, I loved seeing her have fun with her brothers.

"Andy, don't start..." Max's face flushed under his five o'clock shadow.

"Let's make it a competition," George rubbed his hands together and I knew that competing at every little thing was something that's probably been going on between them since they were kids.

"Let's not," Max answered, utterly annoyed. I've seen him aroused, amused, laughing, serious, angry but never annoyed. This was most likely something only George knew how to bring out.

George threw his arm around my shoulder again. "Ginny could be the judge."

Max's eyes narrowed at his sibling's arm around me, and I already knew that he was in it to win it. "Okay, Ginny can judge."

"I don't want to be in the middle of it," I said. "Can't we just style them and be done with this floor swap?" I glanced around; all the visuals were busy taking in the little drama going on between the siblings.

"How much time should we get?" George asked.

"How long does it take to style one mannequin?"

They both turned to me. "About fifteen minutes," I sighed.

George smacked his hands together in giddy delight. "Since Ginny wants to remain neutral, Andy can judge."

"Guys, after thirty years on this planet this gets old after a while." Even as she complained, Andrea finally had a genuine smile on her face.

I handed her the papers. "This is what each mannequin should look like."

She nodded. "Understood."

Each brother stood in front of a naked mannequin. The visuals gathered around to take in the early morning show.

Andrea set the timer on her phone. "On your marks, get set, Go!"

Both men dismantled their mannequins making sure to place each part down gently. If you ever want to know how much a mannequin costs, have a customer break one in an attempt to see what size the mannequin is wearing and tell a district member it needs to get replaced. Not only will you have to wait months for a replacement, but you will be reminded for the rest of your career about the thousands of dollars the company had spent to replace one mannequin.

George threw the clothes on in record time, while Max took his time to not wrinkle the garments as he placed it on. George snatched the page from his sisters' hand, to examine the styling. His large fingers were surprisingly nimble as he manipulated the fabric. Max had just placed the arms back on and began adding his finishing touches.

George threw his hands up in the air. "I'm done!"

Max didn't stop what he was doing. His concentration was amazing. "Okay, twenty seconds left," Andrea announced.

Max narrowed his eyes at a French tuck that didn't want to stay in place. He did his best to manipulate the fabric; untucking and tucking again until he was satisfied.

"Five!" Andrea shouted.

"Four! Three!" Everyone joined in. "Two! One!"

Both men stepped back while everyone cheered at their efforts. Now, it was Andreas turn to step in and examine it all. First it was Georges. "You're missing her accessories and her bow isn't tied quite right."

"Are you serious?" He gave an eye roll.

She stepped over to where Max had been working. "Max..." she glanced at the page. "I think you actually won this one. You hit every detail but the only thing you missed was tucking her tag in the back."

"I win?" his smile went brighter.

"You win," Andrea reiterated with a smile of her own.

The team clapped at the friendly competition that sprouted out of nowhere. "Maybe this is something we can incorporate in morning meetings, a little competition never hurt anyone," Andrea added.

"Something to think about," Max went from intense concentration to quiet contemplation. He looked as if he wanted to get out of there.

"This is the first time Max has won anything in his life," George joked, but looking at Max, I could tell it was hitting a nerve.

Everyone around us laughed. Although everyone was in a jovial mood, Max offered a smile that didn't quite reach his eyes.

"What else has to get done?" I asked bringing everyone to the task at hand.

"We're all done," Meisheko answered.

I looked around and it all looked amazing. "We'll talk about it in the morning meeting, so the sales advisors and managers know how to maintain this throughout the holidays," Andrea informed the team. "What's next?"

All eyes were on me. This was my time to shine, let them know that I can handle this. "The other departments need to be refreshed. Everyone back into their respective departments, evaluate what needs to happen, let me know and we'll see if we can add bodies to where it's needed."

"Do you need anything else from us?" George asked, draping his arm around me. It was hard to be mad at him, especially when I knew he was just trying to goad his brother.

"No, I think the global team has helped enough for today," I said looking up into his handsome face; similar to his brothers but without the stern, hard look that Max was giving right now.

George squeezed my shoulder. "Let me see if Meisheko needs any help." He sauntered off.

"Ginny, this came out beautiful. I'm going to take pictures and send them throughout the company. I'll be in the office if you need anything. Good job," Andrea said. It's crazy but her compliment was the one that I wanted the most. I wanted her to see that I could do a great job. I just think that she has the eye for this company and her opinion mattered.

"Thank you," I muttered instead of curtseying like I imagined.

Then there was Max. He stayed quiet, I lifted an eyebrow. "You good?"

He offered a faint smile. "I'm good."

"What was that whole thing with your brother?"

He trailed a hand down his face. "Something that dates back to when we were kids...always competing. Did it look crazy?"

I shrugged. "If by crazy you mean being ridiculously intense about dressing a mannequin to the point that it looked like you were trying to diffuse a bomb then...maybe."

He offered a bright smile. "Yeah, we could be a little intense."

"A little? I thought I was going to have to blow a whistle and throw a flag down."

He shrugged and kept his eyes down. I knew that he was embarrassed that he let his brother get the best of him. Instead of dwelling on the battle of the siblings, I switched gears. "You guys did amazing. I don't think we would've been done if you guys didn't help us."

"We did nothing. I can't believe you guys do this all the time."

"Like I said, multiple times a week."

"It's crazy, my hands were cramping up from holding onto all the hangers." He gestured with his hand. "I feel like I aged twenty years," he added.

"Imagine doing it for over ten years. I already have arthritis and carpel tunnel from doing this so long."

"Geez."

"Listen, I think while we're here, we shouldn't be near each other for longer than a couple of minutes."

"Because of Maggie?"

"Yeah."

"I noticed her too. I didn't hear her coming in," he whispered while surveying the floor.

"She's a sneaky one."

"We still on for tonight?"

I thought about it. I was upset because of how he scooped into help. Others would be thrilled at the idea of their boss turned lover coming in to save the day.

I didn't want to stop myself from having a good time; I needed time to relax. To rid myself of H. Moda.

"Yes, sir," I answered with a raised eyebrow that I wanted to come off as flirty but instead it felt like I was having a seizure.

"You're okay?" he asked, trying his best to hold back his laughter.

"Yeah, I was trying to be flirty...did it work?"

I saw the corners of his lips briefly tick up. "Yeah, sure."

I rolled my eyes. "Whatever."

"Ginny," He glanced around before bending down to whisper in my ear. "Don't try so hard, you were doing great before."

His breath against my ear, sent goosebumps rising on my arms. If I turned my head only slightly, our lips would touch. But we couldn't do that. "Noted," I whispered back.

"Ginny!" Maggies voice called up from the escalator. "Would you like to walk the move?"

"Do you want me to stick around?" Max asked. Max asking that felt good, like he understood that we need to set some kind of boundaries and that he understood that I could handle these sorts of situations.

"No. I think I should walk with her alone and see if we can get along for once."

The click of her boots were getting closer. "You sure?" His eyes were concentrated on me; his lips formed a grim, stern line across his face.

"I'm sure."

With a quick nod, Max walked away. "Oh, is he not walking with us?" Maggie asked.

"No, just you and me."

Maggie blinked twice and smiled. "Great."

For fifteen minutes, we walked the entire department; mannequin looks, placement of top priority products, replacements just in case things sold down before the holidays arrive. "When will the ladies window get done?"

"The team is prepping it now—"

"Why aren't they prepped already?"

"Because we were focused in setting up the floor move that I told them to hold off the window until tomorrow," I answered.

Her attitude quickly changed from hostile to friendly in record time "I also had another question I wanted to ask you," she lowered her voice.

I glanced from side to side. "Yes?"

"Girl to girl," she shrugged. "Are you and Max Thomas an item?"

My heart sank to the bottom of my stomach. "No," I answered without hesitation. I kept my face dead of emotion. I refused to give her anything that she could ruin.

"Oh, I thought I walked in on something in the stock room." She had a smug smirk on her face that I wanted to slap off.

"No, you walked in on nothing. We were reviewing what we achieved this morning."

"He has a soft spot for you," she insisted. Maggie was trying to latch on to anything, but I wouldn't let her.

"Maggie, I don't date any one I work with."

Her face flushed and I knew she was remembering the love triangle drama that happened. "He's such a good catch."

"So, we'll applaud the girl who catches him, but I can assure you that it's not me." I slid my palms discreetly down the sides of my jeans as I built up the courage to stand up for myself. "I also think that it's inappropriate to insinuate that, so please I encourage you to keep those kind of comments to yourself."

Maggie eyed me slowly the way that the Evil Witch eyed Snow White slowly before sending a huntsman to murder her. If this were a fairytale, I'd be in big trouble. I could see her bite the side of her mouth, calculating. "So, the window? It will be up tomorrow?"

"Yes."

"Okay, then."

My phone vibrated and I peeked at a message Max sent me.

Coffee?

As Maggie walked away, I breathed a sigh of relief. I knew she suspected something was up; Max and I needed to lay low.

> I don't think that's a good idea.

I continued to clean up any leftover racks and garbage that was left behind— I had a feeling that Maggie was going to be paying a lot more attention to Max and I.

15

Rule 76: Try to keep busy! Taking your entrepreneurial spirit in mind will showcase your skills and efficiency!

Four o'clock came at a snail's pace. When it finally came, I practically ran down the escalator.

"Plans tonight?" Maggie called from behind me as I clocked out. "You seem in a rush to leave."

"Yeah, well, being here super early will make anyone want to run home to sleep."

She nodded. "Good job this morning, the store looks amazing. I can't wait to see what everything else looks like." Maggie didn't smirk and I almost believed her sincerity.

"Thank you." I put my finger on the time clock scanner and waited for the beep to tell me that I've officially clocked out. I used to find it amusing, as if I were some kind of spy entering and leaving my secret hideaway; a decade here takes the shine off of that image.

Now, it was just a time clock giving me permission to go home because I didn't have the balls to just walk out.

"Ginny!" George's boisterous yell made Maggie and I look up. George sauntered over, clapping his arm around me; Maggie's curious look made me want to slide out from under there. From the corner of my eye, I could see Max's blurry silhouette, which set me in motion. I laughed at Georges natural playfulness but moved from under his arm.

"What's up?" I asked.

"Ladies' came out great. You should be proud."

"I am. You guys did great as well."

He shrugged. "What we did was nothing."

"What are we talking about?" Max flanked on the other side. I was stuck in the middle.

"Just telling Ginny how amazing she did; She'll be a great Visual Manager," George replied.

"She already knows that," Max said nonchalantly.

"I have a quick question," Maggie began. "Do you all know each other? You two and Ginny seem to get on so easily."

"Of course, we do! We meet a couple of weeks ago at a bar!" George laughed.

"Really?" Maggie asked in surprise while my heart raced a mile a minute.

"Of course not. We just feel like this is our first promotion we want her to do well," George added, although it didn't stop my heart from racing.

I slid my hands down my jeans to dry off the moisture. My nerves were getting the best of me. "I have to go; I don't want to ride on a crowded train." I went to my locker, threw on my coat and finally made my way out. "Have a goodnight, everyone," I zoomed out the breakroom only to be stopped by Andrea.

"Ginny, just a word."

"Hey, Andrea."

"Just want to say that it was amazing to be a part of this morn-ing's move."

"You guys didn't have to, but I truly appreciated it," I said politely.

"Tomorrow we are having a quick meeting with a few manager trainees. I would love for you to come."

"Tomorrow? We're setting up the other departments for the holiday."

"We suggested that Meisheko watch over the team while you're gone. She's been here almost as long as you have."

This felt like an opportunity that I couldn't refuse. Everyone knew that if you said no to this company just one time, you're forever blacklisted and never given another opportunity. This company was so fast paced that they probably already had someone else in mind if I said no. I quickly deliberated, trying to figure out how to not attend and skip off into the sunset with no repercussions. "Why the hesitation?" she asked.

I rolled my neck, trying to release the tension that's been cramping me all day. "No, I just...I really don't want any hiccups or—"

"You don't want Maggie to interfere."

I shrugged. I'm not going to correct her if she said it.

Her lips quirked into a smirk. "Well, Max will be here keeping an eye on things," she insisted.

Andrea was persistent. "Okay, I'll go."

"Good, I'll let Maggie know." Andrea's stacked booties clicked on the linoleum tiles as she gracefully walked back to the break room, leaving only the scent of her crisp floral perfume in the air.

I felt my phone vibrate. It was Max.

Wait for me.

A gust of frigid air hit me, "Ugh!" I yelled like a crazy person, causing passerby's to give me a look. "Sorry," I apologized to no one in particular. I did not break my stride to the subway.

> I'm already at the
>
> station

I lied.

"You really weren't going to wait for me?" Max's voice called from behind.

I glanced around. "You need to lower your voice Mr. Thomas."

He nodded. "You looked like you were in a rush to get out, are you okay?"

"I was in a rush to get out," I shot out angrily. I don't know why my mood had switched so suddenly, but I just wanted to get home and relax.

"So, you're not okay?"

"Max!"

His expression was like stone but his eyes still held a bit of humor. "I liked Mr. Thomas better."

"I just want to decompress. I'm just overwhelmed with everything going on. It's going to be Christmas in two point five seconds, we have all this holiday set ups to get through while Maggie is all over my ass trying to sabotage everything...I just—"

Max's arm shot out as he waved a cab down. "I know what you need."

Although heat began to rise from lower in my belly, I shot it down. "I don't want sex right now," I whispered.

"Although that doesn't sound like a bad idea, that's not what I was talking about."

A cab stopped right in front of him at the corner. "What did you have in mind?"

"It's a surprise."

"Max..." I was just tired, and it was only Tuesday! I felt my mental begin to unravel.

"You don't like surprises?"

I felt the burning of tears begin to form; I began to hate myself. I didn't want this beautiful human being to see me crumble in front of him. His eyes dropped in concern. "Ginny, what's wrong?" His voice was soft, and I let tears come down. He ushered me into the cab. "Get in."

"Eighty second and fifth ave," he directed the cab driver.

On the ride to the top-secret location, Max took my hand in his caressing my fingers with his thumb. "You can talk about whatever's bothering you, I'm open ears."

I let my head fall on his shoulder. "Silence is good for now," I said.

Max squeezed my hand as the hum of the cab and the muffled noise of the holiday traffic calmed my erratic mind. Too much of everything, mixed with no time to really digest anything was a great cocktail to get me to lose it. This thing with Max, whatever it was, this promotion that I didn't even want, my passion that was collecting dust, not talking to my parents, and Maggie's hostility was all enough to get me to crack.

I closed my eyes and let the emotions rain over me. "Hey, we're here," Max gently nudged.

"*The Met*? You brought me to *the Met*? For what?" I asked.

We hopped out of the cab; It was already dark out; the winter chill settling in around us.

The streets were buzzing with tourists, people Christmas shopping and I was here at the museum with the heir to a billion-dollar empire.

"I thought that this would be a great way to get your mind out of wherever it is."

"Siberia," I answered.

"That's far."

"Lonely, cold, and—"

He raised an eyebrow. "You're not alone."

"I know but—"

"But nothing." Max eyebrows furrowed down in annoyance as he pulled me along the massive flight of steps to the entrance. We walked in silence as we passed other visitors who were talking to each other in hush tones. The lighting dimmed as we passed the lobby into our first exhibit.

"Max?"

"Hmmm?"

I caught his eyes through the reflection of the glass case that showcased jewelry from ancient tribes. "Lonely and alone aren't the same thing."

"How so?"

"I know I'm not alone; I have Marvin, the team..."

"Me."

"You," I added. "It's just...sometimes I don't have anyone to talk to about life outside of work and it just tends to get overwhelming."

"Gin." I felt raw, I couldn't bear to look at him. I had offered a tiny piece of my inner workings and I was terrified. Max reached out and gently lifted my chin. "You need to talk? I'll shut up and listen."

"My parents called, and I didn't answer," I finally confessed.

"Why?"

"Because I was too scared."

Max had a look of confusion. "What are you afraid of?"

"I'm afraid of being a continuous disappointment. Nothings changed since their last call. I'm still at the same job that I don't want to be at, I'm still not a successful designer, they aren't any closer to being grandparents. Nothings changed."

I saw the twitch in his jaw. I could tell he was fighting the urge to add his two cents. I reached out and caressed his fiery stubble. "Are you angry?" I asked.

He licked his lips and the different emotions played across his face. I had no idea why he was angry.

"Max, come on. Did I say something wrong?"

He sighed. "Ginny, everything's changed."

I smirked. "Yeah? Like what?"

"You're getting promoted. You're working on a collection. You have friends and colleagues who love you, you're not stuck in a shitty relationship and...you got me."

Maybe it was because I was being defensive but my skepticism couldn't be disguised. "I have you? Do I? We barely know each other."

Max stepped back. "I know you." When I didn't respond, he continued. "I know you, Virginia. You are smart, talented, funny, sexy, determined, commanding—"

"Okay, okay, that's enough."

"It's not, you need to hear it and often. Where's the girl that I met at the bar?"

I let out a small laugh. "She's not real. It was an illusion to seduce you."

Max shook his head. "I don't believe that. She's in there, you're just having a tough time."

I hated that I was being so cynical; I couldn't stop it. It was some kind of weird masochistic pain that I thought I deserved. My life was not what my parents had planned for me; I thought I knew better about my life, love, career and it's turned out that at every possible moment of happiness, I've been proven wrong. Maybe things would have been different if I listened to my parents. I should've gotten that psychology degree and became some kind of social worker. I shouldn't have stayed at H. Moda this long. I should've never gone home with Max. "She's not. I'm a lie. I'm a phony. That girl at the bar saw a gorgeous man and wanted to feel good about herself, so she pretended to be carefree and flirty."

"That's you, Virginia. You are all those things. You don't have to pity yourself."

I felt a rogue tear escape my eye. I quickly wiped it away. "I can't help but feel like a loser. I don't have my family, I'm not doing what I want, and I can't be open about the guy I'm seeing because he's my boss."

"Why are you being like this?" he asked. His eyes searched my face as if the answer was just as easy to find.

"Because that's who I am, Max. I'm tired of being happy all the time or trying to find the good in a bad situation. In the end, I'm the person that everything goes wrong for."

"Is this about Maggie? Is this about today?" he asked.

I scanned the exhibit frantically. I snatched his hand and pulled him along. I wasn't strong enough to really drag him, but he followed along. "Where are we going?" he whispered as we passed through the crowd.

"I don't know," I mumbled. It was the truth; my mind was going in a million different directions, and I didn't want to think. I just wanted to do.

We had walked to a part of the museum that was eerily quiet and dimmed. A velvet rope warned not to go beyond that point, but rules were meant to be broken. "Virginia?" Max whispered. "It says employees only."

"So?" I looked behind me; Max looked unsure. "Are you scared, Max?"

"Not scared, just against the whole going to jail for trespassing."

"We won't go to jail, just probably be banned for life," I scoffed.

"Like that's any better."

I stepped over the velvet rope. "Virginia!" Max whispered frantically, gripping my hand tighter.

I smirked. "Come, Max." I pulled at him. To my surprise he stepped over the velvet rope.

"Okay, I did it. What now?"

"Now? I don't know." I walked away slowly; my heart was racing. I don't know what came over me. The little voice inside my head was yelling at me to turn around. There was nothing beyond the rope. Just an empty part of the museum where another exhibit would go.

Before I could talk myself out of it, I whipped around and pushed Max against the wall.

"What are you doing?" he asked.

My lips landed on his; Max's stubble scratched a little bit as he kissed me back. His hands found my hips; he squeezed one time and gently pushed me back. "What is happening?"

"I want you."

"Here? Now?" The shock was evident in his voice.

"Why not?" I knew why not, but I had adrenaline and false bravery running through my veins.

"Because we could get caught. This wouldn't be a good look."

With my lips set in a firm line, I nodded once and took a bigger step back. "I thought this is the woman you like. The one you wanted."

Max's jaw dropped at my audacity. "Ginny, I want you to be you." His words fell around me. "What do you want, Ginny?"

"I—"

"What are you guys doing here?!" A security guards voice boomed.

My heart started beating rapid fire. Max stepped away from the wall. "We're so sorry, is this not part of an exhibit?"

"Y'all not dumb enough to think that, are you?" The security guard was no dummy. "I'mma give y'all five seconds to get out of here."

I sped walked past him. "Thank you," I said.

"Just thank the Christmas spirits for making me feel all this warm generosity. Now, get the hell out of here."

Max grabbed my hand, and we ran back to the main exhibit.

We stopped in the middle of the crowd, looked at each other and laughed. "I brought you here to get inspired," he said over his laughter.

"Inspired?"

"I know you're working on your collection, and I just didn't want you to lose momentum. Even if you use the inspiration for another collection."

"Oh, Max." I looked down. His meddling was not sitting well with me. I had to put a stop to it.

"What's the matter?"

I shrugged. "I know you mean well but...I have to decide when I'm ready to do all the things. I'm just taking baby steps right now."

"Okay, well, let's look around." He held his hands up in defense when I lifted my eyebrows in his direction. "I heard you; we can walk around...for inspiration or just to enjoy the museum...no pressure."

We walked the massive museum; walking passed artifacts of ancient civilizations; fashion and rooms built for the eighteenth-century aristocrats. Fabrics so fine and soft that it made my heart flutter. Obviously, I rather forgo the corsets and garter belts but I could still appreciate where it's brought us today.

We stepped outside to the dark, wintery night; the city lights shining brighter than the actual stars but it all seemed like magic. I stood rooted halfway down the steps of the museum, holding onto Max's hand. "Are you okay?" he asked.

I closed my eyes, breathing in the cold air. People always have some poetic choice words for New York City autumn but if you truly knew the City like I did, you'd know that nothing compares to the winter. It's freezing cold and the snow changes from sparkling white to dirty brown at the drop of a hat but the lights make it seem like you're living in a snow globe just for the tiniest second and that was my favorite feeling.

Not even the shady Santa's on the corner could take that feeling from me.

I looked over at Max. "I'm good now." I stood on my tip toe to touch his lips when a gust of wind nearly blew me down the stairs. Max reached out to save me just as a big uncontrollable laugh/shout escaped from my belly. That was the only way for my body to get rid of the embarrassment that I felt.

He let out a small laugh. "I feel like I'm asking you a million times but are you okay?"

I continued laughing. "Yes. Yes, Max."

"Good, let's get out of this fucking cold."

His use of a cuss word sent me on another fit of laughter. "Just kiss me one more time."

Max took my face in his hand. "You look like a cold tomato," he commented.

"What?!" I laughed.

"I couldn't think of a better image. You're all red and blotchy from the cold."

"You couldn't say that I looked flushed like a Christmas angel?" I asked.

He shrugged, amused. "I like mine better." He finally leaned down and kissed me. "Are you hungry?" he asked as he pulled away.

"Always."

"Let's go to my place. We can order food."

I rolled my eyes in mock irritation. "Max, if you want to get me into bed you don't have to lure me with food."

He leaned closer to my ear. "If I wanted you in bed, I would of just fucked you in the museum and then taken you back to my place to do it all over again."

His raunchiness sent fire running through my veins. "Good point."

"So, what'll it be?"

16

Rule #34: Be optimistic! There will be stressful times but maintain an optimistic mindset and focus on the good and focus your skills and what makes you happy.

I looked down from Max's apartment. "Everyone looks like tiny ants," I said when I saw Max's reflection pop up.

"New York City is home to some of the busiest ants." He planted a small peck on my neck.

"Busy and lonely," I muttered.

He turned me to face him. "Let's talk." He pulled me over to his bed where he laid back and I sat crossed leg. "Why are you lonely?"

"I don't have a family."

He had the audacity to roll his eyes. "You have a family," he answered.

I sighed. "No, *you* have a family. You see each other every day and you know for a fact that they'll be there if you ever need them. I can't even talk to my parents without it turning into a shouting match."

"My family is a business, we have no choice," he joked.

"But they're there. I want mine just to be...there."

His smile was sadness with a mix of pity. "I want to make it better. I'm here."

"You know in *Home Alone* when he wishes he didn't have his family just to realize that family is what he wanted all along?" He nodded. I continued, "Well, that's the point of the movie I'm in. I just want my parents."

"I get it," he answered. Max placed a hand on my leg. "When my first investment went down in flames, although there was a lot of I told you so's, they were still around to give me words of encouragement."

"That's what I want. Maybe if I get two guys to rob my family home, the Christmas spirit will get to them and they'll reach out," I joked.

He squeezed my leg tenderly. "You know you don't have to do that," he said.

"Do what?"

"Joke about it. You don't have to amuse me. You feel what you feel."

I shrugged. "I just hate that I've been a downer today. I just feel lonely and that's a not so good spot for me."

Max reached for me, pulling me on top of him. "Let's be lonely together."

I laid my head on his chest and let myself relax with every beat of his heart.

I woke up to dark and silence. *What time was it?* I began to panic. *Was it morning yet? Was I late for work?* I had this mixer thing at the support office today, but I still wanted to make it to secure the window. I hurried out of the bed, hurrying to the living room just to find Max surrounded by paperwork and his laptop. "What's wrong?" he looked up and his five o'clock shadow was darker. He began to scrub his face awake.

"I was trying to find my things and head out," I admitted.

"You are always trying to escape this apartment," he pointed out.

"It's not the apartment I'm running from."

"So, it's me?"

I smiled. "No, it's not. I just thought it was morning and I was running late for work."

"It's not even midnight."

Relief washed over me. "Oh, thank God."

"You fell out and I just didn't have the heart to wake you." Max's eyes passed over me. "Come here," he quietly commanded.

"How can I help you, Mr. Thomas?" I tried to play it cool as his arms wrapped around my waist and he rested is chin against my belly.

"You were really going through something. I was worried."

I offered a smile to ease his sentiments. "Just a lot of things coming at me at once, you just happened to be there at the breaking point. Sorry."

Max planted a kiss on my belly. "No, need to apologize, just know if you need me, I'm here."

I wrapped my arms around him, squeezing him tight; this was another magical moment.

I barely knew this man, but I trusted his words. For some inexplainable reason, I trusted him more than anyone. I knew that he would be there for me at the drop of a hat.

Or at least I hoped it were true. The last man to say that to me was a liar and a sneak.

I prayed that my gut was right about this one. I placed a soft kiss on the top of his head as he placed a kiss of his own on my belly. I felt a spasm in my belly as his stubble tickled. Max's hands caressed the bare skin under my shirt. I took my shirt off, letting it slip through my fingers and unto the floor. My nipples pebbled under my lace bra in anticipation of what he would do. Max's hand travelled upwards, cupping me; squeezing me gently in his grasp as if he were savoring the weight of me in his hands. I stepped closer, teasing him— enticing him further. With just a slight tilt of his head, Max took my breast in his mouth sucking and licking. I moaned, holding his head in place.

He stood up, lifting me eagerly and placing me on the dining table where he had been working; papers scattered everywhere. Max had one hand on my hip while the other was secure on the back of my neck, as he held me in place while he devoured my lips as if he hadn't had them only hours before. I felt the need for him all over. The heat of desire spread like wildfire, and I didn't want to tame it. I wanted to burn if it meant I could have him.

His lips conquered mine and I, equally insatiable, conquered him right back.

"Are you kidding me?"

Max and I turned in the direction of the foreign voice that had penetrated our desire.

Until realization hit me like cold water. "George?" I asked a stupid question, knowing full well who it was.

"Shit," Max whispered as recognition hit him. He snatched my shirt from the floor tossing it to me.

"I thought you said it was over?" George, who was always so jovial and playful, was as serious as a heart attack. No warm smile, no playful wink...just a visibly distraught man waiting for an answer.

"It was. It is." Max's answer rain down on me like cold water. I needed to get out of there.

"It is," I answered. I scanned the dimmed living room for my coat, purse and shoes. Methodically putting everything on.

"Max, you can't be this stupid. I thought we agreed this was a bad idea, especially since you're taking over."

"God, George, can you shut up?!" Max ran over to me as my fist closed around the doorknob, eager to get away. He slammed the door back. "Ginny, just give me a second."

"Max, I need to go." I fought against the embarrassment and the lump in my throat. They had all discussed it and he told them it was done. How stupid and foolish I felt. Of course, we wouldn't be. He was a billionaire and I was just some visual merchandiser at the store he owns who barely made enough to pay her rent.

"Not now, let me explain."

"Max, let me go now." I kept my voice low but it struck a chord. It was the only way I could keep from crying.

Without another word, Max stepped back, silently telling me I was free to go. His face was flushed with arousal or anger. I couldn't tell. But his auburn hair and stubble, along with his flushed face made him look like some kind of fire monster.

I hesitated only for a fraction of a second. "Max, she's not the one. You said it yourself," George's voice was low but firm.

I shook my head because I couldn't think of a thing that I could do that wouldn't get me arrested. Without a backwards glance, I ran down the hall bypassing the elevators; Midtown was a blur as I fought against the tears that burned to come down.

I should've known better. I knew that if I waited for a cab, Max would come after me and I didn't want to give him the chance. I threw my arm out and in like New York City movie fashion, a cab magically stopped in front of me, and I hopped in.

"One seventy-fourth and University," I threw out.

I should have known better replayed in my mind as I sat stunned in the back of the cab wondering how I let myself make this mistake.

******

I tossed and turned all night. Sleep? I wish I knew her. I skipped the window installation and put my phone on silent. I wanted to hear from no one. I wanted to hear of nothing. I had enough faith in my team that I didn't think I should check in.

I made it to the support office in Midtown to whatever work-shop or mixer they planned.

I went through the revolving doors, following all the other people who looked like they were deer caught in headlights. Every-one looked around the massive marble lobby. It was obvious that we all worked for the same company. Despite the frigid temperatures, there were some who dressed in short dresses and knee-high boots; then there were those who embraced the winter aesthetic and wore full on fur coats...and I? I wore denim jeans, combat boots and I pulled out one of my own designs, a plaid button-down shirt. It was one of my first designs; I had sewn two different plaid shirts together because I thought the lavender plaid and orange plaid worked well. I cinched it at the waist with a belt, which always made me feel more polished. I threw an oversized leather jacket over it to complete the look. This outfit always made me feel great but today I felt underdressed.

These were the *Miranda Priestly* wanna-be's. The people who believed that they were God's gift to fashion because they worked at this company for two years doing the job I've been doing for a decade. These were people who thought that this job would lead to something greater in the fashion industry. I wish I had the balls to stand on top of the lobby desk and yell to them that this job led nowhere. But then why was I still here?

And then I would have to answer truthfully; fear...laziness...who knew?

The elevator door dinged, and I crammed myself inside. I closed my eyes and tried to ward off the wave off the nausea I felt from all the different perfumes wafting in the elevator.

When we finally filed out, I caught eyes with Max. My heart sank to my ass, and I immediately turned around to escape. Instead, I bumped into Andrea.

"Slow down," she said as she looked up to see who rammed into her. "Ginny? Where are you going?" she asked.

I looked behind me, but Max was nowhere to be found. "Um...I thought I had enough time to get some coffee."

"Don't worry about that, we have breakfast for everyone in the conference room."

I nodded. Turning around I finally got to take in the support office. A spiral staircase sat in the middle of the wide and spacious floor. There was glass encased offices to the left of the staircase while to the right laid a big cafeteria room.

"Wow." I glanced around in awe, like everyone else who had come out of the elevator. This is where everyone wanted to be. No matter what position you held at the store level, the end goal was to work in the support office.

I followed the crowd to where the breakfast station was set up. I went straight to the coffee, filling my cup to the brim.

I sat down at a full table, not one person I knew. "Girl, he is so fine." I overheard one guy say.

"Which one?"

"All three are. But the one with the beard growing in and tattoos, is on another level."

My heart skipped a beat because I knew exactly who they were talking about. "Hey, I'm Carrie and this is Eric. We're from store eight hundred."

"Hi, I'm Ginny, from store one fifty."

"Oh, that's the store that the global team is working from."

"Yeah."

"That means you've seen them, right?"

"Who?" I tried to play dumb.

"The Thomas'."

"Yeah, just about everyday," I answered. I didn't want to conversate with anyone especially about the Thomas'.

"How is he?" Eric asked leaning in closer to get the full scoop.

"Who?"

They both rolled their eyes. "The one with the red beard."

"Max?" I asked. Maybe if I kept answering with a question they'd leave me alone.

"Girl, are you even here right now?" he scoffed.

"They're great. They care a lot about the company, and I really do think they will change the company for the better." I was happy with my answer. Diplomatic, fair...not emotional.

"That's boring," Carrie muttered.

"Well, he is very boring. Doesn't talk much except when he needs to get something done," I added in hopes that they would stop prying.

"Mmmm, sounds like real *daddy* material," Eric said. I felt a tinge of jealousy for no reason. Max doesn't care about them. *He doesn't care about me either.*

The cafeteria hushed down to soft murmurs at the sight of Andrea, George and Max. "Good Morning, we just wanted to say that we are excited to have you all here. We usually don't do things like this during the holidays, but we want to start changing things up a bit as quickly as we can. You all are here because you're the best and we want to get to know you all. We'd like to see which path is more compatible for each and every one of you."

"This is an evaluation?" I whispered to Carrie.

"What did you think it was?" Carrie whispered back.

Something didn't sit right in my stomach. I had that bad feeling, the one you get when you go to *Taco Bell* because you thought you wanted tacos but what they have doesn't even come close to resembling real tacos, so you spend the night depressed on the toilet...that's the kind of stomachache I had.

I locked eyes with George, who winked at me. I looked away

disgusted. The mind games that these men were capable of was disgusting. I couldn't think of a better word for it.

His words to Max kept replaying in my mind. It hurt.

Max and I didn't know each other well; it was all very physical...I thought that our conversations made it deeper than that despite the short amount of time that we've known each other.

It's been three weeks, not a lifetime of knowing someone. I would be screaming at the movie if the heroine fell in love that fast. I would laugh but here I was...in love. And it hurt.

"So, let's all finish up and head into the conference room next door. Ten minutes everyone."

Andrea and George passed me without a backwards glance. Max, on the other hand bent down to talk to me. "Hey, can I see you for a minute in my office?"

His face was only inches away from mine. I didn't want the others to say anything. "Yeah," was the only thing I could say.

I could feel the stares from the others at the table as I followed Max out the cafeteria. As soon as Max closed the door to his office, I was the first to open my mouth. "What is it you wanted to talk about?"

"About last night...the things that George said."

"The things that you said that George just let me know."

Max sat at the edge of his desk, running a tattooed hand down his stubble. "We did speak about you—"

"Did you say those things? It was over? It was nothing. I was nothing?" I hated that my voice cracked.

"I said it was over to get them off my back. They don't think it's a good idea to see you when we both work for the company that my family owns."

"And I agree with them."

I saw as Max's jaw clenched and unclenched. "Don't say that."

"Max this is too much, too fast. We don't know each other, and your family hates me."

"No, they don—"

A knock came through the glass door. "Hey, Ginny. Andrea's going to start soon. I think it's a good idea to go into the conference room," George said.

I rolled my head to look at Max. His face full of annoyance. "I think you need to give us a minute, George," Max spoke calmly but I knew there was a world of anger behind his words.

"I think it's better if I don't." George folded his arms and stood a fraction taller.

I shook my head, walked out of the room. Before I could take another step into the conference room, George ran up to me. "I think we need to talk."

"I don't think so. You made it perfectly clear how you feel."

I scanned the empty hall to make sure there was no one around.

"Ginny, we think you are a great worker. The perfect person to run a store."

"Okay," I shrugged. I was so ready to stomp away. I could feel my face flushed with rage. My ears burned with irritation.

"But it just doesn't look right that you get promoted after fucking the boss." I bit down on my tongue to keep from cursing him out. "You have a history of dating men who you work with and that didn't turn out well." I took a deep breath and looked up to the ceiling hoping that a glimpse of heaven, God or an angel can keep me from hurting this man. "Hey, don't look like that. I am as easygoing as the next guy, but when it comes to this business, the three of us will protect it at whatever cost, understand?"

"Mmhmm," I nodded.

"So, I think that at this time, you can head home, and we can discuss your future with the company tomorrow."

My blood ran hot, then cold, then hot once again. I spun around on my heel, secured my bag across my body and stomped out of the support office.

I had to quit. I just had to. That was the only logical step. George was clearly expressing the family's sentiments.

The next step with the company? Demoted to a sales advisor? Offered a department manager position that I didn't want because I was tenured at this company, and they have to promote me to something. The hours were not as steady as a visual merchandisers.

God! Look at me, I'm panicking.

For no reason.

Is this where I wanted to be? At the mercy of some corporate giant who didn't know my worth. A company who would dismiss me at the drop of a hat because I was in love with the boss and thought I would pose a threat?

I rode the train home crying. But being in New York City, no one batted an eye. They just didn't make eye contact with me or just avoided me all together. I had a two-seater all to myself.

The wind was howling, freezing my tears to my face. I felt my phone vibrate but I refused to look at it. I knew it would be Max. After what felt like the hundredth vibration, curiosity got the best of me, and I glanced at my phone.

My heart began to beat out of my chest. Although my fingers were frozen to the bone, I stabbed the screen and picked up the call. "Mami?" I sniffled.

17

Rule 727: *Be trustworthy! Let your team know that you are a valued and trustworthy team member. Show that you are dependable.*

When I was a little girl, it was instilled in me to work hard and I would be successful at anything I chose to do, even if I wanted to be a fairy princess.

In my teen years, it became evident that all of that was a lie. I rebelled against my parents who fought me tooth and nail. They wanted me to do well in math and science and didn't really show interest when I showed them the new dress I made. When it was time to go to college, I decided that I would do my best to make them happy but even that was tough. I was never doing enough to make them proud; so, I started designing and creating until my grades dropped and they gave me an ultimatum.

I chose my art.

I moved out, got a job at H. Moda and the rest is history. The first couple of years I thought I would be part of the minority who made it. I started to gain a little bit of traction but then I met someone who took me out of that space. That's not right either. I blame myself for letting him affect me the way he did...it's the same as Max.

It's not the same. My inner voice yelled at me.

I pushed that voice down as my mother handed me a cup of coffee. "We were getting worried because when we finally got phone reception, we heard your messages, and they sounded a bit..."

"Strange," my dad finished.

"Strange?" I asked.

"Like you needed us," my mother added.

"I did need you; I do need you," I said as I blew the steam off my coffee.

They shared a look before my dad addressed me, "How much do you need?" he asked.

I looked around my childhood home; the living room hadn't change much in all these years. The floors were refinished, and it looked like new paint...but it was still the same. I knew that behind the closet door was my drawing of a giraffe that I did when I was six and my mother never had the heart to erase. "What makes you think I need money?" I asked, making sure I kept my voice even.

"Why else would you call us out of the blue?" My dad, always being the bad cop, answered.

"William." My mom rested a hand on my dad's knee to calm him down; been doing it for as long as I could remember.

"It's true, Maria. The only time she calls is when she needs us. Remember the thing with the married guy? What is it now?"

My lips quivered as anger turned to sadness. Why couldn't they just be there for me? "Virginia," my mother cooed. "What happened?"

"My life is a mess," I answered. My dad opened up his mouth to speak but I wouldn't let him, "And no, I don't need money. I'm actually pretty good on that front. I just...need my family. I just need you guys to say it's going to be okay and not I told you so."

My dad silently got up and left me with my mom. My mom sat down next to me. "I'll talk to him."

She patted my hand. "What is happening? When Max called, I didn't know who he was, but he said I should reach out to you."

My head shot up. "What?"

"Max...Thomas? Whatever his name, said he was one of your friends and you've been having a rough couple of months and thought we should reach out."

I wiped the tears from my eyes. "Why, mom?"

With a head tilt she asked, "Why what?"

"Why did it have to take someone to call you to tell you I needed you? I called you myself," I pointed out. I hated how my voice quaked, but it hurt from crying.

"Ginny, we've been through this before...you call us when you need us and when you don't, you disappear."

"Because I thought that's what you guys wanted. I always disappoint you."

Her face, so similar to mine; her top lip slightly thinner than her bottom, was set in a straight line. The fine lines became more pronounced as she frowned at me. "We are a family. You are our only child...we love you."

I began to cry. "Then why did you always make it hard for me? Why couldn't I do what I wanted?"

"Because we were scared! We're your parents we want the best for you." Her statement hit me hard. I cried on her lap as she caressed my head. "You'll understand whenever, if ever, you have your own. You want them to succeed. You want them to be okay. You want them to do better than you. Your career choices, your love life, the tattoos...it all scared us. What if you got hurt? What if you failed?"

I sat up straight. "But what if I didn't?"

"Virginia..."

"What?" I swiped my tears with the back of my hand like some sulky teenager ready to rebel again.

"You did fail! Multiple times! That scares us! What if it keeps happening? What if it's still happening when we leave this earth?"

I shook my head so hard I felt a little dizzy. "Mami, stop being dramatic. I've learned from my mistakes."

"Have you?"

"Yes."

"Have you designed anything lately? How long did your career as a fashion designer last? Seeing that you loved it so much." Her sarcasm hit a nerve. My response was to yell at her about how her life had turned out as a seamstress in some dry cleaner that she didn't even own. Was that how she expected her life to go?

Then realization calmed me.

"Mami...what did you want to be when you grew up?" I asked.

She smiled faintly as if dusting off an old artifact lost long ago. "You are so much like me. I wanted to be a costume designer."

"Why didn't that happen?"

"Because things were different back then. It was instilled to start a family, have a successful career, something that paid the bills and made sure the next generation didn't struggle."

"I am the next generation. And guess what? I'm still struggling."

"Not because of us!"

"I didn't say because of you!" I stood up ready to go. "I honestly don't know why I came over here. It's Christmas time and I just thought that you guys would want to be around."

"We do, but you make it difficult."

"Mom, I just want you to be there for me, with no judgment, no matter how many times I screw up." There were many times in my life that I wanted to say these words, and today I just didn't care enough to keep it to myself. "Tell daddy that I love him and it was nice seeing him."

"Where are you going?"

"To take care of my problems, Mom. And to try to survive every-thing during the holidays."

She shook her head. "And you call me dramatic?"

"Mom, it's not dramatic when you feel like you're alone."

"You're not."

"Then where have you been?!" I yelled despite of myself. I had enough. This was it. My mom stood in stunned silence. Her lips quivered but her jaw was set in a stubborn way that I've known all my life. "I gotta go," I whispered. "Tell daddy I'll see him later."

"Virginia," my mom called out to me softly. I stopped in my tracks for what felt like the millionth time. "I got you something for Christmas."

It was my turn to be in silent shock. The last time my parents had gotten me anything for Christmas, I wanted to be the pink power ranger so bad and they got me a costume. They supported my dream back then, why not now?

She walked over to the hallway closet next to the kitchen, I was afraid she was going to pull out holy water and try to exorcise me. I closed my eyes and hoped for the best when I felt a delicate tap on my shoulder. "Merry Christmas," she said.

I stared at the neatly wrapped mid-size box. "Well, aren't you going to open it?" She asked.

"It's not a bomb, is it?"

"Virginia."

I sighed. As I tentatively began to unwrap the gift, I thought of all the holiday movies that ended with family getting back together in the happiest of ways; I prayed that this gift would give us that miracle. When I finally unwrapped it, I was speechless. "Virginia?" My mom nudged.

"What did you get me?"

"Can't you see it?"

"I can," I answered.

"Then I don't understand your question."

"You got me a bedazzling kit?" I asked perplexed, I did my best not to laugh. I wanted one of these so bad when I was a kid, but Santa decided to get me roller blades instead. In response, I began to save the pennies I made at the dry cleaners my mother worked at and eventually bought myself one. I had to hide it from my parents because they didn't want me to be distracted from my studies.

"Yes." When I continued to stare at her, she was quick to continue. "Your father and I didn't know what to get you...you've always bought yourself what you wanted. We just decided to get you this."

"I..."

"You don't like it," she said, her face fell.

"No, I love it...I asked for something like this when I was like ten."

She nodded. "We know."

I hadn't the heart to tell her that I've grown up from this. I have much bigger equipment than this. My bedazzling days were gone. Now it was nights hunched over my sewing machine and printers to create my masterpieces. I knew this was a sign of a truce, even if my father had locked himself in the bedroom.

My brain had malfunctioned, and I couldn't form the words. "What's wrong?" my mother asked. Her eyebrows were low, exposing the faint lines between them. The fine white hairs that laced her dark mane really hit home how much time has passed.

"Please don't ask me that. Everyone in my life seems to ask me that and it's starting to hit me wrong." Her face turned angry, and I rushed in to assure her, "It's not you. Can we spend Christmas together?" I looked at her hopeful. When she took too long to answer I quickly started to stammer. "I mean...I understand...I know you probably are going away."

"We're not going away."

My eyes shot up to meet hers. "You're not?"

"No. We'll see you for Christmas."

I snatched my mom into a hug. "I love you." I held her tight, squishing my present between us.

"We love you too. I'll talk to your dad."

I gave a quick kiss on her cheek and walked out into the cold winter night on a mission.

18

Rule 124: Work/life balance is a thing. So...make sure you keep it a thing.

I knocked and knocked and knocked to no avail. I let my head fall against the door. What was I doing? George had every intention to fire me, there was no reason for me to be at Max's door. I didn't even know what I wanted to say. The fact that he called my parents...I just...my mind was just a jumble of letters and in no way could I form words.

I'll just text him like a normal person. I wouldn't open the door either if some crazy person, holding a bedazzling kit, came to visit me at the god-awful time of...*what time was it anyways?* I checked my phone and the clock hit nine. This was the longest day of my life. It was never ending. I felt frazzled, maybe it was the perfect time to head home and sleep it off.

I waited for the elevator. When I heard the ding, I kept my head low and slammed into a chest.

"I'm so sorry," I apologized and tried to hide in the corner.

"Ginny? What are you doing here?" Max's voice made the hairs on the back of my neck stand on end.

I looked up, speechless. The stunning brunette covered in fur and diamonds standing next to him made me want to shrink into myself and disappear.

"I just lost my mind for a split second. I'm heading home now."

Max turned to the brunette. "Can you give us a sec?"

She nodded, her eyes darting at me with so much curiosity. Beautiful brunette left us in the elevator. "Max, I'm just going home. Don't worry, I'm not going to be a problem."

"She's no one. I needed a date for this company function. She's a family friend."

I snorted. "My family friends tend to have beer belly's or hair on their chin...she looks like she's completely waxed."

"I wouldn't know." The elevator dinged open on his floor again because no one pressed the lobby button.

"Why bring her back to your place? If she was just a date to a function."

"Because..."

"Come on, Max! Enough! I don't need this!" I punched the button to the lobby.

"Ginny! She is no one, I brought her here because I don't want my family to give me hell."

I sighed. "What are you part of the royal family? Do you really have to do everything they want? Keep up appearances? For what? Are you happy?"

He stroked his light beard as a sinister laugh escaped his lips. "Am I happy? Are you in a better position? You don't even talk to your parents? And what's the reason? Because you wanted to follow a dream that you let go of once you found—"

The elevator dinged once again. My hands landed on his chest as I pushed my way out of the elevator. "Fuck you, Max."

His eyes turned to sheer panic. "Ginny, I'm sorry. I didn't—"

I turned slightly, my heels squealing in the empty lobby with a doorman for a witness. "You didn't what? You didn't mean what you said? About what? You're right, I let go of my dream for a stupid reason. But at least I did what I wanted, I'm not scared of disappointing my family."

He tucked a hand into his stylish black suit, accentuating his narrow hips. His lips showed no sign of smile or laughter. His jaw was clenched tight. We stared each other down. It was difficult for me to understand how I could love a man I barely knew, who put his business first...who was someone completely different.

My phone began to ring. I picked it up without looking. "Hello?"

"Ginny, what is going on?" Marvin's voice pounded through my phone.

His panic brought me out of the dark haze that fell over Max and me. "What?"

"As a manager I'm not supposed to tell you this, but as your friend I have no choice."

My heart began to race, and I snapped at the phone. "Spit it out!"

"They're going to fire you."

I looked back at Max. Shook my head and marched out. "What? How do you know this?"

"You weren't there for the meeting. George stopped by to talk to—"

"George? I was brought down by George?"

"I know. I was shocked. He didn't go into great detail, but he said he didn't think you were a good fit. Maggie told him something and he looked deeper into it and...they want you out. But they're not going to fire you tomorrow or anything."

"What do you mean? Are they firing me or not?"

He sighed. "They're going to phase you out."

"Marvin, what does that mean?"

He sighed again as if I was some idiot. "It means that they're going to use any little excuse to write you up until you're on a final that you can't survive."

"Then why stick around. They win." My voice trembled as I held back tears.

"Ginny, are you crying? Please don't cry. Just talk to Max."

"I can't talk to him." The tears began to fall as I finally made it to the lobby of the building.

There was a brief silence. "And?" Marvin asked. I didn't want to talk; I didn't know what to say. There were too many images from the last four weeks that were replaying in my mind. Too much to comprehend at the moment.

"And I don't think I'll be in tomorrow," I sighed.

"Ginny, come over please."

"Are you hosting?"

"Not tonight, boo. I'm all yours."

Because I was a masochist who apparently didn't want this painful night to end, I agreed to go to Marvin's apartment in Brooklyn to spill my guts.

I laid on his couch, drowning in my own tears. "He told George I was nothing!"

"What an asshole."

"And the worst part was I thought George was on our side! He was the one who pushed and advocated for me to have a chance at the promotion."

Marvin adjusted in his seat. "I need to confess something to you."

"Am I going to cry more?"

He shrugged. "Probably."

"Then no."

We sat in silence. "You think he's crying about you right now?"

"No. Max was mad." The memory of his somber, angry face came back in full force. Words that we didn't mean were said and I don't think we could take them back or if he even wanted to.

"I think Max and I were the only ones ever really advocating for you."

I rolled my head over to look at Marvin. "What do you mean?"

"Andrea, George and Maggie didn't even think you would make it this far. Andrea just didn't want to be the one to tell you and George thought that if it looked like they gave you a chance you wouldn't hold it against the company...you wouldn't turn around and sue them or something. Please don't cry."

"And Max didn't know about this?"

Marvin shook his head. "They thought that if they involved him that he would be blindsided and just give you the promotion instead of firing you."

"How do you know this?"

He shrugged. "I sit in on the meetings in a corner and pretend I'm not listening to what they're saying."

I sighed heavy. I screamed causing Marvin to spill the cup he had in his hand. "Dammit, Ginny!"

"Those assholes!" My heartache turned into anger. Anger turned into pure volcanic rage. Ten years of hard work; blood, sweat and tears all down the drain. "Why is it all so sneaky?! I don't cause trouble. I keep to myself. Out of everyone I deserve this promotion."

"I know."

"Do you know what I've been through in this company?!" Every broken nail, bruise, scrape, cut, fractures, mental fuckery and the early onset arthritis and carpel tunnel, flooded over me.

"Yes," Marvin answered calmly. I jumped up. "Where are you going?" he asked. I shook my head and sat back down. "Is this part of your breakdown? Do I need to call a doctor? Priest? Oprah?"

"I want to do something."

"Oh honey, murder is against the law. You'd definitely get locked away and I don't think you're suited for that lifestyle."

"I wish I could make them...ugh! I don't even know."

"Do you wanna crash the H. Moda holiday party?"

That caught my attention. "What?"

"I was invited to the holiday party downtown which..." Marvin glanced at his phone. "...starts in like an hour."

"What holiday party starts that late?"

"One that is being held in the most exclusive club and only managers and people from the offices were invited."

I bit my lip, thinking about what if I showed up there? What would I do? Cause a scene? Then they would be right. But it would feel so good to go out with a bang. "I don't have anything to wear."

"Let's make a quick trip to your apartment. I think you can pull something out of the vault for this one night."

Two hours later we walked down the street to the entrance of *Bisous,* A hot new club in Manhattan's Lower East Side. "What if they don't let me in?"

"You're my plus one, they will let you in."

"What if they don't?"

Marvin's face scrunched in disgust over my doubt. "Oh my God, Ginny. If you don't stop with the questions, I'm going to tell them you followed me all the way here and have a bomb up your cooch."

"Fine. Sorry."

Marvin spun around so fast that I almost slipped on a patch of ice. "What the hell?"

"Listen, Ginny. You look amazing. This dress...I don't know why you've never worn it."

"Because it's barely anything to it," I pointed out as I tried to adjust my coat tighter to keep me from freezing to death. I chose a slip dress I created that had a lace overlay and a high slit. I also chose to wear my highest heels, and vixen makeup with dark eyes and bright cherry lips. My long dark hair came down in loose tendrils...I looked like I rolled out of someone's bed, and I wasn't mad about the look. I knew it was too much for a work holiday party, but I also knew that my days were numbered, I gave zero fucks.

"I just wanted to tell you that I'm as gay as Randy Rainbow at a

Broadway convention, but you just might be able to change me for the night...you look that hot."

I couldn't hold back my laughter; it felt good. Thank God we pregamed at his place, if not I would've talked myself out of it before the *Uber* showed up. "I look good?"

"You look amazing," he gave me a light good luck kiss on the cheek. "Now tell me how good I look."

I eyed my best friend, dark hair slicked back, decked out in an all-black Louis Vuitton suit that fit him like a glove. A gold chain laid against his bare chest. Where he got the money to buy something so expensive was beyond me. "You look amazing."

"Let's give them hell."

I placed a gentle hand on his arm. "Marvin, thanks for everything. I love you." I don't know if it was the drinks, the muffled music or the fact that I was crashing my employers holiday party, but I just felt emotional and needed my friend to know how I felt.

"Why? What's wrong? Are you dying?" He feigned disgust over my dramatics but I didn't care.

"No, but you didn't have to do this. You can get into real trouble."

He shook his head and gestured for me to take hold of his arm. "How do you want things to go?"

"I have no clue."

"What's the plan?"

"I have no clue," I answered honestly as the bouncer checked Marvin's credentials.

"Well, good, as long you got a plan."

The two of us entered the crowded club that was playing Reggaeton as loud as the speakers would allow. There were giant chandeliers hanging from the ceilings, women hanging from large, feathered swings; Marvin tapped me and gestured toward the bar. I nodded and hand in hand we walked over.

We scanned the crowd; many were beyond the point of no

return, women wearing less than I was, men dressed in their best suits, trying their best impressions of Christian Grey. "This looks like more than just managers and corporate," I yelled over the speakers.

"I know, I didn't realize this was a big deal."

I scanned for food, there wasn't much in that department. Just endless bottles. The room was dim with flashes of colorful lights keeping time with the music. We had bypassed the coat check and I could already feel beads of sweat forming at my temples. "Hey! Wait for me here, I'm going to check my coat in!"

Marvin slipped his off. "Do mine too!"

I rolled my eyes and took his coat anyway. I waited in line for coat check, pondering what in the hell I was actually doing here. This day was endless. The rational part of me knew that I should be home in bed licking my wounds because despite whatever happens tomorrow, by the end of the week I will not have a job. The psycho in me wanted to set this place on fire, do a really convincing impersonation of *Carrie* and lock everyone in this club to suffer the consequences...I laughed to myself at the thought.

"Are you serious?" A not so happy Max stopped in his tracks with the same sexy brunette from before.

"You guys really know how to throw a party," I threw out over my shoulder.

"What are you doing here?"

"It's nice to see you too."

He wore the same all black suit from before with just a few buttons undone; a hint of his tattoos were peeking through on his hands and I felt the heat begin to rise. I squashed that bitch down because she had no business making me feel this way about a man who cared more about business.

"Rachel, head inside, I'll check the coats in."

She raised an eyebrow. "Good luck, she looks really mad."

"That's nothing new," he answered.

He stood behind me. "Don't talk about me as if I'm not here."

"Nice dress you have on, I can see what you had for lunch. There's no back to this dress."

"You like it? I made it myself with the intention of picking out a man who's down for a one night stand."

"If that's the goal, I can free my evening." His voice was low, making sure others couldn't hear.

I glance over my shoulder and caught him eyeing me. "In your dreams, Mr. Thomas."

He lowered himself down to my ear, his breath was warm against my skin. "Virginia, you have no idea how crazy my dreams are at this moment." I closed my eyes to ward off the arousal that began to spread.

Because I had no witty comeback, I made it to the window without another word, grabbed my ticket and started to make my way back to the main room. I felt Max's grip on my arm, causing me to turn back around. "Really, Ginny, what are you doing here?"

"I'm Marvin's date."

He nodded. "Can we talk about what happened earlier?"

I shook my head. "No." I spun on my heel, shaking my hips from side to side to give him a glimpse of what he was missing.

I found Marvin talking to some guy. "This is Ginny! Up and coming fashion designer! She made this dress!"

I left for two seconds, and Marvin's face was already red with intoxication. "Oh my god! It's so nice to meet you! Marvin was just singing your praises!" Mystery man was handsome, silky purple hair running just below his ears, tall and slender, but he wore a traditional tuxedo pants and a black shirt rolled up at the sleeves. Small tattoos sprinkled across his hands, the shine from his one earring sparkled against the light. "Nice to meet you...what's your name?"

"Jake!"

"Nice to meet you too, Jake!" I yelled back over the music.

The three of us hung by the bar and kept a pretty low profile. Marvin leaned over to me. "I'm going to the bathroom, I'll be right back."

I nodded, turning back to our new friend, Jake had taken hold of my hand and dragged me to the dance floor. "What are you doing?" I let out a tipsy giggle.

"I saw you eyeing the dance floor. You're sexy. Your body was made to move."

I laughed as he spun me around, my head thrown back, the ceiling with its glittering lights looked as if we were in heaven. He pulled me close, Jakes hand on my hips, swaying together. He threw my arms around his neck, and we grind to the music. I was dancing with this stranger, but I felt as if we were being watched. If that was the case let's give them a show. I turned around and bent my knees, throwing my head back as my backside and his groin danced together.

I felt a hand on my arm, that spun me around, my hands came up so fast to keep from colliding with something, I landed on a hard chest. "Excuse me, but we were dancing." Jakes voice came up.

I looked up into Max's stone-cold face. "Yeah, well, now it's my turn."

"Max!"

"Do you know him?" Jake looked like he was ready to throw down.

I nodded. "He's the new CEO," I said.

Marvin appeared out of nowhere, "Jake, did I show you my biceps? I've been doing this new routine..." he pulled a stunned Jake off the dance floor. Leaving Max and I in a sea of horny dancers.

"I know you were dancing like that to make me jealous," he said in my ear.

"Don't flatter yourself!" Max pulled me close to him, ours bodies flushed as the colorful lights flickered again, smoke and glitter appeared. "What are you doing?"

"Dancing!"

"I'm not dancing with you, Max."

"Why?"

"You have a brunette with you."

His hand on my hips began to move me to the rhythm of the music. "Just one," he pleaded.

Beads of sweat formed against our bodies, as we swayed to the music. I lost myself to this place. Threw my head back as his head fell against my neck, I felt a lick of his tongue as he discreetly had a taste. The music melded into another. I closed my eyes to take it in. "Max? Can we dance?" The brunettes voice snapped me out of my fantasy.

"He's all yours," I said, making my way off the dance floor.

I walked over to the bar. "Water, please!" I yelled at the bartender.

"Ginny? What are you doing here?" all the hairs on my body stood on end in disgust.

"Rafa? How are you?" His hair was shaved off and he was dressed like a low-grade mob boss in all white.

"Well, you know...hanging in there." His eyes roamed my barely there dress. "I wasn't sure if it was really you, but then I caught a glimpse of your back tattoos and knew."

His comment made me feel sleezy. I needed the bartender to come and give me my water. "Why'd you come over Rafa?" I was done being nice. "You know I hate you, I despise your wife, so why'd you come over?"

"You just look really good...it reminded me of old times." I felt his hand on my bare back and felt like I wanted to throw up. I shrunk away.

"Nothing I said warranted your touch. Keep your hands to yourself or I'll be forced to break it off."

"Ginny, I tried calling you so many times throughout these last couple of years."

"Oh, yeah? Does your wife know?"

He sighed. "It's not working out between us."

"Rafa, I don't care."

"I asked her for a divorce."

I rolled my eyes and shook my head. "Again, Rafa, I don't care."

"You might of saw us come in together but it's only for appearances."

I turned red hot with anger. "You came here with Maggie and think it's okay to just come up to me and talk?" The bartender took that moment to hand me my water, without another word I took a step, Rafa put a hand on my arm. "Rafa, let go of me and there won't be a scene."

"Even if I don't let go of you, there won't be a scene. Maggie told me you're holding on like a thread at this company."

"Hey, Ginny." Max dropped an arm around my shoulder. "I was wondering what was taking so long."

"Max, this is Maggie's husband, Rafa." I introduced.

Max held out his hand. "Max Thomas, nice to meet you."

"Rafa Bonilla, store manager of 279." he extended his hand.

"Nice to finally meet you Rafa, now just some sound advice?" Rafa eyed Max wearily, but, said nothing. "Don't talk to Ginny, don't look at Ginny, I don't even want you to sneeze in her direction, got it?"

Rafa's face was flaming red as he walked away. "I didn't need your help," I snapped.

"I know you didn't."

"Have you seen Marvin? I want to go now."

"Let me take you home. I have a car waiting out front."

I rolled my eyes. "Max."

"Ginny."

I was going to tell him that it wasn't a good idea, I had wine running through my veins; the heat from the club made me sweat and I felt sexy. I wanted to be touched, I knew that if Max took me home, I'd let him touch me.

Despite what the smart side of my brain yelled, I grabbed his hand and lead him to a dark corner. "What are we doing?"

"I need to feel your touch, Max."

He looked around. "We can't here. There's a million people here."

"Use your fingers."

I placed his body in front of me, shielding me from the club that paid us no attention. Even with my heels, I could barely see over his shoulder. I saw the hesitation on his face, I grabbed one of his hands, placing it under my dress. His fingers tentatively passed over my silky thong. His hair fell over his face, making this man appear more dangerous than he actually was. His touch was electric. My hips moved with a mind of their own, Max moved the scrap of fabric to the side and his fingers touched my sensitive flesh. My head fell back, exposing my neck, accentuating the low cut of my dress. I felt the sensations all at once—the music, the humidity, the wine, his touch. His fingers rubbed faster until I felt his lips on mine, calming the moan that people couldn't probably hear over the music. When I came down from the euphoria, his soft brown eyes were full of arousal but the rest of his face was as serious as a heart attack.

"Ginny, we can't do this."

"Do what?"

"I want you."

I looked down between our bodies, so close but not touching. "Max, relationships aren't supposed to be this hard."

"Ginny, you can't say things like that after I fingered you in a club full of people."

"Max—"

"Ginny, you can't push me away and then pull me back because you need to get your rocks off. That's not what I want."

"You can't say you want me when your family doesn't like me. You'll always do and say anything for the sake of the business."

He ran a hand through his auburn hair in frustration. "It's obvious we're not going to agree right now. I'll see you tomorrow?"

I didn't want to tell him the truth. I wasn't showing up, I quit. I quit this hamster wheel of a company that has kept me stagnant for almost ten years. I nodded. "Yeah, you'll see me tomorrow. And Max?"

"Yeah?"

"Thank you for calling my parents."

He nodded as I turned to make my exit, caught eyes with George and Andrea, who were dressed to kill like their older brother. Andrea in a sparkling fringe dress, George in a white suit and green tie. I offered a small smile but the two didn't crack. They approached us and George was angry. He was out for blood. "She's playing you, Max."

Max tilted his head. "George, enough."

"Relax, thing one and thing two. You've won." I went to coat check where Marvin and Jake were waiting for me. But George followed behind me, along with Andrea and Max.

"Tell him, Ginny. Tell him that you were seducing him to secure your promotion."

"What?" I turned to him. "What the hell are you talking about?" I was surrounded by the three siblings and at that moment I wished I was in the manager's office sitting in a chair by the door so I could escape if I needed to. Right now, I was trapped.

"Maggie told us how she walked in on you and Max getting close. I had to send an investigator on you. They checked your text messages."

"Is that even legal?" My anger was at a record high. The chill that went down my spine from feeling violated by rich people who thought they had the right to invade my privacy.

Max stood stunned. Not one word escaped his lips. The one time I wanted his help to shut his brother up, he was a statue.

"Ginny was using you to get the promotion," George sneered.

"That's not true!" I reached for Max but he stepped back out of my reach.

George stepped towards me, practically foaming at the mouth. It's as if he took pleasure from this whole thing. "Guess what, sweetie? This is another promotion you won't get because you're fucking around with another person you worked with."

My eyes roamed around the coat check at the small nosey crowd that stood around to catch the drama. I finally found Marvin and Jake and pushed out of the circle.

"Hey, I saw you heading out and ran over to meet you," Marvin whispered. He eyed the Thomas' who began to walk back into the party. Max didn't look back.

"Let's go." I gave my ticket to the clerk.

"What happened?"

"I ran into Rafa."

Marvin's eyes widened. "No!"

"I also begged Max to feel me up."

"No!"

"And he did."

"Ginny...I'm kind of impressed," he said.

"Me too," Jake said from beside us.

"I think Andrea and George caught some of the show."

"What?!" Marvin's eyes practically fell out.

"They think I was using Max to get promoted. I called them thing one and thing two, so I think I handled the situation well."

"What?!" he squealed.

"Marvin, I'm quitting. I quit. No two weeks. I'm over the drama, the hostility, the politics. These positions aren't based on who's best for the job. It's based on likeability and connections. I have neither."

"Wow. This is a lot," Jake said from beside us.

"Sorry, to lay it all on you, Jake. We're a bunch of hot messes."

"She's speaking for herself. I'm pretty stable," Marvin added with a wink. "You can come back home with us," he said to Jake.

"Thanks, but I can't leave just yet. I'm here on business." Jake took my hand. "Ginny, it was a pleasure meeting you. Thank you for the dance." He kissed my hand. "Marvin, give me a call. Maybe we can meet up for a drink."

Jake gave Marvin's hand a quick shake. When he disappeared back into the club, I glanced over at Marvin. "Is...Is he...Are we...are we in a throuple?"

"He's sexy but no Virginia, he's gay."

"Really? I couldn't tell."

Marvin tilted his head and narrowed his eyes in my direction. "Not all gay men are flamboyant."

"I didn't—"

"He's a gay man, who is sexy as hell. I'll tell him to flash his gay neon sign next time."

"I'm sorry, I didn't mean anything."

Marvin sighed. "I know. And we had a lot to drink, let's head back to my place, its closer and I don't want to pay an arm and leg for an *Uber*."

I placed a kiss on his cheek. "I'm sorry."

He kissed my forehead. "You better be." We waited in the lobby for our ride. "So, tell me exactly what happened back there."

19

Rule 55: Don't get emotional. Your name isn't on the door and you won't be able to see clearly through an ocean of tears.

The soft buzz of my phone lulled me out of my sleep. The realization that the sun was shining through curtains that weren't mine made me sit up on a bed that took me a second to realize wasn't mine either. Marvin's studio apartment was extremely small, so one quick turn of my head and I scanned the whole place. "Marvin?!" I rolled out of bed in my slip dress from last night and checked the bathroom.

I heard the soft vibration of my phone and finally picked up. "Good Morning, Maggie."

"Virginia, where are you? There was a mishap with the window."

"I'm not coming in, you can figure it out. You act like you know how to run everything including the visual aspect." The silence on the other end was deafening.

"Are you using a sick day? Do you have any sick days?"

"I don't know and honestly I don't care."

"Ginny, your tone is a tad disrespectful. We can talk about this when you get back in."

"Wake up, Maggie! I quit! I don't want to work there. That

place is a death wish for anyone with dreams! Good luck, have fun and godspeed!" I stabbed the end call button with great satisfaction...and dread.

By noon, I made it back to my building, finding Mrs. Pierce feeding a stray. "Well, haven't seen you in a while."

I turned to this woman who was a pain in my ass since I moved in and began to cry one big cry. "Oh, no." I heard her groan.

I began to hyperventilate. "What's happening?" I placed a hand on my chest.

"You're dying," she said matter-of-factly.

The room began to spin and dull colored spots blurred my vision. "I'm not dying here! I can't die here! Not in front of you! I just need to get a grip!"

It felt as if all the air in the world wasn't enough to fill my lungs. I felt myself fall to the ground. The world went dark.

I woke up on the threshold of Mrs. Pierces apartment, the door was held open by the top of my head. I felt my leg being pulled. "What the hell are you doing?" I said sitting up, the door slammed with a giant thud behind me.

"I was trying to hide the body; I didn't want to be held responsible for a dead hooker being found dead on my doorstep."

"I'm not a hooker," I groaned.

"From what you're wearing, I couldn't tell," she said with her arms crossed.

"I'm not at the age where I want to wear a muumuu everyday thank you very much." I took one hard look at my captor. "No offense."

Mrs. Pierce lifted one bushy eyebrow. "Now that you're conscious...leave!"

"You didn't have to help me you know," I pointed out as I began to rise from my spot.

"Just so you know, you weren't helping yourself looking like a dead fish at my door. Also, you need to lose some weight because I couldn't drag you far."

I finally noticed the apartment. "What is all that?" I pointed past the small hallway to the living room where there were racks filled with endless amounts of clothes; sparkling dresses, colorful trousers, something full of feathers...was that a leather jacket?

Mrs. Pierce heavy eyebrows came down and she began to tap her foot. The soft padding sound of her chancleta was kind of soothing. "You out of all people should know what that is."

"Clothes?"

She began to clap. "Oh, look, she can point out the obvious."

I shook my head. "I don't need this shit, especially from you." I turned but not before I felt a slap against the side of my head. "Oh my God! Did you just hit me?!"

"I did."

"I'm not oppose to hitting you back, no matter how ancient you are."

"I saw you."

I rolled my eyes. "Saw me what?" I crossed my arms and waited for her answer.

"Before I had my heart attack, I went to one of your shows."

"Excuse me?"

"I went to one of your fashion shows...right before you threw it all away for some man."

I felt stiffness in my neck as anger started to settle in the pit of my stomach. "I didn't throw it away for a man."

"Then why'd you throw it away?" she asked with a head tilt.

"Because I wanted to be loved." Who was Mrs. Pierce and why did she attend my shows? This woman grated my nerves, but I'd be lying if I said I wasn't intrigued by how our lives connected.

Her thin, wrinkly lips settled in a straight line. "So, you threw it all away for a man."

"How do you know my business anyway?"

"Walls are thin, you're loud, I could only take the crying for so long until I started listening in on your conversation."

"How...why were you at my show?"

"As a former successful indie brand...I was curious about the next generation that was getting all this buzz."

I gently pushed passed her to look through the racks. I pulled at the leather jackets with its colorful sleeves and fringe. I peeked at the label inside. "You're *Savage Piercings*?"

I looked through the racks in fascination. "The one and only."

"But...how...why..."

"What's hard to grasp?" She pulled a cough drop from her nightgown pocket and popped it in her mouth.

"You're an old hag who always harasses me. How could you be one of my favorite designers? I thought it was a Keith Pierce."

"My brother. He was the face and I was the brains. Are you leaving yet?" she walked to her kitchen and began to busy herself.

I eyed the jacket. "I wanted this jacket so bad. I created pieces with this as inspiration."

I wanted to fan girl because Savage Piercings was the brand that was my go-to. If I couldn't be part of the team in some capacity, I wanted to be in the same planetary system. That brand took risks that turned out to be beautiful and way ahead of its time.

"I applied for an internship with you..." I looked over my shoulder at her. "I didn't get it."

"Good thing, because it turned out my gut feelings were right."

"Why are you always such a bitch to me?" I sighed. I was tired of fighting with the world. I wished I could have a normal conversation with everything.

"Because you gave it all up too easy. That time when you finally left that man, it should've spurred your creativity and greatness. Instead, you pitied and doubted yourself. And the way you're carrying on, it looks like you're going to do it again." She popped another cough drop in her mouth.

"You think I had greatness?"

"I think you need to get out of my apartment."

"I saved up one summer to buy one of your denim jackets."

She sighed. "And?"

"And now I'm disappointed that this is what my money paid for." I gestured around the apartment.

"Get out."

I began to make my exit. "Why'd you stop?" I asked, my curiosity getting the best of me.

"I had a goddamn heart attack."

"That couldn't be it," I said.

"Where you gave it up for the potential at love, I gave it up because I devoted my life for the brand, with nothing to show for it. While I was recovering, I left my business to leeches. They sucked me dry of everything I had, and I just didn't have the energy to start over." A grim look came over her as memories flooded back. To leave your life's work in the hands of people you trusted only to have them destroy it with their greed...that had to hurt.

There was an internal conflict going on within me and I honestly didn't know how to process it. "I want to hate you, but that little tidbit is making me sympathize with you."

"Get out," she said in a flat monotone voice.

I finally opened the door. "I quit my job today."

"Oh, getting too old to be on your knees?"

I sighed. "I thought we really had a bonding moment in there."

"We didn't. Come back to me when you get your head out of your ass and do what you were always afraid to do."

"I don't know what I'm supposed to do." I admitted to this grouchy old woman who, in some weird way could be my Yoda.

"Well, if you don't know, how is anyone else supposed to know."

She slammed the door on my face. I bent down to pick up the purse that was still in the hallway; vibrating as if it had a mind of its own.

I looked down to see I missed a million calls and texts.

Despite what an asshole I thought he was, Max's messages were the first ones I looked at.

What's going on?!!!

I wasn't happy, so I quit. Have a good life.

I saw the bubbles and then nothing.

I walked into my apartment and straight to the shower, stripping off my dress and everything else along the way. I don't know what it is about a good, hot shower that just warrants a cry. I cried until my shoulders drooped from exhaustion and my eyeballs were sore.

As soon as I shut the water off and my toe touched the cool bathroom tile, I heard a knock on my door. "Hold on!" I called out.

It was probably Marvin who came over to tell me about the drama that went on today from my quitting. I opened the door to an irritated Max. His eyes were wide, his hair disheveled and his jaw was pinched so tight I thought I heard a tooth crack. His eyes settled on my towel. "Delivery boys must love you; do you always answer the door with a towel?" his annoyance made me roll my eyes.

"Goodbye, Max." I closed the door before he could stop me.

His muffled voice came through loud and clear. "Ginny, you can't quit." I said nothing. I didn't want to get into this back and forth to taint my decisions. I didn't want to agree to go back just to make someone else happy. I needed to put my happiness first. "Ginny, come back. I'll give you a different position. I'll make it so you're on the design team. More money and you'll be doing something closer to what you really want to do." I didn't answer. "I know what George said wasn't true. That's not you."

I felt the flames rise all the way to my chest. The gull this guy had! I snatched the door back open. "Let me tell you something, Max. You don't know me! Maybe I was using you. And just so you know, I needed to quit. You know why? Because working in that environment was toxic and I wasn't happy!"

"But this can make you happy. This job can make you happy."

"Will it? Are you happy?"

"Virginia, you and I are two different people. I have an obliga-tion to—"

"Make your family happy? Do something that doesn't fill your cup? I've been there, done that. The happiest I've been was when I was stressed out the months before a fashion show when I was cre-ating and editing looks. I'm happiest when someone seeks me out to wear one of my designs. Something I created. I'm not happy when I'm catering to a company who would replace me in two seconds flat. I'm not happy being stressed out because the sell through in fancy jersey is below the country's and somehow that's my fault. I'm not happy working for a promotion that will never come. They will find every excuse to keep me from progressing. We are two different people, I have an obligation to myself. Accepting such a huge offer when I was obviously being phased out wouldn't sit well with me. And you wouldn't know if I stayed with you to get a head and I wouldn't know if you offered me the position just to keep me quiet. I don't like any of that."

I closed the door on his stunned face. "Virginia, I need you."

Through the close door I answered. "You don't need me, Max. You need that thing that sparks you, gives you purpose."

I heard him sigh. "Why did you quit? Tell me the truth. I wouldn't have fired you."

"I was fighting a losing battle. I need to put myself and my mental first...for once."

"Please let me in," he begged softly through the door.

"I can't," I admitted.

"Why not?"

"Because you would make me come back and I would hold that against you."

Minutes passed by and we hadn't moved from our sides of the door. "I know you're still there; I can see your shadow. I have to head back." I heard him clear his throat before continuing, "I got you something, I'll leave it at the doorstep, give me a couple minutes to go."

I looked through the peep hole and watched him give one final look at my door before walking down the stairs.

I finally opened the door, still in my towel, grabbed the small gift, and took it inside. I shook it, just like a kid on Christmas. It didn't make a lot of noise. Should I put it under my small tree? That way I'll have at least one gift to open?

I decided to set the gift aside. The anxiety of not having a job was starting to settle in. Instead of dwelling on it, I did my best Scarlett O'Hara impression and decided to think about it tomorrow. I put on a comfy sweatshirt and dusted off my old sketch book. Maybe it was about time to start something.

I was in deep storyboard mode, sketching things that I had wanted to see in this year's fashion week shows but felt were missing. Bold shoulders, fringed crop tops with pleated wide leg trousers *but maybe we tie dye the fabric?* My inner voice suggested. "Maybe..." I answered the empty room while I jotted down the note. Tomorrow might be a good day to head out into the world and get some new fabric. I heard my phone vibrating for the millionth time. "Hello?"

"The shit storm that you set off is crazy," Marvin said in lieu of a greeting.

I set my sketching pad down. "What do you mean? I've literally been unemployed for a day."

"Do you want to hear what happened?"

I felt the numbing pain of a migraine begin to set in. "Honestly? I don't. I just want to relax and think about how I can only get by for a couple months before I need to find a new source of income—"

"He stepped down."

"Who stepped down?"

"Max Thomas."

"Step down from what?" Although I played as if I was confused, my heart was beating fast.

"Are you that dumb? He stepped down from the company. He doesn't want to be CEO, he doesn't want to be a part of the business." I stared ahead at a blank T.V. not really sure what to say or how to react, which was okay because Marvin had more to say. "It didn't sit well with the others. Max and George almost came to blows."

My heart beat in nervousness at the idea of the two strapping brothers actually physically assaulting each other. "I...I honestly don't know what to say."

"Andrea suggested he head home to cool down, but I...I think his mind is already made up."

A knock sounded on the door and in my gut I knew that it was Max. "Marvin, hold on." I opened the door ready to send Max out on his way, but Mrs. Pierce stood at my doorstep. "What the hell do you want?"

"I wanted to make sure you weren't dead." She adjusted her matronly nightgown.

"Well, I'm fine so you can go to bed with a healthy conscience."

"I wanted to give you this." She held out her bony arms that held a big box that I hadn't noticed before.

"Marvin, if I don't call you back in ten minutes send the bomb squad to my address." I hung up and reluctantly took the box. Best case scenario, it was an actual gift. Worst case scenario, my body parts will be scrapped off the sides of the wall. "What is it?"

"Me losing my mind for a brief second. If you don't want it, give it back." She held her arms out and I clutched the box to my chest.

"I don't know what it is yet."

"Then open the damn thing."

I sat the box down, unwrapping it in the doorway and pulling out the amazing colorful fringe leather jacket that I was salivating over earlier in the day. My eyes flew to the older woman. "Are you serious?"

"I'm surprised too."

I felt the hot sting of tears. "Why?"

She showed her disgust at my emotion. "Please, don't cry. I overheard your conversation with your boyfriend…I think you did good, for once in your life. You told him off and—"

"Ginny?" I looked around Mrs. Pierce to see Max. "I'm sorry to interrupt."

"If you were really sorry, then you would leave her alone!" Mrs. Pierce spat out.

"Excuse her, she didn't take her meds today," I said.

"Don't give up your dream for a good piece of sausage." She gave a nod, scowled at Max and took her time heading back downstairs.

"Ginny, I—"

"Give it a second," I whispered, pointing in the direction that Mrs. Pierce went. "She has a tendency to ease drop."

"Can I come in?"

"No," I answered.

"Good, stand your ground!" Mrs. Pierce yelled from the floor below.

I rolled my eyes, waited for the sound of the door closing

before I addressed Max. "What do you want, Max? I have a pretty busy night."

His hand rubbed behind his neck before coming to the front and smoothing down his beard. "I quit."

"What did you quit?"

"The mob." I didn't give him a reaction. His nerves were getting the best of him. "The family business, Gin. I quit."

"Why?"

"Because you were right! I was living and working for my family. I want to do my own things and I just felt obligated to do what my family wanted to avoid conflict."

"Max—" I pinched the bridge of my nose.

"I...I want to live my life the way that I want to."

"Will you be happy?" He was giving everything up impulsively because I goaded him. I didn't want to live with the idea of this man hating me because what I said pushed him to give up the world he was accustomed to.

"I don't know. Right now, I'm feeling like I just jumped off a cliff...I'll let you know when I land."

Guilt overcame me. I might regret it later, but I stepped aside. "Want to come in?"

He nodded and passed me. He stood still in the hallway, looking at the ceiling. "Ginny, I'm sorry."

"For?"

"What this company has put you through. It wasn't fair. I take full responsibility. There's so much that goes on that I'm not aware of."

"Want something to drink?" I placed my gift from Mrs. Pierce on one of my dining chairs.

"What's that?"

"A weird truce...I think." From the corner of my eye, I could see Max studying me. "What happened, Max?"

"I know," he sighed.

"Know what?"

"I found out about everything. Phasing you out, your talk with my brother. The extent of the drama from a couple of years ago." I handed him a cup of water. His puppy dog eyes fell on me. "You have anything stronger?" I walked back to the kitchen while he took a seat on the sofa, I grabbed a bottle of tequila and a shot glass.

"Max, you shouldn't be here."

He looked up at me like a wounded warrior. "You don't want me here?"

"I don't want you to look back at this and regret this mistake that you made."

"You think I made a mistake?"

I began to play with the ends of my hair because I didn't know where to put my energy. "I think I said some things to you that you took to heart and jumped without really thinking things over."

"I'm a grown man, Ginny. I can make my own decisions."

I took a deep breath because this felt like an argument ready to happen. "What are you going to do now?"

He took a shot and relaxed against the sofa. "I honestly don't even know."

"Well, Max, as much as I'm enjoying your visit, I think it'd be better if you went home."

He sat up straight. "Are you kicking me out?"

"Yes, but in the nicest way possible." When he didn't move, I sighed. "Listen, I think you need to go home and think about all of this. I need to get back to what I was..." I stopped myself because for some reason I couldn't explain, I didn't want to share what I was working on. I wanted to hold on to it.

"What were you doing?" His eyes darted to where mine landed for a brief second. He noticed my sketch pad and picked it up. Every fiber in my being lunged for the book and snatched it back.

"No!" I yelled.

"Ginny! What's wrong? Why can't I see? Were you working on the new collection?"

I felt my anger rise. "It's none of your business."

His lips set a grim line against his face. Max scratched at his beard. "It is none of my business." He nodded slowly. "Is this how we're going to be?"

"Max." My heart ached for this man but if I wanted to get serious about making a living doing what I loved, I knew I had to let him go. "We are a one-night stand that lasted a couple of weeks too long."

Max's eyes darkened, searching my face for any sort of sign that what I said was all in jest. When he didn't find what he was looking for, he cleared his throat. "I'm sorry you think that."

Without another word, Max grabbed his coat and walked out of my apartment. I held my composure until I locked the door behind him. I walked back to the couch in hopes that I could go back to creating. I wanted to lose myself in the process and not think about Max Thomas and his sense of humor, his encouragement, his commitment to those he cares about...*No, Ginny! Don't think about how he makes your body feel. You need to establish your way in the world, and he is a distraction that you don't need.*

I felt a tear fall to my hand. If Santa was real, then he would make this world a place where it's okay to love a man like Max Thomas and still be successful on my own terms.

But my adult brain knew Santa wasn't real, and that world that I wanted was beyond my reach.

20

Rule #38: The customer is never right, you just gotta make it seem like they are.

The holiday set up, came and went and I heard no more drama from my former co-workers because I refused to hear it. Then before I knew it, Christmas eve was here.

I arrived at my parents place just in time for my mom to serve me a plate of pastelles. She practically shoved it in my face as I walked through the door.

I took a place next to my dad on the couch; he was engrossed in a holiday movie marathon. "So, how was your holiday so far, daddy?"

My dad was late-fifties, gone were the days when he used to frequent the gym; he was all polo shirts, khakis and dad belly. He glanced my way briefly before putting his attention towards the T.V. "It's okay. Your mom tells me that you quit your job."

"I don't want to talk about it," I answered around a mouth full of food.

"Was it another man, again? Was this one married?"

I sighed. I knew that coming over here meant that I had to most likely endure my dad's verbal attacks. "Dad, I left because I wasn't a valued employee."

"Virginia, you work in retail, no one is a valued employee! You'd have to make the company millions of dollars to be of any value. What you did was probably secure them a couple thousand."

He had a point, but I wasn't going to let him know that. "Dad, no matter where you work, you always want to feel like you matter. Like you're making a difference, like your ideas matter."

My dad snorted. "That's a bunch of horseshit that your generation created."

"Dad, let's change the subject because we are never going to agree."

"What's your plan now?" he asked, never taking his eyes off the T.V.

I shrugged my shoulder. "I have a plan but it's going to take a little bit of time before it takes off. I'm working part time at—"

"I got her a part time job at the dry cleaners," my mom added as she breezed in with a glass of coquito.

He sat up in his recliner. "What?! A couple semesters in college, a decade at the last job and you're working at a dry cleaner?"

"Part-time there and part-time interning at an indie fashion brand."

"Interning?! At your age?! Interning means no pay. How can you survive with that?!" he asked.

"Daddy, relax, your veins are popping and that means your blood pressure is going up."

"Is it crazy to want something good for my daughter?" he bellowed.

My mother came over and laid a hand on his shoulder. "She is a grown woman with a plan. That's a pretty dangerous combo," she shared a conspiratorial wink with me. This was the first time in a long time I felt a closeness with my mom.

"Daddy, I am interning to gain a better understanding of the industry I want to be in. I'm working on a new collection and until then I am offering ready to wear hoodies and tee's. I have money saved from my last collection."

He looked up at my mother. "You agree with all this?"

"I don't but if she needs us or is in deep trouble, I'm confident that she will come to us." She stared intently as she waited for my sign of agreement.

"Yes! of course! If I'm in trouble you would know!" I added to make her feel better.

"And even if you're not in trouble, you'll come to us."

I took the time to really look at my parents. This is what I wanted; not the arguments because I've had enough of that. What I wanted was the invitation to just pop up at their home and be in their lives. I know that sounds crazy, but I thought that I've screwed up so much in life that they just didn't want anything to do with me.

This moment felt good.

I felt the back of my eyes begin to burn from unshed tears, and I felt that tell-tale knot in my throat. "Yes, I'll stop by even if I don't need you."

We made it through dinner with less hiccups and more food. My dad fell asleep on the recliner while my mother and I sat together on the couch, surfing the channels for a different holiday movie. "Is this Max guy the reason you quit?"

"Maaaa..." I whined.

She held up her hands. "I just want to know. It's been a long time since I've had you next to me like this." I heard the emotion in her voice and immediately felt a daughter's guilt. This standoff was both our fault, I needed to do my part to fix it.

I decided to indulge her a little bit. "Yes and no," I said.

"Can you be any more vague?"

I sighed. "I don't know where to start."

"Start at the beginning, that usually helps."

"Fine." I resituated myself on the couch, getting comfy. "We met on a random night and hit it off." It's my mom so I tried to keep it cute and gave her the PG version. "Then, I found out he was my boss. And not a regular boss but like his family owns the company. We tried our best to keep it under wraps but his family doesn't want me involved with him and they were phasing me out of the company anyways—"

"What? Why?"

"I'm a dinosaur in retail years and they thought I was a problem."

"A problem for who? Do these people even work in the stores or they the kind to keep their hands clean and let everyone else get dirty?"

"I thought they got dirty, but I was wrong."

She nodded knowingly. My parents have also been slaves to their jobs. "What happened?"

"He was really supportive, but once I found out they all were pushing me out from the beginning I decided to quit."

"And you quit him too?"

"Yeah, I can't make the same mistake I made last time. I can't give up on my dream because I'm in love with someone."

From the corner of my eye, I could see her ears perk up. "So, it's love?"

"I think so."

"You don't give up your dream for love. Love is supposed to enhance and support your dreams. Did he know what you wanted to do?"

"Yeah."

"And?"

"And he was great about it! He wanted me to start over even before I knew that I wanted to start over," I looked towards the T.V. "Ma! Look!" I punched the volume up.

She jumped at my shrill voice. "What's going on?"

"Shhhhhh!" I listened to the reporter.

"Things are shaking up at La Moda, inc. Max Thomas is stepping down as CEO just days before he was supposed to officially take over. Andrea Thomas will be stepping in as the CEO of the world's most successful fast fashion brand..."

"That's Max Thomas?!" My mom yelled. "That man is gorgeous."

"Mami, is it okay if I—"

"Go. Just pack up some food."

"What about daddy?"

We both glanced over in his direction. "Your father won't even noticed if the building collapsed. I'll let him know you went home."

"I love you, Mami."

"Love you too."

******

An hour later, I was pushing through the heavy wind and snow fall that had begun. It's been a million years since there's been an actual white Christmas and it had to happen on the night that I decided to wear heels.

The door man looked up from his phone when he heard me approach. His eyes squinted in my direction. "Miss? Are you okay?"

I caught my reflection in the mirror behind his desk. My hair was all over the place, my face red from cold burns. "Yes, I'm Virginia Perez. I'm just here to see Max Thomas."

I shouldn't be surprised that he looked at me as if I've grown another head. He quickly scanned a clip board that he held. "I'm sorry but Max Thomas doesn't have you on the list of visitors."

"You remember me? I've been here a couple times."

"If I had a nickel every time a woman has said those words..."

I narrowed my eyes in his direction. "Listen, I'm not crazy or anything. I'm not going to set myself on fire—"

The door man held up his hand to stop me. I squinted at him

wishing that I had Carrie like powers to cause him pain. "I don't know why you got your hand up for, we all know you're not a traffic cop."

"You can either leave, or I'm going to call the cops."

"Fine." I threw my hands up in defeat. "You know for a door man, you're letting the power go straight to your head."

The ding of the elevator sprung me into action and before I could stop myself, I ran and lunged into the elevator and pressed the button. "Hey!" I heard the doorman yell after me.

My heart was racing, and my hands were shaking from the adrenaline. *What the hell are you doing, Ginny?!* My inner voice screamed at me.

I pressed the lobby button because I came back to my senses but the elevator was already on a mission to the top floor. "It's fine, he won't see you. You'll head back down like nothing happen. And hopefully you get to spend only a few hours in jail," I said to myself. I tried to sound as upbeat as possible which was a sure sign that I was slowly losing my mind.

The elevator doors finally opened. Max Thomas stood there waiting. "Hi, don't mind me. I lost my mind and I'm slowly coming back to it. Merry Christmas." I pressed the close button, but his arm shot out.

"Ginny, what are you doing here?"

He was dressed in a black suit, black tie. "I...I..."

"Max, you can't be serious," George Thomas commented from behind his brother. "She's clearly losing her mind."

"Shut up, George." Max's stern tone stopped his brother from continuing. "Ginny, what's going on?"

"I...Can we talk privately before the cops get here?"

"The cops?"

"Yeah, the doorman made it pretty clear that I'd be headed to Sing Sing if I tried to come up here."

I heard a big cheer come from his apartment; realization hit me. "You're having a Christmas party."

He nodded and pulled me out of the elevator that he had kept open. "Max, we gotta go. You already disappointed the family once—"

"George, I swear if you say one more word I will knock you out," Max threatened.

"Throwing it all away for some girl you don't even know?!" George shrieked.

"I'm giving it away to live my life the way I want to. I don't want the business. I never wanted the business."

The hard set of Georges jaw made me very nervous. He glanced my way. "Maybe I should have a go at you. Maybe your pussy would make me want to—" before he could finish his sentence, Max lunged at his brother knocking him down to the ground.

"Max! No!" I yelled.

The elevator door opened, and two officers pulled the men apart. "Is this the guy?" one asked the doorman.

"No, it's her!" he pointed his stubby finger at me.

"Put that finger down," I growled.

"It's okay officers. She's with me," Max explained. He had hands on his hips, taking in deep breaths.

"See. Told you," I said to the doorman.

"What about this guy?" one of the officers asked.

"That's my brother, he was just leaving." The stony look on Max's face warned George not to stay.

"We'll talk tomorrow," was all George said as he took the stairway down.

"You don't need us?" The other officer asked.

"No, sorry for the misunderstanding."

'They all nodded; the doorman took one final look. "You deserve hazard pay, you did amazing!" I commented.

"Leave him alone." Max kept his voice low but I could still hear the frustrated edge that it held.

He reached for my hand. Pulling me along with him. "Where are we going?"

"Stairs," he answered.

I kept silent because his body was rigid and his grip was tight on my hand. I knew that what just happened with his brother really got to him and I hated that I chose this time to come speak to him.

Max led me to the stairway. The muffled sound of his holiday party behind us. "Now, Ginny, what the hell are you doing here?"

I took a deep breath. "I came to see how you were holding up because I heard that you officially stepped down as CEO—"

"Why are you here, Ginny?" His hands were in his pockets as if he were trying to keep from strangling me. There was a small cut from where his brother had made contact. I reached out to lightly touch.

"You're bleeding," I pointed out. He rolled his eyes, turned on his heels causing me to finally spit my thoughts out. "I came because love is supposed to support your dreams!"

He slowly turned back around. "What?"

I rubbed my hands together to stifle the nervous adrenaline that I had coursing through my veins. "Dreams and love can exist together."

His eyebrows came down in confusion. "I'm trying to follow, Gin."

I closed my eyes, trying to gather my thoughts. "I love you. I thought that if I wanted to reach my goal that I couldn't have it. That you would be too much of a distraction. That I would sacrifice my dream to have you and it would blow up in my face."

"You love me?"

"And I just realized tonight that I can have both." I shook my head. "Scratch that. I don't know if I can have both, but I don't want to miss out on you or my goal. But I want to try and have both."

Max reached for my hands. "So, you love me?"

I nodded. "Yes," I squeaked. When he didn't continue, I began to ramble. "Listen, Max. I get that I said some things. But I said them to keep you at a distance. I...I was too scared. The fact that your family hates me, also was a factor and I think you need to make up with George even though he's an asshole but he's still your brother—"

"Bring it back around, Gin, you're veering off."

"I don't want you to think that we're a one-night stand that lasted weeks too long. I love you." He squeezed my hand but said nothing. "Max, I said I love you three times and if you don't love me that's cool, but you need to say...something. Anything at this point."

"Ginny, as much of a pain in the ass you are...I love you, too." He smirked.

"What about your family?"

"Andrea is happy because she's CEO and that's where she always wanted to be."

I rolled my eyes. "But she hates me."

"She doesn't hate you. She thought you'd put the company in jeopardy."

I rolled my eyes. "Geez that makes me feel better." I sat down on the steps. "I just hate how fake everyone was to me."

He shrugged, taking a seat next to me. "I'm sorry about that."

"What about George? That was some crazy ass shit that just went down."

He smirked. "There was some pent-up aggression from earlier. I'm not going to lie...it felt good." I couldn't hide the shock on my face. "But...it will take some time between us."

"Are you broke now that you left the company?" I asked. Max's laugh echoed through the empty stairwell. "You could've just said no."

"I stepped down as CEO. I still hold a share of the business."

I nodded my understanding even though I wasn't completely

sure what he was talking about. "So, you're not the big boss but you still make a little money if the business does."

"Basically."

"Why now?"

"Someone made me realize that what I want in life matters."

I lightly tapped him with my shoulder. "I wonder who that was, sounds like an amazingly smart person."

"Oh, you two have met. It's my doorman."

"Ha, ha. Not funny."

He tapped back with his shoulder. "How's the collection coming?"

"Just a few rough sketches. I'm actually going fabric shopping with Mrs. Pierce."

"Mrs. Pierce?! I thought you hated each other."

"Hate is such a strong word..."

"You told her she can go straight to hell...that sounds like very strong hate."

I shrugged. "Hey, I'm not listening to you. What do you know? You gave up a billion dollar company."

He laughed. "Wanna get out of here?"

"Max, you have a giant party happening in your apartment."

He pulled his phone out of his pocket, typed something up and placed it back. "It's taken care of."

"Oh, so Batman has Alfred taking care of it?"

"Something like that."

He stood up, holding the door open for me. "Wait, close it back up," I said. Max let the door close.

"What's up?"

"Come here."

Max sauntered over to stand in front of me. "What do you want, Ginny?"

I cupped his face, scratching the beard that was coming in nicely, and brought it closer to mine. "We didn't even kiss."

"Oh, I can fix that." His arms cupped my backside, bringing our bodies close. His lips lightly kissed mine.

I backed away just a tiny bit. "After all that happened, that's all I get?"

His lips crushed down on mine, his tongue parting my lips and exploring. I moaned, pressing my body closer to his. Which was in itself a bit difficult in my puffer jacket. "I need you."

"You got me," he answered with a smile against my neck.

2 1

Rule #29: Don't be afraid to have a work/life balance. We know we've mentioned this before but it's really necessary.

One Year Later...

"Maggie gave her two weeks today." Marvin's voice squealed through the phone.

"Really? I wonder what happened," I absentmindedly toyed with Max's fingers. His soft breathing told me that he had dozed off.

"Apparently, she's getting a divorce and she wasn't happy at H. Moda. The global team had a companywide meeting about the direction we were headed in and she didn't like what she heard. She accepted a district role at our competitors."

Maggie wasn't my favorite person in the world, that's a known fact. That didn't mean I didn't want her to be happy. Everyone deserved some happiness...okay, maybe not all people. I mean the guy who cut in front of me at the coffee cart today could stand a little unhappiness. "Really? Who's the new store manager?"

"You're talking to him."

"No freaking way." Although he couldn't see me, I beamed with

285

pride. I was happy for my friend. He worked harder than everyone and he deserved it.

"Yes! Jake is coming over to celebrate."

"Oooo, so that's a thing? You and Jake?" I pried.

"New year, New me."

I groaned. "That phrase is so overused. Please, say something else."

He laughed. "We haven't spoken in a week, what's up with you?"

Where do I start?! So much has happened, is happening. "Well, the place I'm interning offered me a full-time position."

"As?"

"Designer."

Marvin hollered loud. "Damn, Ginny."

Max stirred against me; I kept my voice low. "Yeah, but I said yes under one condition."

"What's the condition?"

"That they support with my collection."

"Backers?"

"Yeah, Mrs. Pierce gave me the idea. My brand will be under their umbrella for now. I have a majority of the share and they'll have a small percentage."

"Look at you, talking business, is this your boyfriends influence?"

I was proud to answer his question. "Some, but I've been researching and getting my shit together. Just things I've been too lazy to do in the past."

"This is all happening fast."

"Yeah, the company were fans of my designs from before...I showed them what I was working on and they thought it would be a waste to have me interning." It all really happened quickly. I owe it to Mrs. Pierce who connected me with the right people.

As much of a pain in the ass she was to me, she really came through when I needed it.

"We're growing up. Who would have thought?" Marvin laughed.

I sighed and cuddled deeper into a snoring Max. "My collection won't be out for a while but it's a work in progress and I'm happy…"

"And employed."

"Yup."

"Listen, I gotta go and finish getting ready. Happy New Year. I love you."

"Happy New Year, I love you, too."

I hung up and closed my eyes. In a short amount of time my life changed. It was up's and down's and up's and down's and now it felt like I was going up and never coming back down. It felt good.

I sighed, breathing Max's cologne that still lingered from dinner. We went out to have an early New Year celebration with my parents. The time went well, with barely any jabs being thrown. My dad was letting his guard down little by little and my mother understood that I was making a name for myself and that she was there to support if needed.

I moved a tiny bit against Max on this small couch and he groaned.

There's something to be said about being snuggled on the couch on New Year's Eve with the person you love. The T.V. flashed all the tourists who thought it'd be amazing to watch the ball drop in person. It was too cold for that. People born in the city knew the best place to watch the ball drop was in their apartment or at a party where it was warm, there was a bathroom readily available and snacks whenever you want.

"Are you asleep?" I asked a dozing Max Thomas.

"Not at all." His voice was low and rough with sleep.

"Because for a second there it seemed like the T.V. was watching you."

A soft grin appeared on his face. "Seeing that there's nothing on that interests me…"

I looked up at his face ready for a war of flirtation that would lead to the bedroom.

"What sparks your interest, Mr. Thomas?"

I felt his hand slid up my belly to cup my breasts. "I thought I could give you a little present."

"Too many *dick in a box* jokes, so little time." I looked up at him as I felt his hardness against my back. "Just for the record, Max. What you have wouldn't be considered a little present. The postal service would probably charge extra to ship that thing."

I felt his chuckle. This is what I wanted. I turned around to straddle him. Max's hands immediately found their way to my hips as he lightly pressed me down against him. He pulled me down and his lips found my neck, causing my eyes to shut. "God, Max."

"I love you, Ginny."

I rubbed myself against him. His mouth greedily kissed my breasts through my blouse. "It'll be easier just to take it off," I whispered.

He unbuttoned my blouse, painstakingly slow. When he finally tossed it, I ripped my bra off. "My, aren't we in a hurry," he joked.

"Max, I just need you inside me."

I felt his breath against my bare breasts as he took my nipple in his mouth. His strong hands pushed my tits together, letting his tongue run across them. I closed my eyes and savored the pleasure.

"You want more?"

"Mmmhmm."

Max lightly picked me up and laid me against the couch. The restraint he had when he took my blouse was gone. He ripped my bottoms off with no regard. He spread my legs open, looking down, his finger made a trail down my wet slit. I arched, looking for more pressure. "I want to taste you," his said.

Max fell to his knees. Licking every bit of my sensitive flesh. I moaned and arched my back, pushing my pussy further against his tongue. Soft moans escaped the depths of my soul as I savored the pleasure that he provided.

My hands grabbed fistfuls of his hair as I kept rubbing his face between my legs. I felt the buildup start in my belly and kept his head in place while I came all over his tongue and lips.

One of the sexiest sounds to me is this man unbuckling his trousers. I had my eyes closed but I felt him stretch over me. "Look at me, Ginny."

I opened my eyes and I felt him enter me. He groaned deep and rested his forehead against mine. "I love you," He whispered against my lips as his hips drove faster into me. I arched my back to get him deeper.

"Fuck," he moaned.

My cries got louder as I felt the familiar heat. Max began to suck on my nipple, sending me over the edge. He let go of my breast and adjusted himself, grabbing onto my hips tighter. His thrusts were harder and faster. I rode the wave of ecstasy, there was no way to keep my eyes opened.

With one final thrust, he came. His hand trailing down my neck, between my breasts until he laid on top of me.

"Max?"

"Hmmm?"

"I love you."

"I love you, too."

"You weigh a ton. Move back to starting positions," I joked.

Max laughed, but laid back on the couch and pulled me down on top of him. "Better?"

"Much."

We laid silently, watching some popstar sing their biggest hit of the year in the middle of Times Square.

"It's just a weird thing to watch with the volume off. Like...what are they dancing to? Can they only hear the music?" I pondered.

"The way your mind works," Max chuckled. I could feel his breathing begin to slow down.

"Max?"

"Hmmm?"

"Did you hear from George or Andrea?"

He sighed. "Now why do we have to talk about my siblings when we're both naked and sedated?"

I shrugged against him. "I don't know, just wondering. It's been a little strained, I don't want to start another year with family friction...you guys should be able to talk."

"We spoke, we're good. I'm doing my thing and we'll see each other tomorrow at my parents place."

"Was it a normal conversation?" I pushed. I knew that Andrea was a bit more forgiving that George.

"Andrea is great. No hard feelings. You think she's an ice princess but she's a big softy. And George is fine. He's a bit stubborn, so he won't let me live the events of the last year down. But we're good. The holidays are tough for everyone...especially when you work in retail. Especially when it's your family's business."

"We barely survived it," I said it as sleep made my eyelids heavy.

Max kissed the top of my head. "But we survived."

Just a girl from the Bronx living her best life.

J.L. is a wife, mother, and author. After years of working in the fashion industry, J.L. is turning her lifelong dream of writing into a reality. She hopes to inspire readers and make them laugh with her unique sense of humor, one-of-a-kind characters, and hilariously adventurous stories. J.L. currently lives in Connecticut with her son, husband, and extended circle of friends, all of whom help to inspire her everyday!

J.L. enjoys reading romance novels, watching *Gilmore Girls* for the millionth time, hanging out with her friends and family and pretending to be a pop star while singing karaoke.